SKIN DEEP
IS FATAL

SKIN DEEP IS FATAL

by Michael Cormany

An Irma Heldman / Birch Lane Press Book
Published by Carol Publishing Group

An Irma Heldman / Birch Lane Press Book
Published by Carol Publishing Group
Birch Lane Press is a registered trademark of Carol Communications, Inc.

Editorial Offices: 600 Madison Avenue, New York, N.Y. 10022
Sales & Distribution Offices: 120 Enterprise Avenue, Secaucus, N.J. 07094

In Canada: Canadian Manda Group
P.O. Box 920, Station U,
Toronto, Ontario M8Z 5P9

Manufactured in the United States of America

10 9 8 7 6 5 4 3 2 1

Carol Publishing Group books are available at special discounts
for bulk purchases, for sales promotions, fund raising, or
educational purposes. Special editions can be created to
specifications. For details contact: Special Sales Department,
Carol Publishing Group, 120 Enterprise Avenue, Secaucus, N.J. 07094

Library of Congress Cataloging-in-Publication Data

Cormany, Michael.
    Skin deep is fatal / by Michael Cormany.
       p.   cm.
    "An Irma Heldman / Birch Lane Press Book."
    ISBN 1-55972-110-3
    I. Title.
PS3553.06525S57   1992
813'.54—dc20   91-47055
                                                        CIP

SKIN DEEP
IS FATAL

PROLOGUE

Detox Ward. The third morning. My nerves screamed like Sam Kinison. The Valium might as well have been M&M's for all the good they did. I begged for more. Was told I was doing fine on the maintenance allotment.

Like hell I was doing fine. Dryheaving, shaking so hard it felt like my bones would snap, and no sleep for three nights running was not doing fine by my definition. Especially when I knew one drink would take it all away.

I hadn't seen Heather since she trashed the cafeteria the night before. I didn't know where they had her, what they were doing to her. All they'd tell me was she was still in the building detoxing.

An hour ago a quiet IBM salesman named Josh dropped to the floor like a sawed-off dead branch and then flopped like a fish on a pier. The nurses took it in stride, but it pushed my anxiety right over the top.

I had to get out of here. But I couldn't call Marvin. Nobody has phone privileges in Detox Ward.

I stood near the front desk when two nurses brought a stocky woman whose blond hair looked like filthy wet straw up the stairs. I hadn't seen her before, which meant they'd just sobered her up and did the tests and now she was ready for Detox. She wore baggy jeans and a purple blouse that looked like a huge bar rag. Her face was bloated, her eyes scared. She looked at me and said, "Can we get out of here if we want?" in a voice of total panic.

I shook my head. "I think we're in hell. And you can't get out of hell."

One of the nurses said, "Come on, Amy, we'll show you your room."

Amy lost it. Went berserk. Started screaming and fighting.

The nurse at the front desk left it to help her co-workers subdue Amy.

I reached over and quick punched Marvin Torkelson's office number. He answered the first ring. I said, "Marvin, if you love me, you got to get me the fuck out of here."

He said, "Dan, that's exactly why you're staying in."

ONE

Dr. William Eli, Heather, and I sat in high school desks in a fluorescent-bright room.

Dr. Eli was a shrink. Thick wire rim glasses sat in front of intelligent, friendly blue eyes. He had a generous Roman nose and a trim reddish beard. He wore what he wore every day: faded jeans, grungy lowcut Reeboks, and a white oxford shirt with an assortment of food stains down the front. Heather and I share a mutual antipathy for people in authority and Eli was the head honcho around here. But we'd found after a few days we actually liked Dr. William "Call-me-Bill" Eli. It's hard not to like a guy who genuinely likes you no matter how screwed up you are.

Dr. Eli said, "Okay, you two. You got here June second. Today's June twenty-nine. You know what that means."

I said, "It means time flies when you're having fun."

Dr. Eli laughed. He laughed a lot for a substance abuse shrink who worked at a county sponsored rehab like Mercy Mother's Alcohol and Drug Dependency Unit for half what he could make at one of the area's spa type rehabs. He said, "Means tomorrow you hit the streets. I think you're both ready, but we have got a small problem we should talk over. The last day or two of the program we like to bring a patient's employer or immediate supervisor in for an informal session. See how they feel about having you back, how much support they're willing to give." He looked at a piece of paper in front of him. Said, "No employers."

Heather said, "I got no problem with that, Bill."

Eli smiled. Few people in Chicago smile at Heather. Heather shaves her head and wears only black. Including the Doctor Marten brogues on her feet and the oversize leather jacket she wears everywhere except to bed. Even in Mercy Mother's. Her accessories include studded leather collars and bracelets, six silver earrings, three on each ear, and occasionally a gold nose ring. Her look is the most important part of her life. You mess with it you invite peril. They'd taken away her PILLS ARE HEAVEN T-shirt the second day we were in. Her temper was on short fuse because she was coming off the speed and that's why she trashed the cafeteria. Between the screams and the bangs and the shouting of the nurses and orderlies it sounded like a DC-10 was crash landing down there. That was twenty-five days ago and she was mellowed out now, but the nurses were still scared to death of her. Eli actually seemed to enjoy her.

Dr. Eli said, "This kind of echoes the family situation for the Large Therapy sessions involving loved ones. Dan, you had no family to bring in. Heather, yours, in your own words, wanted nothing to do with you."

Heather said, "All we got is each other."

Dr. Eli said, "Staying clean and sober is tough outside these walls. You obviously won't have the support groups out there you have here. You *will* have temptation. For two recovering abusers who live together, who have no families to lean on and no regular jobs. Well—"

I said, "I read that even if I wanna stay sober—and I really want to—odds are less than fifty-fifty I'll go a year without a drink. Doesn't matter if I'm working or not. I mean, lots of people with regular jobs relapse."

Heather said, "You know what they say. Detox-retox."

Dr. Eli said, "We don't say that here, Heather. And you have to *fight* the odds, Dan. You think you can?"

I said, "Yes," firmly.

"Do you want to?"

"Yes."

"You didn't when you came here."

I said, "That was then, this is now."

Heather said, "Technically speaking, Dan is my employer."

Dr. Eli raised his eyebrows.

I said, "You know she works with the band I play in."

"Yes, but Full Frontal Nudity's not your band. So they're her employer."

"Right."

"You never did explain what you do with the band, Heather."

"Help set up and break down the gear, run the sound board, keep the guitar player sexually satisfied."

Without missing a beat, our Bill asked, "Dan, how do you advertise to fill a job like that?"

"You don't advertise, you beg."

"We've discussed this before, but I want to reiterate the two jobs you do have are more than a little risky. Playing guitar in a rock band is a tough job for a man coming off twenty years of substance abuse. Both of you think you can handle the atmosphere of a bar or club?"

"Yes," we said in barely audible unison.

"Can you play a gig sober?"

He used the musician's word. It flashed on me that many a musician had no doubt passed through here. I said, "If I can play life sober, I can play gigs sober."

He said, "You've heard us talk many times about dry time as opposed to sober time. You are going to be socializing with substance abusers as soon as you get out of here. You strong enough to handle that?"

"I have to be. I need the income."

"I'm gong to be with Dan." Heather said, and took my hand.

Dr. Eli said, "The one-man private eye operation. You've indicated you don't work often."

"Sad but true. People prefer the bigger agencies."

He leaned forward, hands on knees, face concerned and intense. "You see what I'm getting at, don't you? As things stand now you're going to have a lot of time on your hands. You'll experience boredom, frustration, depression. In the past you relied on alcohol and other drugs to get you through times like that. Now you need something to get you through those times sober. Support groups. In the absence of an employer proper, I've asked Marvin Torkelson to come in tomorrow morning. You share an office with him and he's paying for your treatment. I don't think he wants to see his money wasted. Or see you again in the shape you were in June second."

Marvin Torkelson had been my best friend since high school. Was convinced I'd been put here as his cross to bear. Definite love/hate relationship. I said, "He offered to come in?"

"Said he'd come in and once you're out he'll help any way he can. But most important, you and Heather are going to have to help each other. And you'll go to the meetings of course."

We both said, "Of course," although that was one part of the deal I wasn't so sure about. I hate meetings, always have.

He said, "Okay, I want you two to think about life outside Mercy Mother's for a while. It's imminent. Go over potential problems. Situations you'll encounter that might be particularly stressful that we haven't discussed before. We'll talk about strategies to combat those situations." He stood. "We'll meet back here in, say, one hour."

Heather and I left the room, went down a flight of stairs, then down a short hall to the small kitchen area. Poured coffee from the pot that always sat on the stove. The stuff tasted like liquid tar but everybody drank it constantly.

I sipped from the styrofoam cup. Heather said, "I need a cigarette." She headed for the Day Room, the only place in here you could cop a smoke. We both spent a lot of time in the Day Room.

I leaned against the refrigerator door watching the coffee traffic.

A soft voice beside me said, "Mr. Kruger?"

It was Amy, the scared-to-death blonde who'd asked about escaping my third day in Detox Ward. She'd turned out to be a quiet, loner type. Hadn't talked much except at therapy sessions so I didn't know a lot about her except her horror stories. And we hadn't been in that many therapy sessions together. But she was one of the few people here who was friendly to Heather, which made her an automatic friend in my book. I very often judge people by how they react to Heather.

Amy couldn't have looked more different from the first time I'd seen her. Her hair was combed neatly to one side and tucked behind her ears like a little boy going to first day of kindergarten. She wore black jeans and a pressed white shirt. Her face was less puffy.

"Your girlfriend told me yesterday you're a private detective," she said nervously.

I said, "That's right."

"Could I hire you?"

"Amy, anybody can hire me. And I do mean anybody."

"What do you charge?"

"Hundred a day. Expenses."

"Can I talk to you tonight? Seven o'clock in the Day Room?"

"I'll talk to you too."

One hour later Dr. Eli, Heather, and I sat in the same chairs in the same fluorescent-bright room. I said, "Guess what, Bill? I might have a job and I haven't even hit the streets yet."

Dr. Eli's smile showed pearly white teeth. "Splendid."

Easy for him to say.

TWO

I remembered Amy's initial "speech" during her first Large Therapy session. She told us, in a voice so soft the whole room leaned forward to hear, that she had woken up five days earlier on her basement floor, covered with vomit, her live-in lover towering over her. She was told either she quit drinking or she was out the door. They had a two-year-old son, Alan, who would be raised without her if she continued to drink.

After her story Heather leaned to me and said, "God, I hope somebody could realize they had a problem if they wake up in their own puke. Dan, you and I weren't so bad off." But Heather said that every time someone told a hit-bottom story. It hadn't been Heather's idea to rehab. Of course, it hadn't been mine either. But that's another story.

But now since Heather and Amy were kind of friends, I asked Heather what she knew about Amy. She told me not much. They talked mostly about how things were going in rehab. Amy was pretty close-mouthed about her personal life. Heather knew she missed her son terribly and she lived on the near North Side.

There's a privacy nook in the Day Room. Four orange contoured plastic stack chairs partitioned from the rest of the lounge by a clear plexiglass floor-to-ceiling divider. The nurses could see us but couldn't hear us. The nook and your tiny sleeping cell is all the privacy you get in a rehab unit.

At 7:00, Amy and I sat across from each other there. She'd changed into a lemon yellow tank top, acid-washed jeans, and sandals. She smiled a nervous smile, ran one hand through her hair and said, "I've never done this before. How does one hire a private detective?"

"One states the problem, suggests a course of action, hands over a check. Easy as ABC. Third part is the most important, by the way."

"My problem isn't—normal."

"It was, you'd solve it yourself, right?"

"Actually the problem doesn't concern you."

"What does concern me?"

"Heather must be quite a handful."

"She's a wild child, but so was I. It's why I understand her so well."

"She seems a little out of control, but she's nice. She told me you play in a rock band too. I imagine you two live a lifestyle that's a little—"

"Peculiar?"

"Unconventional is the word I was looking for."

"Unconventional works too."

"What do you know about me?"

"You're addicted to alcohol. You have a son you miss a lot. When your boyfriend threatened to kick you out of the house, you came here. You have a problem that isn't normal and actually doesn't concern me, but you want me to solve it anyway." I shrugged. "That about covers it."

Looking away, Amy said softly, "Why do you assume my lover is a man? At no time during my stay here did I refer to my lover as 'he.'"

"Your lover is a woman?"

"Her name is Kay." She looked at me, started curling the hair behind her ear with her fingers.

"I apologize for jumping to conclusions."

"The part about Alan probably confused you. Kay and I wanted a family of our own. I went to a feminist health center in

Atlanta that has an insemination program for unmarried women."

"Don't they have screening programs at those places?"

"I'd been clean for five years at that point. I had a drinking problem in my teens. My father was a very domineering, unforgiving man. Then I married a man who was abusive, to put it mildly, and it snowballed. I drank the whole time I was married. He drank even more than I did so it was easy to be in denial. I didn't like myself then. I knew something was wrong, I wasn't sure what. I was a total mixed up mess. No self-confidence, zero self-esteem. After he and I divorced, I realized my sexual orientation and acted on it. I gradually stopped drinking and stayed sober, although sometimes it was difficult."

"But you started drinking after Alan was born?"

"I got very depressed. Postpartum blues. I started drinking to deal with it. All my life that's how I've dealt with depression and this was the first major one I had in five years. Within no time I was drinking—well, you heard the stories."

"And you heard mine."

"Do you believe a gay lifestyle is against nature?"

"Life's too short for me to bash people 'cause they don't think or act like I do."

"So it wouldn't bother you to work for a lesbian couple?"

I shook my head. Lady, I work for anybody whose check don't bounce.

"You've given off those kind of vibes. Like you'll help anyone. Like anybody *can* hire you. Even if their lifestyle is irregular or frowned on by most people."

"Sometimes I think those are the only people who do hire me."

We both smiled. She said, "And I think I knew because of Heather. Most people would run the other way the first time they saw her. You're the type who looks beyond the outer core to see what's inside a person.

"Bo Diddley says, 'You can't judge a book by looking at the cover.' And Bo should know."

Amy said, "If you don't mind my asking, the age difference between you two? What is it?"

"If I'd known Heather's mother when I was seventeen I

might be her father instead of her boyfriend."

She nodded sympathetically. "I'm twenty-eight, Kay is forty-four."

"Friends say Kay's old enough to be your mother, right?"

She blushed, said quickly, "There's this woman who used to be our friend. Kay's and mine? She has something of ours, she refuses to give it back."

"She steal it from you?"

"No."

"You and Kay give it to her?"

"It's not like that. Not something you give or take."

"It a gift?"

"No."

"Why don't you call the police?"

"We can't go to the police."

I said, "Amy, there's a certain gray area between legal and illegal called shady. Whenever I hear people say they can't go to the police when they have a problem, shady's the first thing comes to mind. This shady?"

"I don't think so."

I tried to read her face. She blinked, lowered her eyes. I said, "The ex-friend's name?"

"Shannon Harper."

"What is it she has?"

"Don't worry about that. She'd never give it to you and I don't expect you to take it from her."

"You don't want me to get the something back?"

"No."

"What is it I'm supposed to do?"

"Talk to Shannon Harper."

"Just talk to her."

"Yes."

"What do I say?"

"Tell her if she doesn't stop what she's doing and return what's ours, Kay and I will give the videotape to the police."

"Thought you couldn't go to the police."

"The videotape would be sent anonymously and would harm Shannon, not us."

"What's on the videotape?"

"I can't tell you that."

"What is it she's supposed to stop?"

"She'll know what you're talking about."

"But I won't."

Amy looked at the floor again, said nothing.

I said, "You won't tell me what she's supposed to stop doing, what she has that's yours, or what's on the videotape?"

"It's not that I won't. I can't."

"Amy, I'm a detective, not a mushroom."

"What's that mean?"

"Means I can't work in the dark."

"All you have to do is deliver the message. None of the rest concerns you."

"Hire a messenger service. Be cheaper."

She hesitated, still looking at the floor. "I also would ask that you identify yourself as a private detective. And maybe act— threatening? In your line of work, you've done that before, right? Imply you might be back if she refuses."

I said, "The clouds are breaking a little here. Amy, you've seen too many old Bogie movies. Look at me."

She raised her eyes reluctantly.

"I pretty much flunked Threatening 101. I weigh a hundred fifty, sopping wet. I don't even own a water pistol I could wave around. Besides, I come on like a goon, she calls the police."

"I guarantee she won't do that."

"What's all this gonna accomplish?"

"A private detective is the next best thing to the real police. It can make her believe we mean business."

"You really can't involve the real police?"

"No."

"Still you'll send the real police the videotape if she doesn't come across."

"I know it sounds confusing."

I said, "No more so than Bush trying to explain why he picked Quayle."

I removed the pack of Kools from my shirt pocket. Lit one up. I was smoking three packs a day in rehab. If I was lucky and stayed sober maybe I'd get to die from lung cancer instead of cirrhosis.

Blowing out smoke I said, "Where do I find Shannon Harper?"

"She lives on Astor Street."

I raised my eyebrows. "Rich people live on Astor Street."

"Shannon Harper is extremely rich."

"Not just regular rich?"

"Harper Cosmetics? Shannon Harper is an heiress to that fortune."

I'm no expert on the cosmetic industry, but I knew Harper Cosmetics was up there with Revlon and a few others I could name after watching a little daytime TV. "You should hang on to extremely rich friends. Never know when they might come in handy." Amy twisted and tugged her hair some more.

I asked, "Who else in the family lives there?"

"No one. Her parents and sisters live elsewhere. The family has owned the mansion since 1950 or something, but only Shannon lives there now."

I collected my thoughts. She watched, trying not to look apprehensive. I was getting out of rehab. I was broke. This woman wanted to pay me one hundred bucks to speak two sentences and flex a bicep. Upon sober reflection, something I was starting to get the hang of, I concluded I could work with blinders. I said "Okay. I'll give your message to Shannon Harper."

Amy smiled, stuck her hand out. We shook. She said, "Great. When do you get out?"

"Looks like tomorrow."

"You'll see Shannon right away?"

"Within twenty-four hours."

She lifted a little off the chair, removed a piece of paper and a BIC pen from her back pocket. Wrote two addresses on the paper. Said, "Bottom address is Kay's and mine. I'll call Kay tonight. She'll have your check ready when you stop by."

I walked back to my room, swinging squared shoulders, my stride slow and firm, repeating, "Listen, ya mug, they want what's theirs," in my best Edward G. Robinson voice.

THREE

Marvin came to Mercy Mother's the next morning. At 10:00 A.M. he sat between Heather and me in Dr. Eli's cramped, cluttered office on the top floor.

Eli was on the other side of his black metal desk. A pile of papers six inches high sat next to a coffee mug that said DON'T KNOCK THE DOC. He leaned forward, elbows on desk, his fingers making a temple in front of his face. He said, "Mr. Torkelson, Dan spends a good portion of his time with you. You've indicated you'd be willing to put forth an effort to help him stay sober. It could be important because Heather and Dan don't have as extensive a support group outside here as some of our other patients."

Marvin said, "I'll do everything I can."

Eli said, "Dan didn't call you to get him out except that one time during detox week, did he?"

Marvin said, "No, but he got pretty abusive during that conversation."

I said, "It was *detox*, Marvin. You can't get out during detox. You can't get off the damn floor. It was like being in prison and I was hurting big time and I wasn't sure I wanted to be sober in the first place."

Dr. Eli said, "At that point."

I said, "Once I got over the shakes I realized maybe I had a problem and this was my chance to do something about it."

"Maybe you had a problem?"

"Okay, I *had* a problem."

Eli said, "Marvin, he hasn't called you since?"

Marvin said, "He called sometimes when he had phone privileges, but he never asked me to sign him out."

"You're sure?"

"Positive."

Dr. Eli said, "I ask that to see if you've been blowing smoke at me, Dan. Telling me what I want to hear, then running to a phone asking him to come sign you out or smuggle in some booze or drugs."

Stricken, Marvin said, "I'd never do that."

Dr. Eli smiled his friendliest smile. "I know you wouldn't. It's Dan's commitment I'm checking here, not your integrity. But we've had so-called *friends* smuggle every drug you can think of in here. We've found residents snorting coke in the stairwells, toking up in the john stalls. Bottles turn up in waste baskets. People who've been here two weeks, haven't left the building, you give 'em a urine test and it comes back loaded with tranquilizers or cocaine." He looked at me. "What do you think about coming here now?"

"I think it was the best thing I ever did. Or the best thing Marvin made me do." Again, I meant it.

"And you, Heather?"

"I feel the same way." I was pretty sure she didn't.

Marvin gave her a quick look. He wasn't too sure either. There was a bit of coolness between the two. They tolerated each other because the other was so important to me, but there was more than a little jealousy there for the same reason.

We listened a little more. At 10:30 A.M. Dr. Eli said, "Okay, good luck to you both." Everybody stood and shook hands. Dr. Eli said he was coming to see FFN the first gig we played. I asked, "Gonna check up on me?" He smiled, didn't deny it.

Heather and I signed release forms. Eli gave us a booklet with the addresses and phone numbers of North Side support groups.

As we bounced down the stairs to the patients' floor, Marvin said, "Did you mean that back there?"

I said, "What?"

"That coming here was the best thing you ever did?"

"Marvin, I'd of said I'd dance naked down Michigan Avenue at high noon to get the fuck out of here."

Marvin made a face.

I smiled and elbowed his ribs. Said, "But yeah, I meant it." And I did.

Marvin dropped us at our apartment on Fremont Avenue. It's four blocks west of the lake, three blocks east of Wrigley Field.

Heather and I missed the pets. She has tropical fish; I have Bugs, my black-and-white lop-eared French rabbit. Bugs was ecstatic to see me and ecstasy is not an emotion rabbits show very often.

Marvin had stopped by every day to feed him, but Marvin refused to talk to Bugs. He said people shouldn't talk to rabbits because it was weird. I've talked things over with Bugs from the day I rescued him from the dumpster in an alley behind a bar on Milwaukee Avenue. Bugs expects to be consulted. That may be the difference between Marvin and me. He thinks most things are weird, I think nothing is. Still, outside of Bugs, Marvin remains my best friend. This is more weird than Marvin cares to admit.

We checked on Bugs and the fish, then Heather pulled me into the bedroom. What followed wasn't the most tender, slowhanded romantic session we'd ever shared. There was no sex allowed in rehab and we'd been in rehab four weeks. Sex sure would've helped that first week.

And wouldn't have hurt anything the other three.

At 2:00 P.M. I drove Heather to Shake, Rattle, and Read on North Broadway. It calls itself Chicago's only rock 'n' roll record and book store. It's one of Heather's daytime hangouts. At night she cruises the North Side rock clubs, once in a while dragging me with her. Heather is from a town called Johnson City. I met her on my last case. You can imagine the rock scene in a town called Johnson City. In Chicago she'd been like a kid in a candy shop. The results: she'd lived with me only a few months, but she was already as well known on Chicago's rock scene as I was. And I'd been part of it off and on for twenty years. But at my age all I want to do is show up, do the gig, pocket the check and go home.

We kissed goodbye and I headed for the Gold Coast to make one hundred bucks.

FOUR

The windows were down. It was a pressure cooker June day. Humid air, saturated with the smell of car exhaust, loosening tar and scorched concrete, smothered everything like a soggy blanket. The sun bounced off glass and chrome like long white needles, piercing my sunglasses. Tempers were short. Horns honked all around me; everybody was a son-of-a-bitch.

But I couldn't stop grinning. In more ways than one I felt like a canary free of its cage.

Best thing was I had no desire for a drink. I'd worried about that. I knew a certain percentage drive straight from rehab to the closest liquor store.

Astor runs north and south a few blocks west of the Lake. A short, impossibly narrow street, it's full of landmark-status stone mansions crammed next to ultra-modern highrise condos. Old, established money mixing with those running the fast track. You can cruise it for days and not see a parking spot. I didn't even try. I parked six blocks away, on Concord, walked over.

I always think of Astor as a sleepy, shaded street with a string of Beamers and Benzos at the curb and tall, snooty blondes walking snow white dogs on the sidewalk.

But it's not a neighborhood I spend much time in. So imagine my surprise when I turned the corner from North Ave and discovered Astor Street resembled a boom town. Scaffolding covered the fronts of five mansions. Construction vans were parked everywhere, bare-chested men wearing toolbelts crawled all over the place. Electric saws growled, hammers pounded, men shouted. Rehab, rehab. Another five years and most of Astor's mansions would be divided into condos too. I wondered where the old money was going.

The Harper residence was a turn-of-the-century, three-story, clean-lined graystone behind a black wrought iron fence. Front lawn the size of a throw rug. Ropes of emerald green ivy crawled along the sides and upper stories of the house. At the right side of the house was a porch with a vault ceiling. A flower motif carved on the curve of the porch matched the carvings on the spikes of the fence.

A stout Latino girl answered the door. She had wide-set eyes and black hair tied in a bun on top of her head. She wore a "maid's uniform": black linen dress, white apron, black hose and pumps. Beads of sweat made a bubbly mustache along her upper lip. I said, "Miss Shannon Harper?"

She made a pretend laugh. "The designer clothes must of give me away? You think I look like Miss Harper, do you?"

I gave her a dazzling smile, said, "I never met the woman, but I was told she's very pretty. I thought you might be her."

As usual the Kruger charm went over like a new tax bill. Face sullen she said, "I jus' work for her."

"That's fine, Miss—"

"Lucy Miranda."

"Lucy, is Shannon Harper home?"

"Might be she is."

"I have a message for her."

"I'll take a message."

"Gotta see her myself. That's part of the message."

She looked me over. I imagined not many men wearing faded to white bluejeans, black Keith Richard T-shirts, and beat up hightop Nikes came calling on Shannon Harper of the Harper Cosmetic family. Lucy said, "What's your name?"

I told her.

She said, "Miss Harper know you?"

I said, "The message is from two friends of hers, Kay and Amy."

She made a face. "Those names won't getchu very far, Mr. *Dan* Kruger."

"Listen, Lucy, I speak one, maybe two sentences to Shannon and I'm outta here. You never see me again."

She debated a second, said, "Come inside. I'll see what Miss Harper says."

I stepped into a foyer with a black-and-white marble floor and gold leaf ceiling. An ornate fan made lazy swirls, creating a soft swishing sound. It was dark and cool here and it smelled like luxury.

Lucy left. I stood there, my eyes adjusting to the shadows.

Suddenly an angry voice shouted, "Dammit Lucy, what am I going to *do* with you?" The voice came around the corner of the hallway that ended in the foyer and its owner was striding toward me. Lucy tagged behind like a tin can on a Just Married car. The woman with the angry voice was taller than me and health club slim. Moved like a cat. She had a curly mass of bright orange hair. Freckles plastered the woman's face and neck and arms. She appeared to be twenty-five or so. She wore black pants and a red-and-black striped polo shirt. Her feet were bare.

She'd built up a good head of steam. For a second I thought she intended to run me over, but she stopped on a dime and we stood nose to mouth. She leaned into my neck, made a long sniff. "A carnivore," she sneered.

Lucy cowered behind the woman. I looked at Lucy around the woman's shoulder. Lucy's face indicated this had not been a good idea.

I stepped back and said, "Miss Shannon Harper?" Her eyes narrowed and bored into mine like a high speed drill. I could almost hear the whine.

Then the woman whooped a laugh, clapped her hands. "So Kay and Amy socialize with carnivores now? Christ, what next? I understand you have a message for me. Let's hear it."

I handed her one of my PI cards.

Part one accomplished.

She took the card, but kept staring at me. Her hostile eyes seemed to focus and detach in rapid succession. Like a mean man's eyes at the end of a long bender. The kind of demented stare that says, I'm such a crazy bastard even I don't know what I might do next. I forced myself to meet it.

I said, "They want you to stop what you're doing, return what belongs to them. You don't, they send the videotape to the police."

Part two accomplished.

Part three was acting tough. I hitched my shoulders and grimaced like Bogart.

She yelp laughed again. "This a threat? They trying to threaten *me*? Tell those two dykes to go fuck themselves. It's all they're interested in anymore anyway."

I said, "They're serious about the videotape."

"Did you see the videotape?"

I debated for a second. Said, "No."

"They won't even show it to you. They'd never send it to the police and you know it."

I didn't know much of anything at the moment.

She read the card, relocked her eyes into mine. "What next, you gonna rough me up?"

"No goon stuff. My job was finished soon as you heard the message."

Shannon poked at my nose with the card. "It better be, Kruger. This card means I know where you live, I know where you work. Now I got a message for *them*. You tell *them* to stay off my back, off *our* back. You tell *them* nothing is going to stop us. They wanna wimp out, fine, but the rest of us? No way. And if you, Dan Kruger, and those—*people* keep fucking with me, you're all dead meat. You tell them that, okay? Perhaps you don't know it, but they'll know that is no idle threat. Now get out of my house."

She turned and glided away, arms swinging like a model on a runway. Lucy and I stood there. Lucy looked mortified. I said, "What the hell was *that*?"

Lucy shook her head. Whispered, "Miss Harper is—*intense* about things."

I said, "Mention Kay and Amy and she goes off like a roman candle. Why is that?"

"I don't know. When I come to work here just six months ago Kay and Amy were like her closes' friends. All the time I heard, 'tonight I'm visiting Kay and Amy.'"

"They ever visit here?"

"Amy sometimes. Kay never. I never met her, jus' hear a lot of talk about her. I use to think Miss Harper admire her."

Shannon Harper's voice screamed from above us, "Lucy, I want that man out of this house. Now!"

Lucy's eyes rolled back in her head and she pushed me toward the door.

FIVE

I was not grinning as I walked back to the Skylark. Didn't feel so free and happy. Maybe because I do not like people using "dead meat" and "Dan Kruger" in the same sentence.

Kay and Amy and Alan lived in a large two-story brick house on a street of large two-story brick houses in Lincoln Park, a couple of miles from the Gold Coast. As I walked across the street a horde of teenage skateboarders with long-on-top, shaved-around-the-ears haircuts, wearing baggy T-shirts long as dresses, whizzed past me.

Kay answered my knock almost immediately. She was a big, solid woman with a handsome, dignified face under graying auburn hair cut short and combed straight back. She wore navy sweats and white Keds. Alan stood behind her, peering around the back of her thighs, clutching a tiny handful of pants.

I said my name and she nodded. She led me into a living room tastefully decorated in soft colors. Two mauve and gray sofas with lots of oriental-print throw pillows, a Boston rocking chair, walnut tables, colorful Turkish rugs on a polished wood floor. Small impressionistic bronze statues sat on the tables. One wall was floor to ceiling bookshelves crammed to overflowing with books and magazines and videotapes. More books were stacked on the floor and lay open on the sofas and end tables. Symphonic music played softly on a small stereo in the corner.

Kay said, "Mr. Kruger, how did things go with Shannon?"

"Not well."

She frowned, said, "Wait here," and left the room.

I sat on the sofa in front of the window that faced the street. Alan stood ten feet away and stared at me, chewing his index finger. I picked up the closest book. It was *Green Eggs and Ham.*

I grinned at Alan, said, "Can't go wrong with Seuss, kid." He grinned back, finger still in mouth.

Raising my voice I said, "I have some questions to ask you, Miss—"

"Thornberg," I heard from another room. "Kay Thornberg."

Kay Thornberg came back into the living room, stood in front of me. She said, "Amy's last name is Barrow."

"I know. Like the gangster."

She smiled a tight, cold smile. "Yes. Like the gangster."

I recognized the music. I said, "That's the song some airline uses in its commercials, right? How'd you get a tape of that?"

"It's 'Rhapsody in Blue,' Mr. Kruger. George Gershwin? One of the most influential composers of the twentieth century. Would you describe the William Tell Overture as the Lone Ranger's theme song?"

I usually do, but I grinned like I'd been making a funny.

Alan said something that sounded like Amy.

I nodded at Alan, said, "Your son's cute."

Kay Thornberg's smile turned genuine. "Isn't he? And he's so bright."

"Amy told me how she was able to have him."

"I'm proud of Amy. I know she told you about our relationship."

I nodded.

"That's wonderful. I've tried to get her to become more positive, more assertive about being lesbian. She sometimes acts— almost ashamed. So often there's ridicule. And it's getting worse, what with the current political climate and AIDS and all. Gay-bashing is 'in' again. Not that it ever went away. She's not good at facing that."

"I told her I'm not a basher."

"She *said* she felt comfortable with you. Amy's closet has a revolving door. I don't believe in closets. It's not healthy. Don't get me wrong, I don't believe in outing either. Forcing people to admit they're gay."

"I don't get you wrong."

"It's only been four years since Amy realized. And sometimes the consequences of coming out are unpleasant. Of course, I'm

older. The older I got, the more open I became. Nothing to lose
I guess."

"That why you never visited her at rehab?"

"No."

I was curious, but didn't ask.

She handed me a check. It was for five hundred dollars.

I said, "Miss Thornberg—"

"Please, address me as Ms. or Kay. I am not a single woman."

"Kay, I expected a check for one hundred dollars. I did not
expect Shannon Harper to threaten my life. What gives?"

"She did that?"

"Emphatically."

Kay bit her lip, clasped her hands together. She went to the
rocking chair and sat down. Alan followed her, buried his face in
her lap. She stroked his hair and made tiny, almost impercepti-
ble rocks. After some seconds she said, "I'm afraid Amy was not
entirely truthful when she talked to you."

"I came to that very same conclusion as soon as Shannon
Harper opened her mouth."

"What exactly did that woman say?"

"That woman started the conversation by smelling my neck
and calling me a carnivore. Said it like she couldn't think of a
worse insult and like she couldn't believe you and Amy have
sunk so low you'd associate with one. She ended it by threatening to turn all three of us into dead meat if we don't back off."

"That's deplorable."

"I couldn't agree more. It's happened to me before. But I
resent being included this time because I don't know what the
hell is going on. Why don't you tell me?"

"The carnivore part? We're all vegetarians."

"That part was fairly easy to deduce."

"Shannon Harper is an unbalanced individual. Unbalanced
mentally, unbalanced morally. She's compulsive, obsessive—
other things."

I said, "I don't need a psych degree to know that a woman
who smells strangers to determine their dietary habits might be
a few beers shy of a six-pack."

"What else did she say? Will she give us back our—property?"

"I'm making progress here. It's gone from 'something' to 'property.'"

Kay forced a smile that vanished immediately. She said, "Did you see anyone else?"

"The maid. She said Shannon Harper used to admire you."

"Yes, she did. I forget about that sometimes." She gazed at the bookshelves.

I said, "Shannon says if you wanna fade away, fine with her, but she's not. What're you fading away from?"

Kay shook her head.

I said, "She says nothing will stop her. Not me, not your threat of sending the videotape to the police. She says if we keep fucking with her—"

She covered Alan's ears with her palms. "Mr. Kruger, I do not appreciate foul language around my son."

"I apologize, but there's things *I* don't appreciate." I leaned forward. "One of those things happened today. Amy sent me into a situation that was a lot more volatile than she led me to believe. Amy made my participation sound pretty harmless. From what she told me I expected Shannon Harper to blow me off, I did not expect her to threaten to blow me away. I don't appreciate that Amy did that. What's the extra four hundred bucks for?"

"We want you—what term do you people use when you follow someone?"

"Us people term it a tail."

"We want you to tail Shannon Harper."

"Why didn't Amy tell me about the tail?"

"We hoped your visit would be enough to persuade Shannon to return our property."

"Baloney. You knew Shannon Harper wasn't going to give anything back just because some skinny PI she didn't know from Adam showed up and told her to. This was a classic bait and hook. You baited me with a hundred bucks to deliver a message you knew would accomplish zilch. But it *would* get me involved. And once I got *involved*, you'd wave more money in front of me to do what you really want done."

Kay Thornberg said nothing.

"Why do I tail her?"

"Couldn't we hire you without you knowing the whys?"

"Not a second time."

"All we want you to do is tell us what she does during the day. Where she goes, who she sees."

"Kay, I know what a tail entails."

She sighed.

"And I could do that. *If* you told me why."

"Do it on faith, Mr. Kruger. Please?" She leaned forward, hands folded tight, knuckles white. "We *need* you. We need your help."

"I do not work on faith, Kay. You just assured me a woman who threatened my life is mentally unbalanced. Now you ask me to get even more involved with her, but wear a blindfold while I do it."

She looked down at Alan's head resting on her lap.

I said, "Follow her yourself."

"Mr. Kruger, you're a professional at this, we're not."

I said, "Last call. Tell me why you want Shannon Harper followed and what this is all about."

"Mr. Kruger, I simply can't do that. Amy and I discussed this when she called. We want you to work for us, we *need* you to, but we just can't explain why. The money's the same whether you know or not. Later, perhaps, we can tell you everything."

"Later, perhaps, I might be in no condition to hear the story or spend the money. I'd like to trade this check for one that says one hundred dollars on it."

Kay Thornberg blew out a lungful of air, looked at me like I had betrayed her, then stood and left the room.

Came back with a check for one hundred dollars.

SIX

At 3:30 P.M., having cashed the check, I parked the Skylark just north of Addison. As I exited, two men got out of a brand new black van parked in front of LeMoyne Elementary School, across and down the street from the apartment. I walked toward my house. The men walked toward me. When I was in front of the house I stopped and watched them approach. When they got to the sidewalk I said, "Me?"

One said, "You Kruger?"

I nodded.

"Then you."

Both were my size, I was happy to see. They wore pastel colored shorts, white knit shirts with poloplayer pocket logos, canvas boat shoes, no socks. One had short blond hair, thinning in front, and a sun-pinked baby face. The one who said, "You Kruger?" was olive-complected with thick features, droopy eyelids, and curly black hair cut in a trim Afro. Dense five o'clock shadow covered his jaws and chin and neck. Coils of hair corkscrewed out of the V-neck of his shirt. He wore red hornrimmed glasses. He came up close to me. The blond man stopped a few feet behind him.

Hairy Man said, "You talked to a friend of ours about an hour ago."

"Doubt it. I haven't been to the Yacht Club in weeks."

He said, "Our friend got to thinking about the conversation. She didn't like what she came up with."

"I'm truly bummed."

"We're here to discuss the situation."

"What situation is that?"

"You and Kay and Amy."

"Goon union got a dress code now?"

He said, "We're no goon squad. We just wanna know how you

tie in with Kay Thornberg and Amy Barrow."

I studied the men's faces. I've stood face to face with hired toughs before and these boys sure didn't fit the stereotype. And it wasn't just their size and the preppie clothes. Your average hired muscle looks about as bright as a dead tree. He's too stupid to do anything but hire out as a thug. The two faces staring at me now showed some intelligence.

And something else. After a second I realized it was the cast in the eyes. They had the same stare Shannon Harper had. That scary focus-detach stare. A stare that fell somewhere between intensity and insanity.

I said, "I got no tie to Amy Barrow and Kay Thornberg."

"You implied otherwise."

"That was then, this is now."

"Meaning?"

"Meaning Amy Barrow hired me to deliver a message to Shannon Harper. I delivered the message, went to Kay Thornberg, got my money. End of story."

"We're thinking maybe that isn't the end of the story."

"I never saw you two bozos before in my life, I'm supposed to care what you think?"

Blond Man stepped forward, pointed a finger at me. Said, "Listen, loser, I don't know who you are, but you ain't nothing to me. You—"

I put my arms out and pretended to shake. I said, "P-p-p-please don't hurt me, Biff."

Hairy Man put his arm across Blond Man's chest, gently pushed him back. He said, "Relax, Boyd, we're here to talk to Mr. Kruger."

"But, Sorrento, she said—"

"*Relax*, Boyd."

Boyd grimaced, but stepped back.

Sorrento said, "We just want you to put our minds at rest, Kruger, that we don't have to worry about you."

"Pal, I think your mind is already at rest, and that's the major problem here."

He blew out some air.

I said, "Shannon worried about that videotape?"

Sorrento turned, looked at Boyd. Boyd made a face, twisted his hands up in a "See?" gesture. Sorrento turned back to me, said, "You seen the tape?"

"Just heard about it."

"Know what's on it?"

"No."

"They tell you what this is about?"

"They didn't tell me Jack. That's why I got no tie to them anymore."

Boyd said, "What if he's lying?"

Sorrento stared at me for ten seconds, trying to read my eyes. I wiggled my brows like Groucho checking out jailbait.

After a bit he said, "Kruger, for your sake you best forget about all this."

"Best I?"

"About Shannon Harper, about the two of us, about this visit. If you've got no idea what this is about, don't find out now. Thornberg and Barrow want any more messages delivered, tell 'em to call Western Union."

"They still in business?"

"If they aren't, tell them to find someone who is."

"Or I'm dead meat, right?"

"I didn't say that."

"Didn't have to. Your boss already did."

"Shannon's not my boss. She's my friend."

"If it waddles like a duck, and quacks like a duck, it's a duck."

Sorrento frowned. "Translate, buddy."

"She sent you here, you came here. Means she's your boss because that's what bosses do. Tell people to do stuff and the people do it. And when a boss sends two guys to spout or-else threats to one guy, it makes the two guys the boss's goon squad. You can deny it all you want, you can dress like preppie pukes, but you're just a couple of punk goons. And your boss can live in a million dollar mansion on the ritziest street in town, but when she threatens people and sends goons out to threaten them once more for good measure, she's just another lowlife slimeball. Tell her I said that."

I love it when goons are the same size as me.

Boyd stepped around Sorrento, grabbed the front of my shirt. Said, "You're the only lowlife slimeball in this scenario and when I get through with you—"

The apartment door flew open. Heather leaped from the porch to the lawn. She had a long knife in her right hand. A long knife with serrated blade. She made a bee line for Boyd who let go of my shirt and stepped back. Way back. Sorrento did too. Heather fluttered the knife two inches from Boyd's belly button. She said, "Keep your fishskin white yuppie hands off him."

Sorrento and Boyd stared at her with a mixture of terror and fascination. Neither said a word, neither breathed.

I said, "Scenario, Boyd?"

He kept his eyes on Heather.

I said, "Guys, consider this a valuable lesson. A good goon dresses the part. It's hard to put the fear of God in people when you look like you're stopping off on your way to a pool party in Winnetka. But shave your head, wear black leather and studs, wave a knife around and people will pay *attention.*"

Boyd made a production of his next swallow. Sorrento looked quickly at me, then at Heather. The knife wasn't staring at his stomach so he said, "Relax burrhead, we just came to talk to the guy."

"And you did that, so get the fuck out," I said. "And tell Shannon Harper two can play this game."

They walked with haste back to the van. As it pulled away Heather said, "What game is that, Dan?"

I said, "I haven't the slightest idea." I smiled. Said, "Fishskin white yuppie hands?"

Heather blushed. "It just came out."

Still smiling, I put my arm around her and we walked inside.

SEVEN

Heather and I sat at the kitchen table, drinking coffee and smoking Kools. I told her how I spent my afternoon. Why Boyd and Sorrento showed up on our front lawn wearing country club duds, pretending to be Elisha Cook, Jr.

I said, "I don't think those two have much experience in that line of work."

Heather kept grinning. "Man, the look on that blond dude's face. I should hire out as a laxative."

"You were the last thing he expected to see charging out the door."

"The girlfriend from hell. Thing is, I really wanted to stick him."

"And he knew it."

"You honestly don't know what goes on?"

"Not a clue. I don't know if I should find out or drop it. Why were you home anyway?"

"I ran into Maria Leary."

I winced. Maria Leary had been Heather's main pill connection.

"Right off she says, 'Heard you got stuck in rehab, wanna cop some bams?'"

"With friends like that."

Heather stubbed her cigarette, nodded.

I said, "What'd you say?"

"Told her no, but I miss it, Dan. I really do. Not the booze, the pills. I got so freaked I had to come home so I could talk to you. I almost called her ten times waiting for you."

"We knew it wouldn't be easy."

"I only went in because of you. To help."

"And you know I appreciate it. I only went in because of Marvin."

"You got to stay high for twenty years before you cleaned up."

"It wasn't always a real fun twenty years, Heather."

"You know what I mean."

I moved the cup in clockwise circles for some seconds, watching drops of spilled coffee change shapes. I said, "Heather, you relapse, it don't change us. You know that. Make it a little rough on me, I see you buzzing around here like a Geiger counter, but I never judged anyone by their lifestyle when I was drunk and I don't plan to start when I'm sober. For one thing, it'd take a whole lot of gall."

"It'd make things difficult for you."

I said, "You never promised me a rose garden." I smiled and batted my eyes.

Heather made a face. She said, "You ever say *that* again I swear I go straight to a pusherman."

"One day at a time," I said. "We'll keep ODing on caffeine and nicotine. Maybe we can fake the body out."

She said, "You really wanna stay clean, don't you?"

"I gotta try it. If life isn't a better deal this way, then fuck it, but I gotta try. Last twenty years I didn't get a damn thing done."

I called Priceman, the bass player for Full Frontal Nudity, the only guy in the band I actually liked. He said we had a gig at the Cubby Bear Lounge next weekend. Nothing till then. He asked did I think I could make a practice the next night? I said he should chill on the sarcasm, but I thought I could.

At 5:00 I sat on the living room couch, Bugs on my lap, a Metallica tape cranked to max on the boom box. Heather rattled pots and pans in the kitchen.

The only problems so far in this relationship had been divvying up kitchen duty and music time. KP was easy. Heather said she'd deal with it so long as she wasn't working. Heather's idea of haute cuisine was opening a can, heating the contents till it bubbled, then dumping it on two plates and yelling, "Soup's on." Which is roughly my idea of haute cuisine, so in that area we were very compatible.

Tunes were another matter. Music played a dominant part in both our lives. Heather was hardcore punk, thrash, and speed-metal. In my dotage, as Heather put it, I favored blues, funk, and roots bands. We agreed to a nightly coin flip to determine who chose tapes. Tonight I lost and now I was listening to what happens when white boys with an attitude get their hands on electric guitars, stacks of Marshalls, and lots of speed. But at least I wasn't living with a Top 40 fan. Metallic sure as hell cut Michael Bolton or Wilson Phillips.

I guess part of me will always be seventeen, saying "Fuck you, world."

I massaged behind Bugs's ears and said, "What would you do, wabbit? Check into this mess or forget it? Remember, I got offered five hundred clams and we aren't lighting Kools with dollar bills around here. I get very negative vibes from Shannon and Boyd and Sorrento. Those three have the same eyes you see on religious fanatics. Or presidential candidates. I worry when people with that look start spouting phrases like 'nothing will stop me, if you try you're dead meat.' And there's plenty I'd like to know about Amy Barrow and Kay Thornberg. What's the connection, Bugs? Why were they such good friends with Shannon? Why aren't they now? What's Shannon got that's theirs? That they *say* is theirs? What's on the videotape? What's Shannon Harper doing that Amy and Kay quit doing? Why'd she send the yuppie goons after me?" I put my hand under Bugs's stomach, lifted and turned him so our noses touched. I said, "Bugs, what's the meaning of life?"

Bugs twitched his nose.

I cocked my head. "Bunny chow? And what's that? You say that by asking myself this barrage of questions, I'll only pique my curiosity to the point where I *have* to check into it? Bugs, you know me too well."

The decision got made thirty minutes later when Kay Thornberg called, interrupting a gourmet meal of Dinty Moore stew, Wonder Bread, and Diet Pepsi.

Her voice was panicky, close to hysterical. She said, "Mr. Kruger, I have to talk to you. Immediately." Alan cried his head off in the background.

"I told you I wanted no part of this, Kay."

"Mr. Kruger, a brick just shattered my living room window."

Her voice rose. "A brick! Alan was playing on the living room floor. It missed him by inches."

I said, "It could've been random." Knowing it wasn't.

"A note was tied to the brick."

"Read me the note."

"It says 'You three are dead if you speak a word.'"

"You call the police?"

"I'm going to, but I can't mention the note."

I said, "Note doesn't say who the three are?"

She said, "Probably me, Amy, and Alan."

"Come on, Alan can't tell anybody anything." I said, "Dammit, you know they mean me. I come over this time, you're gonna have to talk."

No answer.

I said, "No talk, no visit."

I started to count silently. I was at twelve when she said, "I'll talk."

EIGHT

At 6:00 P.M. I parked the Skylark on Willow Street, walked to Kay and Amy's house. Two double-parked blue-and-whites and a small crowd of curious neighbors were out front.

Kay answered the door. She held Alan tight to her chest like he'd shatter if she dropped him. Three cops stood in the living room, looking at the sparkly shards of glass on the sofa and rug. One held the brick like it was a loaf of bread, tapping it against his thigh. They were telling Kay what a shame it was, vandalism in nice neighborhoods in broad daylight. They told her who to call to get the window boarded and left.

She left the room with Alan, came back with two pairs of gloves, a broom, a large black Hefty bag. Together we cleaned away the glass while Alan watched from a playpen. She vacuumed, I sat on the couch.

When she was done I said, "You didn't mention the note to the cops?"

"Amy agreed we shouldn't," she said, like that ended any discussion on the matter.

"You talked to Amy?"

"It's why I called you. She said to." Kay sat in a chair in front of the bookshelves with Alan once more in her lap. Her legs jiggled from delayed fear. "Amy wanted to leave Mercy Mothers, come here."

"You said?"

"I wouldn't hear of it. No matter what happens here, Amy has got to be cured once and for all. She's had a serious problem the last year and a half."

"She said it was a postpartum thing."

"It's more than that. That was just the trigger. Amy's family has a history of two things—depression and alcoholism. Her parents were reactionary Christians, both alcoholics who died before they were forty. Mean, extremist type people—especially her father. She had a miserable childhood and a worse marriage.

"Her husband was the typical hard drinking, a-woman-is-good-for-only-two things type. Consequently she drank all through her teen years and all through her marriage. She got straightened out about the time we met and she let her real self come out. She wouldn't admit it, but I think all along she's felt tremendous guilt about being lesbian because of what she was taught as a child. She'd have these horrible spells of depression. When the depression hit after Alan was born, it was so major she couldn't deal with it. She did get some counseling, but she also started drinking. Just a little at first. A couple of glasses of wine at night. That helped, but within six months she was drinking a bottle of gin a day. Did it for a year. She kept saying she could quit on her own, she did it before. Eventually I had to threaten to kick her out of the house to get her to go for help."

I said, "I hit bottom too."

"Nothing to be ashamed of. Nobody slides through life without ordeals."

I said, "Sending me to Shannon Harper backfired bigtime. All it did was freak her out."

Kay pressed her lips together.

I said, "Long as it was just you two bugging her about getting your property back she shrugged it off, but when you hired me she started thinking you really might go to the police."

She kissed Alan's cheek, said, "Yes." She caressed his head, murmured in his ear. She said, "The brick came so close to him." Hysteria crept into her voice again.

"But it *missed*, Kay."

She took a deep breath, held it for some seconds, let it out slowly. Said, "Yes, it missed. Mr. Kruger, Amy assures me you march to a different drummer. She says you do not perceive the world in conventional black-and-white terms. She says we can trust you."

I said, "I appreciate gray. I appreciate lavender. I appreciate oddballs, misfits, loners, anybody who gets pushed aside or around by somebody bigger or richer. I not only appreciate, I empathize, and when I can I help. I evaluate everything in life case by case and I never apply hard, fast rules."

"Most people consider us lunatics."

"Immoral maybe, not lunatics."

"I'm talking about something besides sexual orientation."

"I hope so."

"Amy also said if telling you is the only way you'll work for us, then we have to tell you. I must admit I'm not entirely convinced, but we have nowhere else to turn. I've lost one, I can't bear the thought of something happening to Alan."

"What did you lose, Kay?"

"Mr. Kruger, I'm going to tell you things nobody knows. You have to promise me you'll reveal nothing of what I'm about to tell you."

"We talking crimes here?"

"Some would call them that. I don't."

"I'm not a priest, Kay. PIs aren't bound by an oath of confidentiality."

"You have to promise before I'll talk."

"I won't promise if it involves murder."

"No harm was done to any person."

"Then I promise. What does Shannon have that's yours?"

"In a minute, Mr. Kruger. I need to explain some things."

"You can start by telling me what's on the videotape."

"Shannon Harper engaging in criminal activity."

I nodded.

Kay said, "But if we turn the tape in, there's the possibility she could incriminate Amy and myself. Turning the tape in was only a threat. A last gasp, born of desperation. I couldn't think of what else to do, to say to her."

"Kay, never make a threat unless you're prepared to go through with it."

"I'm not very experienced at things like this."

"Obviously."

"Mr. Kruger, what do you know about the animal rights movement?"

"Nothing."

"Amy and I have been active in animal rights for years. It's how we met. After we became a couple we joined several groups. They all served good purposes, but none was as aggressive as we wanted. So two years ago we organized our own group. Animal Sanctuary. Shannon Harper joined Animal Sanctuary a year and a half ago."

"What was the purpose of Animal Sanctuary?"

"We picketed fur salons on Michigan Avenue, we marched out front of the research labs at Northwestern University. We sent protest petitions to other research labs, organized boycotts, raised funds for AR groups. As we became more knowledgeable, we became more aggressive. Last winter and spring we conducted three raids on laboratories that experiment on animals."

"Raids?"

"Modeled after military commando strikes. We entered the labs, liberated the animals, destroyed the torture machines."

"You broke and entered, you committed grand larceny, you vandalized and destroyed personal and or public property."

Kay smiled tolerantly, like I was a child announcing I'd just discovered how to make bubbles in the bathtub. "Mr. Kruger, I don't care one iota what other people think about this. I don't care what society's opinion is of me. Animals have the same rights as humans do when it comes to decent food, adequate shelter, and unnecessary pain. Someone has to maintain those rights. Someone has to speak for animals, someone has to act for them. The purpose of this conversation is not to secure your approval. I couldn't care less what you or anyone else thinks."

I said, "I get the point. Tell me about the tape."

Kay put her hand up. "In a minute, Mr. Kruger. Our first raid was unsuccessful. We got inside the building, but not inside the lab. We later learned the university we raided had just spent one hundred thousand dollars to upgrade their security against groups such as ours. On February seventeenth we conducted a second raid. It was a success. We liberated twenty rabbits and scores of mice and rats and gerbils from the Harper Cosmetics research lab north of Milwaukee. We destroyed research data and lab equipment. The animals were taken to a farm owned by a sympathizer where they'll be able to finish their lives with dignity. Amy recorded the raid with a camcorder."

"Harper Cosmetics?"

"Yes, you see what Shannon has at stake?"

"Why would she go along?"

"It was her idea. She led the raid."

"Why did Amy tape it? Why tape yourselves committing a crime?"

"Everyone wore disguises of course. And we wanted to document the torture going on. Also, it was for my benefit. I didn't actually participate in the raids."

"Why not?"

"There are reasons we won't go into now. I plan, I research, I communicate with other animal right's groups around the country."

"What other groups?"

"The two best known are Band of Mercy and the Animal Liberation Front. They've been active since the early eighties. I've learned so much from them."

I said, "This is like the ultra-violent radical left in the sixties, right? Underground network type thing."

"Kind of, yes. I planned the raids utilizing tactics I picked up from the other groups. Shannon led the commando unit. Amy and three men comprised the rest of it."

"The Amy I knew in rehab was as meek as a mouse. It's hard to picture her involved in this."

"There's another side to Amy. Especially the Amy who drank."

"No doubt."

"At one point at Harper Cosmetics, Shannon became so enraged at what she saw, she removed her mask and made a speech directly into the camera denouncing her family, in particular her father, swearing vengeance. But next day she had second thoughts and asked us for the tape."

"You give it to her?"

"No. We convinced her we could never use it to harm her because it would harm us too. She saw the sense in that. But things have changed."

"One hundred eighty degrees, I'd say."

"By editing that tape we could send the incriminating clip to her family and the police."

"And she'd risk disinheritance *and* jail."

"That's right."

"But she'd say you and Amy planned the raid and Amy participated in it."

"I told you my threat was from desperation. I couldn't think of anything else to do. That tape is all I had to bargain with." I started to talk, but Kay said, "Wait, there's more. Amy and I preached liberation of research animals and destruction of torture chambers. Are you familiar with Jeremy Bentham, the eighteenth-century philosopher?"

"Wouldn't you know? The one eighteenth-century philosopher I'm not familiar with."

"His famous quote is 'The question is not, can they reason? nor can they talk? but, can they suffer?' Think about that, Mr. Kruger. That was our guiding philosophy. But we never wanted human animals injured or maimed or killed. Violence toward people does not help animals. Amy and I stressed that constantly."

"A good thing to stress."

"Our third raid was also a success. A biology lab at Dickson University. A research student was in the lab. It was two A.M., he shouldn't have been there."

"*He* shouldn't have been there?"

"He was conducting a test called LD 50 for another cosmetic

firm. Not Harper. Have you ever heard of the LD 50?"

I shook my head.

"It's a toxic test. LD stands for Lethal Dose. Say a new color dye or chemical is developed that could be used in lipstick or mascara. To ascertain it's toxicity a group of experimental animals is gathered. The poisonous substance is then introduced into their eyes or onto their shaved skin or force fed into their mouths. Dripped onto them from tubes. The animals, rabbits or rats usually, but sometimes mammals, are placed in boxes from which only their heads protrude. They cannot move. If the chemical is being tested on their eyes their eyes are kept open by metal clips. They cannot blink. They do squeal, Mr. Kruger. And when an animal squeals, it means it is suffering. Just like when a human squeals. The fifty stands for fifty percent. The entire point of the LD 50 is to learn what amount of the substance will kill fifty percent of the animals. When fifty percent have died the test is stopped. Of course the remaining fifty percent are sick and will eventually die too. This is done so a woman may safely wear *lipstick*. Living, feeling creatures are tortured to death for *lipstick*, Mr. Kruger."

No fear showed in her face now, only rage.

I said, "The man in the lab?"

She took another deep breath, hugged Alan tighter. "Yes, we caught a student making notes about an LD 50 experiment. How can a man dispassionately take notes about suffering?" Kay shook her head, was quiet for a few seconds. She said, "Some in the group wanted to tie him to a chair, clamp his eye open with the chemical dripping into it. Leave him there till he was discovered. Amy persuaded them not to. They freed the animals, destroyed as much of the lab as they could, tied the man to a chair, gagged him and left."

"How's this tie in with Shannon Harper and the rest of it?"

"Shannon was the person who argued hardest to torture the human animal. Emotionally I sympathize. A life form is a life form. I understand where she's coming from, but intellectually I cannot endorse it. I cannot condone it. If we did things like that, we'd be as evil as they are. Shannon became increasingly radicalized on this issue. Maybe in part by the guilt she feels being a Harper. Most cosmetic firms have curtailed their animal research and almost all have discontinued duplicate testing, but Harper and a couple of others refuse to even discuss the matter. Shannon now advocates much more than liberating the animals and destroying the instruments of torture. She no longer wants to just save animals."

"What's she want now?"

"She wants to avenge them. She wants to retaliate."

"Meaning?"

"That's the question. Because of Shannon a rift had been growing in Animal Sanctuary for some time. Six weeks ago, two weeks after the Dickson raid, Amy and I were told Animal Sanctuary was no longer our group. Shannon claims it's her group now, that the rest of AS agrees with her. Amy and I are no longer welcome members because we're not hard core enough. I'm not sure what her plans are. Judging by things she's said, I wouldn't put murder past her."

"Who would she murder?"

"Anyone making animals suffer. She's become so radical I honestly believe nobody is safe from her. Not just people engaged in medical and cosmetic research, but heads of veterinary schools, hunters, even farmers or fur owners. Butchers for all I know. She draws no line."

"Veterinary schools?"

"They use live animals from city pounds to teach surgical techniques."

"In other words, she co-opted your group and took it to the lunatic fringe?"

"Yes. I have to admit she has persuasive leadership qualities. I was a professor at Roosevelt University. I talked to students for a living. But that's what I did. *Talked.* Shannon radiates a kind of zeal when she speaks. Plus, I can't prove it, but I'm certain she's seduced some members."

"Sex?"

"Yes, she has a sexual hold over them."

"The men?"

"Perhaps the women too. The strange thing is I don't think she *likes* people. She uses them physically. She has a kind of contempt for the human race. Maybe because she finds it so easy to get them to do whatever she wants."

"I still think you should go to the police."

"Oaths have been taken, Mr. Kruger. Vows. You can't possibly understand the secrecy and loyalty, the *commitment* to one another a group like this needs. It would be like turning in family. Some are members of the gay community. Friends of mine for twenty years who because of Amy and me became interested in the movement and eventually chose to help. I must protect them. I *will not* inform on them. Or on myself and Amy, because that's what would ultimately happen. Besides, Shannon hasn't done anything yet."

"Sounds like it's only a matter of time."

Kay nodded.

I said, "How many people were in Animal Sanctuary?"

"Eight."

"How many follow Shannon Harper?"

"I don't know. Four won't speak to me anymore, so those I'm sure of."

I said, "Sorrento and Boyd talk to you?"

Her eyes narrowed. "Sorrento Gallo and Boyd Fuller. How do you know those names?"

"Shannon sent them to talk to me this afternoon. They told me to stay away from you. Boyd wanted to get tough about it, although it's hard for me to believe he knows how. I assume the brick was from them."

Kay said, "Boyd, I was sure of. Sorrento swore to me just last week he thought Shannon was going too far. But he introduced Shannon to AS and he's infatuated with her, so I'm not shocked. You see, Mr. Kruger, it's easy to become impassioned on this subject. If you could witness the things we've seen. And Shannon is so intense, so *into* anything she believes in. People follow her because she makes them feel the same way. They feel *alive!* Like they're involved in a great and noble cause. Which they would be if only they'd respect the sanctity of life in all its forms."

"We're talking zealots here."

Kay made a perturbed face. She said, "Will you follow Shannon? We need to know what she plans to do. Like I said earlier, we need your help. Desperately."

"What's the point? I can't bring your group back."

She didn't talk for almost a minute, then she said, "This is so hard for me to say. Mr. Kruger, I want my daughter back and I think she's with Shannon."

"You think or you know?"

"I'm almost positive."

"Your daughter's name?"

"Tricia Lynn. She's only sixteen. She worships Shannon Harper. Or maybe more than that."

"More?"

Kay said, "She might be in love with her. At the very least she admires her fiercely. She left two weeks ago. I'm certain she's with Shannon and I've called there scores of times. Shannon won't talk to me of course, she keeps having the maid tell me she hasn't seen her, but I'm sure she's there. I need you to find out for sure and bring her back."

I digested this development.

Kay said, "I encouraged Tricia's interest in causes. Most sixteen-year-old girls care only about boys or clothes. But Tricia's been active in causes since she was old enough to understand evil and injustice. And she loves animals so much. Animal Sanctuary was very important to her. That's another reason I'm so sure she's with Shannon."

"Did she participate in the raids?"

"Of course not."

"Did she know about them?"

Kay hesitated, then said, "Yes."

"When did you notice her growing so close to Shannon?"

"Over the last year or so she started to withdraw from me. Became rebellious, sullen, uncommunicative. All I got from her was anger and hostility. The last few months before she took the group away, Shannon was increasingly vocal and angry. Tricia responded to that, being in an angry and hostile mood too. She paid too much attention to her. She'd sit at her feet at meetings. Talked about her constantly. With Amy anyway. She almost totally stopped speaking to me. But I never thought—this. It's embarrassing to admit I lost my own daughter."

"Happens in lots of families. And nobody can ever figure out why it happens to them. You two were close before a year ago?"

"Yes."

"The way she acted the last year. It have anything to do with you and Amy?"

"Our being gay?"

I nodded. "She's becoming sexually aware."

"Mr. Kruger, all teenagers rebel to a certain degree. Would you ask that question of a heterosexual parent?"

"Not in so many words, but I always try to find out why a good parent-child relationship falls apart. Sometimes you gotta ask questions that hurt a little."

"If she's having problems as a teen adjusting to life and she uses that as an excuse, she's copping out."

"She doing drugs?"

"I don't think so."

"She know her father? She in contact with him?"

"No."

"Are you?"

"No. Last I heard he was in California. Mr. Kruger, I can't say for sure what caused it. Maybe she just fell under Shannon's spell."

"What do you want me to do?"

"Bring her back. I don't want any harm to come to Tricia."

I leaned back, took a deep breath, locked my fingers behind my neck.

She said, "Now you know why I can't have the police involved. It's not just intimate friends, comrades. It's my daughter. If they're planning radical activity—felonies, Tricia could end up in prison."

I said, "The fact you have a daughter confuses me."

She said, "In my twenties I was person attracted. Bisexual, you would call it. As I got older, I became exclusively gender attracted. Lesbian."

"Why didn't you or Amy mention Tricia right off? Why'd I get sent after 'something' and 'property'?"

"We didn't know how much to tell you. Can't you appreciate the position we're in? You're an outsider. I didn't know if we could trust you. I was afraid if you found these things out and Shannon did something, you'd go straight to the police and Tricia would be arrested with the rest. I'm still not one hundred percent sure about you, but I'm desperate and I'm scared and Amy trusts you. I want Tricia back. I want to build a relationship with her again. I don't want her involved in crimes." She sniffled. Alan brushed at her tears with his tiny fingers.

I said, "She's not being held against her will."

"Mr. Kruger, she just turned *sixteen*. If Shannon told her to come home, she would." Kay's voice got quieter. "I also hoped if Tricia learned I was so concerned I sent a private detective to talk to Shannon, she'd return on her own. Doesn't look like that'll happen."

"You realize you and Amy didn't exactly set a perfect example for her when it came to respect for the law."

Wearily, she said, "I'm not going to argue with you, Mr. Kruger. In my eyes what we did was not a crime. What Shannon plans probably will be."

"What if we all got to decide what is or isn't a crime?"

Pretty high road talk for a two decade drug user, but I've always been a do-as-I-say-not-as-I-do kind of guy.

"I told you, I will not argue this."

I looked at her for a long time. I said, "Give me a check for four hundred bucks. Also some photos of Tricia. And the addresses of Sorrento Gallo and Boyd Fuller." I said, "You wanna stay at my place for now?"

"No. Why would I?"

I jerked my thumb at the shattered window behind me.

Kay said, "That was a warning, that's all. What we did backfired and Shannon wants us to know it. If you talk to Shannon again tell her I'll never go to the police. I was scared and confused. I said I'd do something I regret. I just want Tricia back."

NINE

That night at 3:00 A.M. I woke up covered with sweat. I crawled to the end of the bed, switched the fan from low to high, sat in front of it. The sweat evaporated and I started to shiver.

I'd dreamt Bugs was inside a box with his head sticking out, eyes clamped open, poison dripping in. He made little whimper sounds.

I got up, fetched Bugs from his cage and brought him to bed. I spent the next three hours petting my sleeping rabbit, thinking about what Kay Thornberg had told me, and wondering how in hell I was going to get her daughter back.

At 6:00 A.M. I silently pulled on jeans, an oversize black tank top, and hightop Nikes. I lightly kissed Heather and Bugs good-bye. They slept like babes.

At 6:30 A.M. of what promised to be another smothery, sun-baked day, armed with a pack of Kools and giant-size container of 7-Eleven coffee, I parked the Skylark down the street from a two-story narrow brick row house on Cleveland Avenue. Like Kay and Amy's house, it was in the middle of a tree-shaded block of identical houses. It had bright white trim, a high stoop and tall front door, bay windows on both floors. A nice house in a nice neighborhood. Sorrento Gallo and Boyd Fuller lived there. The black van was parked in front of the nice house.

While lying awake I had devised a strategy. Given my druthers I'd stake out the mansion, but I had a better chance of passing for African-American than of passing unnoticed if I loitered for any length of time on Astor Street. And Kay knew nothing about Shannon's daily routine, so I couldn't wait elsewhere and pick her up.

Which meant my only chance was to hope Sorrento Gallo and Boyd Fuller would lead me to her. And Tricia.

Around 7:30 A.M. young men and women dressed for success

started to pour from the houses on Cleveland Avenue. They hurried to Civics and Corrolas and Escorts. All carried briefcases and mugs of coffee. Folded *Tribunes* and *Wall Street Journals* were pressed under their armpits. The looks I received ranged from curious to decidedly hostile. A fifteen-year-old olive green Skylark with rust sidepanels and more dings than a demolition derby beater tends to stick out in neighborhoods like this. Especially when a sun-glassed longhair sits behind the wheel. I made a show of raising my arm like I was checking a watch, made impatient faces. Some fool on this block was gonna catch twenty kinds of hell for making me wait like this.

By 8:30 A.M. the last of the upwardly mobile folk had left for work but the van was still there. I removed the five photos of Tricia Thornberg from the envelope on the seat next to me. Looked them over for the umpteenth time.

Tricia was a pretty girl, was going to be prettier. Auburn hair like her mother's with a blond tint, worn long and thick and wavy and moussed to a moist shine. Freckled pug nose. Skinny as a rake. Braces.

And zero self-esteem. In every photo she slouched and wore a distracted, hangdog expression. In none of the photos did she look directly into the camera. Her face seemed to say, "Why would anybody want a picture of me?" Just the kind of person who'd religiously follow anyone who showed her some attention, told her she was somebody. I put the photos back in the envelope.

At 9:30 I started wondering what kind of hours animal rights people kept. My 7-Eleven coffee container had become my pit stop, only four Kools remained in the pack on the dashboard. I started thinking of alternate options.

And came up with none, so I was extremely happy to see Sorrento Gallo and Boyd Fuller tromp down the stairs at ten minutes to ten. Gallo wore a pair of madras print knee-length shorts and a white tank top. Fuller wore green and blue striped shorts and a Hard Rock Cafe T-shirt. Both wore scrunched down white boot socks and black canvas hightop basketball shoes. Their faces were stern. Maybe it was the early hour.

They went north. I followed. They turned east on Belden, south on Clark. Stayed on Clark until they hit North Avenue in front of the Historical Museum. They blinked to turn left. We were five blocks from Astor. I assumed that's where they were headed and I tried to decide what streets I could duck down and over so as to stay out of sight, but not lose them. But then the van swerved to the curb just before Dearborn Street, three blocks shy of Astor. I stopped at the entrance to a service alley, flicked on the distress blinkers, waved cars around. Some schmuck had the nerve to call me an asshole when he went past.

Shannon Harper and two men, one tall and dark with a short ponytail, the other short and wide with brown hair, stood against the wall of a building that had a tan stone bottom floor and red brick upper stories. A sign standing where the two sidewalks met said "The Parkway, a Residence for Career Women."

Four black suitcases stood in front of the three of them. The men lifted the suitcases, one in each hand, and the three people walked fast to the van. The men grimaced from strain. Shannon slid the side door of the van open. The men heaved the suitcases in one at a time, both men lifting and chucking, and then the three people scampered inside.

The van pulled from the curb. So did I.

They went north on Lake Shore Drive. It was a nice morning for a ride on the Drive. Rush hour was over and traffic was light. White flares of sun shimmered on the lake, scores of brightly painted sailboats bobbed in Montrose Harbor, neon-colored bikinis and tan skin covered the beaches.

But I doubted animal rights fanatics appreciated beautiful scenery. From what I'd learned so far these people were as drunk as I used to be, their perception of life as fogged as mine had been. I never appreciated things like bobbing sailboats or sunshine on wavy water or girls in bikinis when my mind was consumed with the single passion of staying high.

Well, maybe girls in bikinis.

The Outer Drive ended. They took the turn at Hollywood and continued up Sheridan Road past apartment buildings and blocks of small businesses. Just before we entered Evanston they made more turns and ended up on a drab residential street named Cyprus.

The van stopped in front of a six-story brick apartment building constructed around a court. Courtyard apartment buildings must have been the highrise condo's of the 1920's. They're all over the North Side. I kept going, pulled to the curb a few hundred feet ahead, tilted the rearview to look back.

The five people exited the van. Each man lugged one suitcase. They used both hands and listed to the side the suitcase was on. They took awkward, tiny steps, like Chinese women with bound feet.

I hurried to the apartment building. Peeked around the corner of the west wing. Watched the last of the group, Sorrento Gallo, enter the building.

I counted to thirty, walked to the door. The courtyard grass was ankle deep and the garden on both sides of the entrance looked like untouched prairie. The smell of dry earth and sweet flowers was heavy.

The building had a buzz-in security system. I made fans of both hands and pressed every button on the wall. In seconds a chorus of "Who is it?" and "Who's there?" and "Yes?" came out of the tiny speaker above the buttons. I said, "It's me," and there was a cascade of raspy buzzes. You'd think Chicagoans would be more security conscious but it works most every time.

In the entryway an elevator was on the left, a plaster-walled stairwell with threadbare gray carpet on the right. I took the stairs two at a time. At each floor I hustled the twenty feet from the stairs to where the hallway started, looked left, then right.

I heard them on the fourth floor. I walked quickly to the hall, stuck my head around the corner. The five people stood in front of the last door before the hall turned into the right wing. Shannon Harper inserted a key into the lock.

I went back to the Skylark, lit my last Kool and waited.

And waited some more. By noon I was suffering severe nicotine withdrawal. A corner grocery store sat a block ahead, but I didn't dare leave for smokes. When I came back I'd know if the van was gone, but I wouldn't know if all five people were. So I suffered and swore. Felt sweat flood my armpits and ribs. Listened to beetles drone loud then soft all around me.

At twelve-thirty the five people climbed into the van and left. I whispered, "About fucking time."

I beelined to the store, purchased a carton of Kools and a can of Pepsi. I inhaled half a cigarette, drained the pop before I stepped away from the cash register. The obese Mexican woman behind the counter smiled and said, "It ees soo hot, no?" Hard to argue with the obvious, so I smiled back.

I got past the security door of the apartment the same way I had earlier, although this time I made sure not to press any numbers starting with four.

I expected a deadbolt but there was only a standard key lock under the doorknob. I own a decent collection of passkeys. The third one I slipped in snapped the lock open.

The apartment was a far cry from a mansion on Astor Street. Or even a row house on Cleveland Avenue. Hell, it was a puny whisper from my crib on Freemont.

The room I stepped into was littered with old newspapers and torn-up cardboard boxes. There was no furniture. It smelled like overripe garbage and cat piss. Along the left wall of the room were four rolled-up sleeping bags. Stacked next to the sleeping bags were four inflated ribbed mattresses, the kind you use as floats in a swimming pool. An orange and white kitten sidled up to me, rubbed against my leg. I kneeled and scratched behind its ears. The kitten purred and flopped on its side.

I stood and went to the wood-framed window that overlooked the courtyard. A mottled gray film covered the glass, filtering the sunlight, making it seem like late afternoon. I looked back at the room. On every wall waterstains made spidery brown designs on faded rose print wallpaper.

To the right of the first room was a kitchen and off it a tiny bathroom. Rust blotches the size of dishcloths stained the basin of the kitchen and bathroom sinks. The inside of the toilet bowl had thick lines of burnt orange. You couldn't have paid me to get into the bathtub naked.

The suitcases, along with four others, were in a second room, slightly smaller, left of the main room. Seven suitcases were locked, one wasn't.

Inside the unlocked one were packages of night-bright flares, two heavy duty wire cutters, thick rolls of heavy strength cord, a five-way fluorescent flashlight, and two kerosene powered camping lamps. Also a square metal padlocked box. I lifted the box with both hands, could barely raise it from the bottom shells of the suitcase. No wonder the men looked like they were giving themselves hernias carrying these things.

On the wall above the suitcases FRIENDS OF THE WILD was spray painted in red. In green paint below that, along the entire length of the wall, was written EQUAL RIGHTS, EQUAL TREATMENT, EQUAL CONSIDERATION, EQUAL PUNISHMENT.

The kitten had followed me through the apartment. It rubbed against my leg again, squeaked a meow.

I said, "Yeah, puss, I'm not so sure I wanna know what it means either."

TEN

Before I left I checked closets, cupboards, the fridge. Nada. No clothes, no blankets, no towels, no dishes, no food except a rolled up half-empty bag of Meow Mix under the sink. I poured some of that into a plastic bowl on the floor by the refrigerator.

I left the apartment and knocked on the door of the adjoining unit. A tall black man wearing baggy white terry cloth shorts and mirror sunglasses opened the door. He had a washboard stomach, long, clean-sculpted arms, and shoulder-length dreadlocks thick as hawser ropes. The smell of pot and the sound of reggae danced out the door.

I said, "My name's Kruger." I handed him a card. "Mind if we chat a minute?"

The man shrugged, didn't look at the card. He said, "That depend, mon."

I said, "You know the people next door?"

He glanced in the direction of the door, back at me, said, "What if I do, mon?"

"Seen a teenage girl with them? Skinny, reddish-brown hair, braces."

"What you want wit dis girl? You a pervert?"

"Not since the electro-shock. Just wanna talk to her."

"I not fix to inform on me neighbors. I maintain cordial relations with all me associates."

I said, "I'm not a cop. Nobody's gonna end up in jail."

The man laughed, showing large white teeth. He said, "I hip to that."

"The girl's underage. Her mother would just as soon she didn't run with this crowd."

"Her mother should say, 'Come home, girl, and stay home.'"

"It's not that easy."

"Life never be easy. But like I say, I don't fix to inform."

"But you have seen her?"

"What I just say, mon?"

"I'd hate to do it, but let's say I told the police I know she'll show here, have 'em stake the place out. Long as they were hanging around they might be interested in a drug bust if all they had to do was step next door. You know, two birds with one stone."

The man slid the sunglasses down his nose, looked me in the eye. Said, "You a asshole, mon, you know that?" He pushed the shades back up.

"You're the second man today come to that conclusion."

"What you fix to learn? I not knowing such about these new next door people. They only been here two weeks. See dem in the hall sometimes."

"How many people've you seen?"

The man thought again. Shrugged. "Don't know. Sometimes four show, sometimes more."

"The girl I described one of 'em?"

He nodded.

"You talk to them?"

"I say, 'Hello, neighbors.' I say that to everybody."

"Didn't say it to me."

"You not a neighbor. You a asshole."

"They answer when you greet them?"

"My neighbors? Sure, they reply 'hi—'"

"The new next door people?"

"They smile, but don't say nothing. Except the one woman."

I described Shannon Harper. Said, "She the one who talks?"

He smiled. "The long freckled thing? Sure. She talk fine. She and the schoolgirl you want? Thought dey be mother and daughter, but you claim this not be the case."

"Those two women, they the only women you see?"

He shook his head. "Two others. Not as fine as Miss Freckles and the schoolgirl. One short, one tall. They wear flannel shirts even when it's hot, frowning faces, man short hair. I'm thinking dey don't appreciate the menfolk, dem wimmen."

"How many men you seen?"

He thought for a bit. "I'm thinking four."

"Eight people all together?"

"If four put with four makes eight, and I think it do, then I see eight."

"They stay here at night?"

He shook his head. "Nobody be complaining when I crank the high explosion."

"The high explosion?"

"A spliff, man, and the tunes, you know, they got to be loud. My box be next to their wall. But only at night. High explosion no good in the day."

"You talk to your other neighbors?"

"Of course, mon, I tell you, I say hi to everybody."

"Except assholes."

He grinned.

"Heard any gossip about the new next door people from your other neighbors?"

"Nope."

"You ever wonder why eight people go in and out of a one bedroom apartment and none of them sleeps there?"

"I don't wonder about nothin', mon. I take everything as it comes. My neighbors do what they want, I do the same. Now, asshole, I think I talk about enough to keep your big mouth shut about drug busts. Peace." He made the sign and closed the door.

I left the building. Called Kay Thornberg from a pay phone outside the Mexican woman's grocery store.

I said, "Here's what I know so far. Like you suspected, Tricia is with Shannon. So are at least six other people. With Amy out and Tricia in, we'll assume all of Animal Sanctuary follows Shannon."

"You've seen Tricia?"

"No, but I talked to someone who has. And he saw her with Shannon."

"Is she okay?"

"She's okay." I hoped. I said, "They call themselves Friends of the Wild now."

"How do you know that?"

"They've rented a dumpy apartment up by Evanston and that's spray painted on one of the walls. Just below something about equal rights—"

Kay cut in, "Equal treatment, equal consideration. It's a slogan of the movement."

"Well, these guys've added equal punishment to the slogan."

Kay said, "Oh, God. See? I told you that's what she was up to. Mr. Kruger, you've *got* to get Tricia back."

"It's not gonna be a picnic getting next to Tricia if she's running with seven fanatics."

"Why did they rent the apartment?"

I had my suspicions, but I didn't need to get Kay any more worried than she already was, so I said, "I'm not sure. We'll find out as time goes by."

Kay's breathing got shorter and faster.

I said, "I'll be over this afternoon. I wanna see photos. All you've got of these people. I want addresses and phone numbers."

This time she said okay before I started counting.

ELEVEN

I drove south on the Drive, shades on, windows down, smelling the heat and exhaust and the tang from the lake, looking at the tall buildings up ahead that seemed to rise out of hot, wavy air.

I hadn't wanted to tell Kay what I though about the apartment because the place resembled a Mafia mattress factory. A hideout used when heavy shit like gang wars came down and the wiseguys didn't want to have to worry about getting whacked coming out of their own homes. My initial hunch was Friends of the Wild was up to something so heavy they needed a hideout. The sleeping bags and mattresses and suitcases supported that hunch. But why no food or supplies? I hadn't even seen a roll of toilet paper.

And why hide out in a multi-unit apartment building? Lots of nosy neighbors to notice your eight people traipsing in and out. Not everybody on that floor would be as laissez faire about eight scowling new tenants as the Rasta Kid. It'd make more sense to rent a house or the bottom floor of a two-flat with an alley behind it so people could come and go front and back to dilute attention.

Before going to Kay's I decided to make a quick cruise of Astor, see if the black van was there.

I did Astor, then the rest of the Gold Coast. Lake Shore, Burton, Schiller, Ritchie, Goethe, North State Parkway. I passed more mansions of red brick and greystone, more towering glass and metal highrises, more townhouses with ornate trim and ivy-covered walls, some posher than posh hotels. And the archbishop's mansion. The one on State and North that has nineteen chimneys. Or is it twenty-nine? I know there's a nine at the end, but I can't remember the first number and I'll be damned if I'll waste my time counting them.

I saw lots of people, places, and things, but no black van containing off-the-wall animal lovers.

I got back on Astor. Half a block north of the Harper mansion I spotted Lucy Miranda up ahead, walking three white poodles on the sidewalk. When I stopped even with her I saw that even though this woman was dressed in a maid's outfit like Lucy's and strongly resembled Lucy, it wasn't Lucy. But I wouldn't want her to take me for a perv so I said, "I'm sorry, I only stopped because you look like someone I know."

The woman who was a little heavier than Lucy and a little older smiled and said, "Lucy Miranda?"

"That's right."

She pulled the dogs to a halt. "People on this block always confused us. Her and I would talk on the sidewalk and people would ask us if we were twins. Even in Logan Square people think we are."

"You live by her?"

"A block away. I work at the Jefferson place across the street from the Harpers'. I got her the job there. I regret it. The Jeffersons are wonderful people to work for, Shannon Harper was—" Her voice floated away.

I said, "You don't have to explain anything to me about Shannon Harper. If you'd been Lucy I was gonna talk to her."

"You won't talk to her here no more."

My stomach sank.

The woman said, "She got fired yesterday."

I muttered, "Damn!" Said, "Was she told why?"

"Miss Harper said she was unhappy with her performance. Didn't need her anymore."

I really wanted to talk to Lucy Miranda now. I said, "Give me her address?"

The woman wasn't so sure she should.

I said, "I need to talk to her. And I'm not gonna hurt her in your neighborhood. Hell, I'm the one might get hurt."

She thought for some seconds, saw the logic in that and gave me the address, which was on Cortez Street. Said, "It's a big pink house across from Valdez Park."

It took twenty minutes to drive over. Lucy stood on the edge of Valdez Park across the street from the big pink house. She stood with a group of ten women around two modified lowrider Buicks. The cars had tiny wheels and the undercarriage sat inches off the ground. The women wore day-glo color shorts and tops and had high hair. Lucy wore a yellow shirt that had IF MAMA AIN'T HAPPY, AIN'T NOBODY HAPPY across the chest in black. The two cars were having a hop-off. First the front of one would vault into the air, then the other. Back and forth. The women watched with intense faces.

I parked, walked up to the group slowly. I wanted to talk to Lucy Miranda, but there was a good chance she didn't want to talk to me if I was the reason she got canned. I stood off to the side and watched until it was determined the burgundy Buick could hop highest.

The drivers got out and the group went to the trunk of the winning car. I said, "Lucy?"

They all looked at me. Suspicion was on every face, but I was happy to see there was no hostility on Lucy's.

I said, "I'm sorry you got fired. It wasn't because I came by yesterday, was it?"

She shook her head, said, "No. And don't be sorry. I planned to quit anyway. Things were getting too weird there."

"Weird, how?"

One of the drivers, a tall, lithe kid with lots of hair and tattoos said, "Wait a minute here. Who the fuck is this dude?"

Lucy said something to the guy in Spanish. The kid wasn't having any of it. He straightened up and looked at me hard. I said, "You know, I've always wanted to know how you guys did this."

The kid's face changed a little, but his eyes stayed hard, waiting to see if I was mocking him. I happen to think lowriders are kind of silly looking, but I *was* interested in how they did it. When he saw I was serious his look changed completely. He smiled and said, "Come here, man." This car was his life and he'd show even a *quero* how it worked.

I walked to the trunk. Inside it were eight batteries with a lead extending from the batteries toward the front of the car. The kid said, "It's real simple. It uses a hydraulic system with dump valves. There's a button up front I push and she hops up and thumps down. Look." He led me to the side of the car, pointed inside. The floorboards and seat cushions were red plush velvet. The steering wheel was the size of a dinner plate and looked gold plated. *Campeon* was scripted in black just under the window on the passenger side. Champion.

I said, "How much you got tied up in this baby?"

He said, "From the day I bought her until now, I've spent twenty-five grand. I'll spend more."

He beamed at my expression. I said, "She's a beauty, no doubt about it."

I looked at Lucy, said to the two drivers and the girls, "Don't mind if I talk to Lucy for a minute, do you?"

The kid who wanted to send me back wherever I came from at the end of a boot two minutes ago said, "No, man, you guys step over there and have your talk."

Lucy and I walked toward the backstop of a baseball field. She said, "My brother. Ricky. You figured out real quick how to get on his good side."

"Lot of money to put in a car."

"He works for that car."

"Tell me about Tricia."

She leaned against the backstop and looked toward the group, busy checking out Ricardo's *Campeon*. She said, "What's to tell? I went to work one morning two weeks ago, she was there, told me she was living there now."

"You know she's Kay Thornberg's daughter?"

Lucy shrugged.

"You know she's only sixteen?"

"So what?"

"So she's a kid and her mother wants her home."

"What was I supposed to do about it? Is not my kid."

"Why didn't you tell me she was there yesterday?"

"You didn't ask."

Good point.

She said, "Besides, she wasn't there when you came by."

"Where was she?"

"I don't know. Maybe at Amanda Truitt's."

"Who's that?"

"An old friend of Miss Harper's. The only one of her friends she still sees who isn't weirder than shit. She's weird enough, but the rest of them are out and out loco. Amanda and Tricia got along okay. None of the rest liked Amanda."

"Where does Amanda live?"

"Sandburg Village, I think."

"How's Tricia doing?"

Lucy shrugged. "Doin' okay. Why wouldn't she be?"

"What's going on that's so weird?"

"I don't know. Miss Harper don't discuss many things with the help." She said "help" like it was the most distasteful word in the English language. "But everybody was getting so uptight.

And Shannon, she be blowing up at the drop of a hat. Like yesterday when you come by."

"They talk about animal rights while you were around?"

"Animal *rights*?" A look of complete bewilderment clouded her face. "She never say nothin' about animals and their rights to me."

"You know two men named Sorrento Gallo and Boyd Fuller?"

She nodded. "Recently they come over all the time. Them two and George, who's the weirdest of all of them."

"George?"

"George Kemp. Short musclebound guy never says nothing. A creep."

"These guys all acted stressed out too?"

She nodded. "Very tense people."

"And you got no idea why?"

"None."

"Shannon say anything about leaving town for a while? Vacation maybe?"

"Like I *said*, she never discuss personal stuff with me. All I know is last night I was getting ready to head for the bus stop, she give me a month's pay and told me not to come back. I ask why and she says my performance is unacceptable. I told her it's fine by me because she was one ignorant, slut bitch. And now that I didn't work for her I might just kick her ass for all the shit I had to put up with."

I smiled. "What'd she say to that?"

Lucy grinned. "Yelled, 'George, would you come down here right away?' I got out of there. George is too fucking weird."

I had new names. I interpreted Lucy's firing as meaning something would be happening soon and Shannon didn't want anybody not involved around when it did. All in all a good conversation. I said, "Hope you find a new job soon."

Lucy said, "Don't worry about me. I'll find me a whole lot better job than cleaning house and answering doorbells for that *puta*."

I nodded at Ricardo, the other driver, and the girls and headed for the Skylark.

TWELVE

Two sheets of particle board covered the front window of Kay and Amy's house. Out front a group of children pointed at the wooden window and talked it over.

A stack of photos waited for me on the chrome and glass coffee table in front of the sofa. Because of the lack of sunlight, a reading lamp on high beam sat next to the photographs.

On top were pictures of two women who fit the description given me by the Rasta Kid. Kay told me the tall one's name was Cornelia Haas, the short one Susan Chapman. Lovers for ten years, with an apartment in Rogers Park, they'd been acquaintances of Kay's since the late sixties. They were the first recruits in Animal Sanctuary. Eventually their commitment to the cause became greater than their commitment to their friends. Kay said she understood that, even though I didn't.

In every photo Cornelia and Susan were together, there were no shots of either one alone. In group shots they stood together. "They're inseparable," Kay said. "To a degree I think is unhealthy."

Haas and Chapman had short, severe haircuts and dressed in a uniform of sorts. Checked flannel shirts, blue jeans, and high-top canvas basketball shoes. Cornelia had graying blond hair, a large Roman nose, wide shoulders. Susan was short and dark and petite, a mere wisp next to her friend. Her lips were thick and purplish in color.

In every photo the two women looked like they were on their way to a funeral. I said, "They always so glum?"

"They are serious people. Hardly ever smile. When they do it's like a private thing they share only with each other. They have two passions in life: each other and animals. Both possess brilliant minds, but the last year or so they've had no other outside interests."

"Going on the descriptions I got, these two definitely are with Shannon."

Kay looked sad, nodded.

I flipped through more photos. At the bottom of the pile were shots of the two men I'd seen entering the van with Shannon. The short, brown-haired man had more muscles than the Incredible Hulk. His pockmarked face was devoid of expression. His eyes zombie-like. I showed his picture to Kay.

"George Kemp," she said.

She told me the tall, skinny man was Frank Kelson.

"Tell me about Kemp. Lucy says the guy is weirder than shit."

Kay nodded. "George Kemp is one of the strangest men I've ever known. He made a fortune trading currency at the Merc. Swiss francs and yen. He sold his seat six months ago and retired so he could devote all his time to Animal Sanctuary."

"Age?"

"Thirty-five maybe."

"Retired at thirty-five? Lucky bastard. He married? Gay?"

"George Kemp's social life is not something he shared with anyone else. He lives alone with three pets in a walkup studio apartment on Clark Street, six blocks from Sorrento Gallo and Boyd Fuller. But he made it clear none of us were to visit him there. Ever."

"A Merc trader in a studio apartment on Clark Street?"

"I told you he's strange. Admirably eccentric in some ways, scary strange in others. He has no use for financial trappings like lakefront condos or Lotus cars or designer clothes. No interest in any of the toys most yuppies find necessary. He lives a very austere life."

"By no social life you mean no girlfriends, no friends period, what?"

"I never heard him mention an activity outside of Animal Sanctuary. Before he joined us his life consisted of the Exchange floor, weightlifting, and the dog and two cats. No friends, no family. He told me that once. I'm not sure why."

"Think hard. Anything else?"

"I'm not sure. Like I said, he never talked about himself, his past—anything like that. He was so walled in he scared me to death most of the time, to be honest. Yet he could be extremely personable, charm your socks off. But that was equally scary—it was so . . . so classic. Most times he'd stare at you like you were a piece of furniture. A totally anti-social person. One thing he said that stayed with me was that if he were the last male human being left on earth, even if there were a million beautiful women, the human race would die out because he would not be responsible for singlehandedly keeping it going."

"*That's* creepy."

"He detested the human race except for people like us who wanted to save animals. He said many times the perfect world would be no humans, lots of animals. But I've never forgotten one time he said to me when we were alone, 'You know,' he said, 'I've killed people who deserved it. I'd do it again, because they all deserve it.' Then he smiled. Actually smiled."

"What did you say?"

"I couldn't think of anything to say. I assumed he was joking but he just kept smiling and shook his head a little, put his finger to his lips. Then he said, 'But it's okay because fate decides everything that happens, so why worry about your actions? You can't do a thing about what you are, what you do. It's all been decided eons before you're even born.'"

"How'd he join Sanctuary?"

"Through a man named Arthur Irwin, who was a member at the time. They were walking their dogs in Lincoln Park. Arthur wore a *Meat Is Murder* T-shirt. George asked him where he got it. George made several comments about how much animals meant to him, how he preferred them to people, how much he admired groups who risk jail to help them. He seemed sincere, so Arthur gave him my phone number."

"Wasn't that risky?"

"He didn't tell him about Animal Sanctuary, just gave him the number. George and I talked on the phone a few times and I invited him to a meeting. That night we worked out a schedule where half of us picketed Northwestern Technological Institute—they experiment on cats there—and the other half of AS would hand out leaflets in front of the fur salons on Michigan Avenue. George asked if he could go with us. As time went by, I trusted him more and I asked him to join us. He, Sorrento Gallo, and Frank Kelson were the three men who raided Harper Cosmetics with Amy and Shannon."

"How'd he relate to Shannon?"

"He worships her. Like the rest."

"She have a sexual hold on him?"

"I'm sure I told you he's the most walled in person I've ever met. People like that can become emotionally dependent on someone very quickly if they let their guard down."

I looked at photos of Frank Kelson. He had long black hair, wore black clothes and, in most of the photos, mirror sunglasses—even indoors. I said, "What about Kelson? Kid looks like he's barely old enough to shave."

"He's twenty-one. Another one of Shannon's lovers. There's not much to him that I ever saw. She insisted he join. I don't know what he did for a living, or if he even earned a living. He's a street-wise type. Always smirking. Struts when he walks, preens when he's standing still. Whatever Shannon says, he does it or thinks it. From day one he was a Shannon Harper follower rather than an Animal Sanctuary member. I never felt comfortable with him, but he never scared me like George Kemp did."

"Doesn't look like the animal lover type."

"He never said so, but I got the impression he thought most of what we believed in silly. These looks he used to make. He never talked much, but whenever Shannon suggested something he was the first person to argue in favor of it."

"Like Tricia and Kemp, he idolizes her?"

"His eyes never left that woman."

I shook my head. "Sounds like this is more of a cult of personality than a noble cause to these people."

"It's both. That's why I'm so scared."

Alan started crying in another part of the house. Kay stood and hurried from the room.

I said, "Another fine mess you've gotten me into, Kruger."

Kay and Alan came back. She carried him hitched on her hip. He rubbed red eyes, looked at me like I was responsible for waking him up.

I said, "Think hard, Kay. Did any of these people ever mention anything that'd give us a clue what they're planning now?

Anything at all. Make the wildest assumption."

"Mr. Kruger, I've replayed entire conversations, arguments, reconstructed meetings. I can't suggest a thing."

"Nothing?"

"The last great 'idea' Shannon presented before she dissolved Animal Sanctuary was we'd go to the woods when deer hunting season started and hunt hunters. See how they liked being stalked prey. And of course we'd dress like they did so it would be a guerrilla infiltration thing. The hunters'd end up shooting each other, not knowing who the real killers were. George Kemp thought that was the greatest idea he'd ever heard. Genius, he called it. But hunting season is months away."

I said, "Jesus."

"That's how her—their—minds worked the last few months. She became obsessed with revenge. All she talked about was death threats, murder plots, stuff like that. 'Let human animals feel the terror for a change,' she used to say. And she was so persuasive that the rest of them picked up on it too."

I spread out one photo each of the members of Friends of the Wild on the table. I looked at Cornelia Haas and Susan Chapman, George Kemp, Frank Kelson, Shannon Harper, Boyd Fuller, Sorrento Gallo. I was struck again by the tense, stiff postures and the angry faces. Not a speck of humor in the eyes. People on a mission. John Browns freeing four-legged slaves.

Kay said, "There are some brilliant minds in that group, Mr. Kruger. Cornelia Haas has three degrees, Susan Chapman is a published poet. Gallo and Fuller are law students. Except for Frank Kelson they're all quite intelligent and successful in one field or another."

"And they're all crazy as hell."

Kay let out a long breath.

"I want the addresses of all these people. Did George Kemp stay friends with Arthur Irwin?"

"I don't know."

"Why'd Irwin quit?"

"I'm not sure. Philosophical differences perhaps. He just stopped showing up. I called him, but he never gave me a reason. Some people get more and more impassioned, some cool off after the initial enthusiasm."

"Give me his address too. You know an Amanda Truitt? Friend of Shannon's?"

"I don't know her, but Shannon and Tricia talked about her. Why?"

"I talked to Lucy—Shannon's ex-maid. Amanda Truitt visited Shannon recently. She active?"

"With us? No."

"Sympathetic?"

"I couldn't say."

Kay set Alan on the floor. He continued to stare at me with accusing, sleep-fogged eyes. She went to the bookshelf, removed a leather address book. She sat next to me and flipped through it, stopping at different pages and writing addresses in a 3 × 5 notebook. She said, "You don't know how much I abhor doing this, but I *have* to get Tricia back. Just remember you promised not to go to the police."

"I promised."

I looked at the John Brown faces some more. Chills shivered my backbone. I said, "Might be a good idea to keep the wood window for the time being."

Her face jerked toward me. She looked behind us, back at me, then she nodded briskly.

"I think I will," she said. She ripped the page of addresses from the notebook and handed it to me.

THIRTEEN

Arthur Irwin lived in a flat-front Italian style row house on Lincoln Park West in Old Town. Sun-waxed, Jello-colored sports cars lined the curb the length of the block.

Being a man on the cusp of middle age who has yet to experience the phenomenon of disposable income, I envied these upscale bastards. Yuppies with a cause. Make a good flick. I felt a smidge of admiration too. I applaud people with so much conviction they put their balls on the chopping block. Been a long time since I felt that way about anything. I even respected this cause to a point. Torturing rabbits so women can have Red lips with names like *Cherries in the Snow was* a disgusting commentary on mankind. But if only these people would put their time and money and energy into helping the poor and the homeless.

I laughed at myself. Said aloud, "Christ, Kruger, you sound like a social worker. It's their time, their money and their energy."

Arthur Irwin opened the door and said, "What do you want?" before I said hello. He was tall and bony and his skin was white as milk except for his cheeks, which were a shiny pink like he spent his spare time buffing them. He was either color blind or dressed in the dark. Or maybe I wasn't keeping up on fashion. He wore a baggy mauve shirt printed with purple license plates, copper and yellow striped slacks, and khaki deck shoes. His wheat-colored hair was as short as an FBI cadet's. His hands and arms shivered like we were outdoors in January.

I said, "Mr. Irwin, I work for Kay Thornberg."

His eyebrows arched, he said nothing.

"She gave me your address."

"That wasn't a very good idea." His voice was like dry ice. He said, "Why'd she do that? Who are you?"

I gave him my card. He frowned while he read it, the card vibrating in his hands.

I said, "She said you were a member of Animal Sanctuary, but you're not now."

The frown deepened. "What else did she say?"

"Relax, I'm not interested in you. I wanna talk about George Kemp."

"Why?"

"You still friends with him?"

A noncommittal shrug.

"I'd like to find out what he's up to?"

"Kay sees him more than I do."

"Not anymore. Animal Sanctuary splintered. He aligned himself with the radical wing."

Arthur Irwin smiled. Said, "Kay *was* way too—soft in her approach."

Good God, another one. I said, "Have you talked to George the last month?"

The smile died. He said, "Why is Kay—more, why are *you* so interested in George Kemp?"

"We think the new group is planning illegal activities. You know Tricia Thornberg, right? Kay's daughter? Tricia's with the new group and Kay wants her home before she ends up in jail. Kay hired me to get her home. Surely you can appreciate a mother wanting to extricate her daughter from a dangerous situation."

"Perhaps the situation isn't nearly as dire as you perceive."

"Why take chances?"

"Tricia could turn right around, run away again."

"That's up to her and Kay."

"You got a job to do and couldn't care less what happens afterward, right?"

"Something like that."

"Shannon Harper's with George?"

"More like he's with her."

Arthur Irwin bobbed his head like he approved of that.

I said, "You talked to George?"

"He's not a man who encourages friendships."

"Mr. Irwin, have you *talked* to the man? That's all I'm asking."

"I don't see what business that is to anybody except George Kemp and me."

"Don't you have any feelings for Kay Thornberg? What she's going through."

He wrapped his arms around himself. Said, "Sure, I like Kay fine, but she should remember Tricia is *her* daughter. Kay's been active in a lot of causes for a lot of years. Suddenly it's not right for Tricia to be?"

"Tricia's barely sixteen."

"Come on, to you Tricia's a payday. You couldn't care less if she's sixteen or sixty or if she ran off with a criminal group or the circus."

"Can the cynicism, Irwin. I got enough for both of us. All I wanna know is have you talked to George Kemp the last thirty days?"

Arthur Irwin shrugged. Suddenly there was a faraway, distracted look in his eyes. Like I was no longer of any interest to him. He said, "If she gave you my address, she gave you others. Talk to them."

"I'd get nowhere with the others because they follow Shannon Harper. I hoped since you didn't you could help me out."

"But I can't."

"Shows just how wrong a guy can be, don't it? Sorry I took up your time."

Arthur Irwin smiled like he had a secret, said, "Not at all," and shut the door in my face.

I walked back to the Skylark. Sat behind the wheel and pondered. I was not off to a real auspicious start here, and I had the uncomfortable feeling things weren't going to get better any time soon.

And I was pretty sure Arthur Irwin could've shed a whole lot more light on the situation than he chose to. I wondered if I'd said too much. Or had I said enough? Wouldn't be the first time for either.

I pulled from the curb, headed for Sandburg Village.

FOURTEEN

Sandburg Village is a sprawling collection of high and low rise apartment buildings. It's a short walk from the Gold Coast. In the late 60's and 70's it had a Swingersville reputation. Every unmarried flight attendant, secretary, stockbroker, commodities trader, drug dealer, and lawyer in town lived in Sandburg Village. The rest of the city considered it Sodom and Gomorrah. And wished they were single and affluent enough to live there.

Sandburg Village doesn't have that rep these days. Everybody's too scared of social disease or too bushed from grubbing for money all day to throw bashes at night. I never have figured out how piling up money and possessions supplanted sex and drugs as the national pastime of young adults. Seems unAmerican to me.

I stopped at a White Hen, flipped to the T's in the phone book the kid at the counter shoved at me. A Truitt, A. was listed on a street five blocks from the Harper mansion. I was close, so I drove over.

The address was a three-story stone building. Sorrento Gallo and Boyd Fuller's black van was parked out front.

I said, "Hello."

I squared the block, pulled into a Safeway supermarket parking lot across the street, parked so I could watch the van. I digested this development. It was so unexpected I didn't know how to play it. Until I saw Shannon Harper and Tricia Thornberg leave Truitt's building.

I exited the Skylark, trotted across the street, dodging cars and waving cheerfully at the honks and swear words. I came around the rear of the van as Shannon put her hand on the side door handle. I said, "Yo, Harper."

Both women looked at me with blank faces. Shannon recognized me and stepped in front of Tricia, wrapped her arms backwards around her. She said, "What are you doing here?"

"Wanna talk to Tricia."

"How'd you know we were here?"

"I'm a detective, remember? Maybe I followed you."

"I warned you about this."

"That's always been a problem for me, following instructions from people who got no business giving me instructions."

Tricia was almost as tall as Shannon. She peered at me over Shannon's shoulder. She looked very confused.

I said, "Tricia, your mother sent me."

Tricia said, "My mother?"

Shannon cut in, "Tricia wants nothing to do with her mother. I take care of her. Tell Kay that's the way it is."

I said, "I want Tricia to tell me that's the way it is."

"She doesn't need to."

"Let me talk to her just two minutes."

"Forget it."

"Her mother—"

A high-pitched man's voice said, "What's this jackoff's problem, Shannon?"

I looked to my right. The four men in Friends of the Wild stood at the bottom of the apartment building stairs. Frank Kelson was in front. He was the one called me jackoff.

Sorrento Gallo said, "That's the PI Kay and Amy hired." He sounded amazed. I didn't know if it was because he hadn't scared me off or I'd found them here.

Kelson walked toward me. The others followed. Kelson wore mirror sunglasses and a black longsleeve shirt untucked over skintight black jeans. His black slouch boots had silver metal toes. His spritzed hair was pulled back in a knobby ponytail. Steven Seagal Kelson.

He said, "You got yourself a major problem, you know that? You been told twice to stay away from Shannon. You got problems compre*hend*ing the spoken word or something?" He said comprehending proudly, like he'd just learned the word from *Reader's Digest's* "Expand Your Vocabulary."

I said, "I got a problem with kidnapping."

Shannon said in a disgusted voice, "This is no kidnapping and you know it. Did you tell those two what I said?"

"I told Kay." I nodded at Gallo and Fuller, said, "They did too."

"And she still wants you to stick your nose in this?"

I looked around Kelson, said to her, "Tricia's her *daughter*, Shannon. For Christ sakes, put yourself in Kay's shoes." I pointed at a bus stop bench fifteen yards away. "Let me talk to Tricia just two minutes. Rest of you can stand right here, close enough to rush me if you think I'm here to snatch her."

Shannon started to speak when Tricia said, "I'll talk to him. It's okay."

Everybody except Shannon turned and looked at her. Tricia nodded briskly, a flustered look on her face. "Really, it's okay."

"Shannon said, "Trish, it's not wise." Her voice was hard. Her eyes didn't leave my face.

I said, "Come on Harper, what're you afraid of?"

Kelson put his hands on my shirt. I slapped them in the air, shoved his chest hard. He stumbled back five steps, waving his arms to keep balance. He stood there, cheeks flushed, clenching and unclenching his fists. He wanted to come at me, but wasn't sure he should. He had the Attitude and he talked the talk, but deep down he wasn't a tough guy. More important, he didn't know I wasn't either.

I said, "Keep your hands off me, Kelson."

Sorrento Gallo and Boyd Fuller watched with interest but said nothing. Probably afraid Heather was close by. George Kemp, the one guy in this crowd who could for sure clean my clock one on one, acted like the entire incident was of absolutely no interest to him. He stared across the street at the Safeway like he'd been hired to security guard it.

Kelson sneered. Said, "A tough guy."

I said, "You don't know the half of it. I'm only the second toughest person in my own house."

Kelson said, "I heard about your burrhead sweetie."

I said, "Come on Tricia, let's talk."

She moved from behind Shannon and walked toward me, passing through the knot of men. She wore white running shorts, a lime green tank top with *We Are All Noah* written across it in pink, and white sandals. Her hair was wrapped with a violet scarf. She was even thinner than she looked in the photos, with long legs and scrawny arms. She walked with downcast eyes and a newborn foal's nervous, wobbly gait. It was obvious she hated being the center of attention, even in front of only six people.

We went to the bench. She sat gingerly on one end. I sat on the opposite end, hoping space between us would put her more at ease.

Shannon said, "The two minutes start now, PI." I felt ten eyes bore into my back.

A squad car pulled into the parking lot of the Safeway, parked in front of the display window. I pointed at it and said over my shoulder, "What you gonna do if I take three, Shannon?"

Tricia said, "You said two minutes." Her voice was soft, but indignant.

I said, "I know, but I can't help needling that bunch. They're too damn serious. You heard one joke since you been with these guys?"

Tricia stared straight ahead, said, "There's not much in this world to joke about."

"Jokes are one way to cope with a world like this."

"Fighting wrong is the only way to cope with a world like this." She sounded like me when I was sixteen and saw wind-mills everywhere I looked.

"If you have the energy. And you'll never have enough time."

"You're Dan Kruger, aren't you? Shannon told me about you."

"What'd she tell you?"

"That—" She let it drop as she realized it probably wouldn't be a good idea to tell me what Shannon told her.

I wanted to ask about the Cyprus apartment and the words on the wall and the suitcases and what was in the suitcases. Say, "Tricia, tell me what the hell is going on." But I couldn't let them know what I'd discovered. I took the threats seriously and if they thought I was hip to the agenda, Kruger and dead meat *would* be synonymous. I said, "Why'd you leave home?"

"To be with my friends."

"You can't live at home and see your friends?"

"No."

"Your mother's frantic."

"I doubt it."

"Why?"

"She's got Alan and Amy. She doesn't need me. My friends do."

I put my left arm on the backrest and turned slightly to face her, lacing my fingers together. "Maybe your mother needs you too, but temporarily didn't realize it. She's been through a lot because of Amy. I know. I have the same problem Amy does. I've put people through a lot of—"

"Maybe you're full of shit."

I nodded. "There's always that possibility."

She scooted back a fraction on the bench, made a nervous glance past me at the five people who watched us. Two globules of sweat rolled down her forehead into her eyes. She blinked, then pulled the shoulder strap of her shirt up, vigorously cleaned the salt away. She looked like a little girl rubbing sleep from her eyes.

I said, "Your mother says you never told her why you ran away."

"I just *said*. These people need me and I need them. We have important things to do. And I didn't run away, I moved out."

"What important things?"

"What do you know about us?"

"Not a damn thing. I don't know what you all have in common or what important things you've got to do or why you're running around together in this van or why Shannon doesn't want me to talk to you. All I know is your mother wants you home. She wants to start over."

"I'm sure."

"Then why'd she hire me?"

"I don't want to go home. Shannon takes care of me fine."

"Move in with her when you're eighteen."

"That's two years from now."

And to a teenager two years might as well be twenty. I said, "Do me a favor. *Think* about going home, okay? I don't know why you left, I don't know what the problems were. That's between you and your mother. I don't know why you and that crowd over there need each other so bad. But your mother needs you too. She's upset and hurting—"

Tricia said, "I *told* you. She's got Alan, she's got Amy. She doesn't need me. She made that very clear."

"She said that?"

"She didn't have to *say* it."

"We must be talking about two different people here, Tricia. Because the woman who hired me to bring you back is worried sick. How do you explain that?"

"I don't have to explain anything."

"Why did Shannon threaten me and your mother?"

"She'd never do that."

"Not only did she do it, she sent Gallo and Fuller after me, and they did it too."

She sneaked a look at me, suspicion and doubt on her face.

After some seconds she said, "Shannon wants you to leave me alone. She'd never hurt anybody, but she wants to protect me. Maybe she thought she had to scare you to do that."

"She wants to protect you from your own mother? I doubt it, Tricia. I think she's protecting herself."

Tricia looked at me full on for a bit then jerked her head away. She said, "Protect herself from what?" Her voice was quieter.

I said, "Why don't you get away from these guys tomorrow? I'll pick up your mother and she can meet you somewhere for lunch. You two can talk."

Tricia forced a laugh. "You don't know a lot about my mother, do you?"

"Just met her yesterday."

"Ask her what agoraphobia is. Ask her where she wants to meet for lunch." She turned to face me and her voice rose. "She's so into shrink BS. Ask her why she's so concerned with correcting everybody else's problems, but ignores her own. And mine. Ask her why she analyzes everybody she knows, but never herself. Ask her why she spent hours telling other people how to change their lives, but ignored her own daughter and refused to listen to anybody who wants to help her. Ask her about that, why don't you? Ask her why, if she's really so upset I'm gone, she didn't do anything to prevent it? Ask her why none of my friends come over anymore."

Then a basso profundo voice next to me said, "Two minutes are up, friend. Come on Tricia Lynn, we have to go now."

I shifted, looked up into George Kemp's impassive face. He gazed past me at Tricia. He didn't pose tough or sneer or stare me down or flex his muscles, which made me realize he *was* tough. The genuine article never has to advertise. The seams of the red knit polo shirt he wore strained against his shoulders and pecs and biceps. I said to Tricia, "Go on. We'll talk more later."

George Kemp said, "I doubt it, friend," in a voice so hard it was like a punch to the stomach.

Tricia reddened, started to talk, stopped. She stood abruptly and they walked back to the van. She was half a head taller than he was. Everybody got inside and the van pulled away. I sat on the bench saying the word agoraphobia over and over. A lot of things about Kay Thornberg fell into place.

FIFTEEN

I stayed on the bench and smoked a Kool. Thought things over.

I wondered if I'd ever get close to Tricia again. And did I want to? I kept hearing George Kemp say, "I doubt it, friend," in that frozen rope of a voice. Kept seeing the mound of muscles trying to rip his shirt apart.

I jaywalked to the Skylark, pointed it toward home.

Maria Leary trucked down Fremont at Irving Park as I waited for a gap in traffic to turn the corner. She moved fast for such a sultry day. But Maria Leary, pill freak and pill pusher, moved fast every day. Her face was a maelstrom of motion—eyes blinked in four-four time, mouth twisting this way and that as she chewed away the insides.

I said, *"Damn!"*

I took it slow to the apartment, dreading what I'd find. Heather met me at the door. She was wired tighter than a spool of sewing thread.

The tip of her tongue flicked around her mouth. She had Charlie Manson eyes. Her face and arms were luminous with sweat. She said, "Dan, I'm sorry. Maria was here. I'm only gonna do it this one time. Honest."

I said nothing, walked to Bugs who slept on a corner of the couch. I sat on the edge, scratched behind his droopy ears until he stirred a bit.

Heather followed. She stood over me, spewed out sentences and fragments of sentences, all of it boiling down to this was a one time high and she was sorry. Her voice was shredded, the words shot out like machine gun bullets. Everything rammed together, no space between words, no pause between sentences. No one else on earth would have understood what Heather was saying. But I had lots of practice.

Keeping my voice calm I said, "It's cool. I just stopped by to—stop by. On my way to the office."

She said, "Don't be mad, Dan. It's just one time, I swear it. Just a taste."

I said, "A day and a half, Heather?"

I started for the door. She yelled, "Dammit, it wasn't my idea to go in there in the first place. Some very unreal expectations were set up here."

I quietly said, "Detox, retox, right?" and left. I punched the roof of the Skylark, left a dent.

But driving to the office I thought about what she said. Asked myself why was I so bent out of shape? The night Marvin said he'd pay for both of us to rehab, Heather signed herself in. For me. She didn't care she was a pill freak, she had no desire to stop. She checked in to be there for me. If she got off the pills, fine. If not, oh well. It was absurd to expect a twenty-one-year-old speed freak who figured she'd live forever to quit a habit she'd barely started and still loved because her thirty-nine-year-old boyfriend had to quit one that would kill him if he didn't.

And who was the smug bastard who said he never judged other people's lifestyles? I muttered, "She didn't get cranked to spite you, you self-centered jerk."

It was after five, but Marvin was still there. I went to my desk, called home. I said, "Heather, it's okay. I'm fine now."

She exhaled into the phone, said, "I'm so glad, Dan. I felt sick after you left. I threw up even. I swear it's just one time. It won't happen again. Maria came by and she was wired so tight she was shivering like an Eskimo and it brought back all the feelings and I thought, like, one time can't hurt anything, you know? I bought enough for a taste. I swear that's all. I told her to stay away from me from now on because I guess I can't handle temptation so well." She kept talking.

I said, "We'll talk about it later. I just wanted to tell you it's okay. And it won't make things difficult for me."

I hung up the phone, looked at it. Said, "I hope."

Marvin said, "She's fucked up already."

"She's a kid, Marvin."

"I spent a ton of money to keep your punk straight for one fucking day?"

"Who twisted your arm?"

"Jesus Christ. What about you?"

"I'm okay."

"Sure?"

I shrugged.

"You got urges?"

"We all got urges, Marvin."

"You know what I mean."

"Haven't had time to dwell on it."

"You working?" He sounded surprised.

"Wanna call Ripley?"

"Don't be so touchy. Tough case?"

"If I knew then what I know now—"

Marvin eyed me up. Said, "You pissed at Heather?"

"No."

"You oughta be."

"I was at first."

"Honestly Dan, what do you see in her?"

"A sensitive, caring person who feels totally out of place and time. Who feels a camaraderie with almost no one. Who feels like she fits in nowhere. Who's scared to death she never will fit in anywhere and deals with that fear by getting trashed and saying fuck you to all the round pegs who found round holes." After a second I said, "Like me at twenty-one. And thirty-one. And thirty-nine."

"A rebel without a cause?"

"Just a scared kid."

Marvin faked a laugh.

I said, "You never felt like an outcast? Like you're totally alone? Nobody on earth gives a damn if you're dead or alive?"

"I think you're trying to relive your youth."

"Maybe I genuinely fell for the girl, Marvin, you ever thought of that?"

He shrugged again.

A minute passed. I said, "Why'd you take me to Mercy that night?"

"You would of died if I hadn't. You were one sad sonofabitch when I got to Lounge Ax."

I shook my head. Said, "I don't know what happened. I hardly ever go on binges. I'm the type of lush who keeps a steady buzz going, breakfast to bedtime, day after day."

"Well, that weekend you binged."

Did I ever.

I remembered very little of that lost weekend a month ago. I was stone cold sober when Heather and I climbed into Priceman's Econoline at two o'clock Friday afternoon. Driving to Milwaukee, our singer Justus Walker, Heather, and I sat in the back surrounded by guitar cases and amplifiers. We passed around a bottle of blackberry brandy, smoked half a baggy of homegrown. Nothing special about that. Justus, Heather, and I always got numb on the way to a gig.

But something was different, because about the time we hit Milwaukee events started swimming together, the chronology got skewed and I recalled only bits and pieces of the next thirty-six hours.

The two-night gig was at the Kiwi Club. We'd played there before. Owner loved us. Comped pitchers of beer and shots of brandy kept materializing in the dressing room and on stage. I grabbed more than my share. Friday night we were hot. Audience was rowdy.

The band got invited to a party at a huge house on the Lake, a party that still rocked when Heather and I left at 7:00 A.M. We grabbed a few hours sleep, headed back to the same party, bigger and louder now, stayed all day.

I remembered eating speed in the dressing room before the Saturday night gig. I played on automatic pilot. The last set seemed about ten seconds long because I was out on my feet, speed or no.

Priceman brought a tape of the Saturday night sets to Mercy Mothers during my second week. I cringed listening to it. A deaf man had tuned my guitar. A man with ten thumbs played it. He did songs in the wrong key. Blew changes left and right. And then songs where he didn't play at all. Priceman said, "I wouldn't hear anything so I'd look over and you'd be slanted against the amp, eyes closed, flipping wrist up and down, but missing the strings." My solo on "Madison Blues" sounded like I'd laid the SG on the stage and kicked it around. Priceman said, "I seen you fucked up before, Dan, but this was the worst. I never seen you where you couldn't *play*."

And the rest of that night's fog. The ride home early Sunday morning—I ate more speed to stay awake, knowing it was a mistake, because Heather wanted to visit a private club in some North Side alley. Justus twisted a joint the size of a Polish red hot. Insane laughter. Another bottle. Something brown that scorched when it went down.

At some point the world started to spin off its axis and next thing I knew I was puking my guts out in the curb in front of a crowd of dawn patrollers on North Lincoln. I was vaguely aware I'd crossed way over the line. I drank like a fish most of my adult life, but that was the first time I puked from booze in ten years.

It scared Priceman too. He called Marvin, who to his credit crawled out of bed and drove right over. He and Priceman took me to Mother's Mercy.

Where, on TV, they claim they can help even those who don't want help.

Like me. I blew a .32, the whole time insisting I wasn't drunk. They ran a blood test, the results of which Eli said looked like Elvis's autopsy report. That alarmed me because I could only remember ingesting booze, pot, and white cross. In reality I must have swallowed anything anybody handed me that weekend.

All of which meant Marvin probably saved my life. Whether I wanted him to or not. Right now I was glad he did. I said, "Thanks, Marvin."

He knew what I meant. He made a face, said, "Who the hell would talk to that damn rabbit of yours if you weren't around?"

I smiled at the way Marvin and I always dance around the edge of our friendship. Must be a male thing.

That night I blew off FFN's practice and did something I never really thought I'd do. Attended an AA meeting. A cinder-block-walled room painted pale yellow in a community building on North Broadway. The floor was dirty, the walls dingy, the room thick with smoke and sweat and regrets.

I didn't say anything. I sat in the back next to a video game and watched and listened and chain smoked.

When I got home the apartment was cleaner than it had been in years. Heather sat on the living room floor, snapping gum, a box of 48 Crayola crayons next to her, a Yosemite Sam coloring book open on her lap. She was beyond the motormouth stage now, deep into the artistic phase. She meticulously colored Sam's mustache bright orange, careful not to color outside the edges.

I remembered my own go-fast nights when I'd spend four hours tuning my guitar and it still wouldn't sound right, or use the entire night to draw and color DAN KRUGER, PI posters complete with stars and moons and planets and all kinds of psychedelic designs to put in the window at the office.

I bent down, kissed her head. It was covered with a soft black down. She looked up, eyes wild, and grimaced a smile, but didn't speak.

I grinned, said in my best Yosemite Sam imitation, "I ain't a goin' down there again, rabbit!"

And then I wanted to get away from it all. Everything. I didn't want to think about Heather and her pills or AA meetings or detox-retox or runaway teenagers or revenge-minded animal rights activists.

I didn't want to play this game any more.

I went to the kitchen, found my baggy of Valium in the sugar jar, swallowed two with a glass of V-8. I leaned against the counter for awhile, let my mind go blank. Okay, blanker.

I went to the bedroom, stripped, and stretched out. The V's kicked in. I felt the calming sensation start in my belly, glide up and down my backbone, seep into my nervous system. The sedation and the murmur of the fan on low put me in something like a trance.

Valium only gives you calm of body, not peace of mind, but that night calm of body was enough to make me fall asleep.

SIXTEEN

The next morning at 9:30 Amy Barrow was discharged from Mercy Mother's. At 9:45 she was shot and killed as she walked from the building to a waiting taxi. At 10:15 Kay received a phone call. A female voice she didn't recognize told her Amy was dead and if she didn't keep her mouth shut Tricia was next. At 10:25 an Area Six Violent Crimes detective came to the house to verify the anonymous phone call.

Kay called me at 10:45. She told me what happened in a voice that was way too controlled. I told her I'd be right over.

I got there at 11:15. Kay sat on the sofa below the boarded-over window. Two detectives sat, one on either side of her. An old one who had seen it all, a young one who looked like a teenage hearthrob circa 1959. They sat half-facing her, their knees making a V to lock her in place. A psychological ploy to make her feel they were there to protect her; she could trust and confide in them.

A uniform cop stood in front of the bookshelves, his arms folded. Two women—one ash blond, thin, and delicately beautiful; the other a raven-haired, bosomy Earth Mother—sat in other chairs. The women wore blue jeans, untucked white silk shirts, and running shoes. They'd been crying, but weren't now. Alan sat on the blond woman's lap. He didn't take his eyes off Kay. She held a wadded handkerchief to her mouth and stared at the floor. She seemed oblivious to everyone in the room.

The cop was Randy Crawford. He started out in Area One same time I did in the early 70's. He's known to friend and foe as Atlas. I belong in the latter category. Atlas is a hardass cop. A throwback to the '40's and 50's when there were as many thugs on the force as on the street. He's called Atlas because all he's done for fifteen years is pump iron and eat steroids. Consequently Atlas looks like a walking tank. The steroids also caused

Atlas to lose all his hair and gave him the worst case of acne in the U.S. of A., but he sure could pose nice at the beach and not many punks lipped back, so maybe it was worth it.

He cocked his head and strolled over when I stopped just inside the living room. When he walked his shoulders rolled like a gorilla's. He whispered, "Kruger, the fuck you doing here?"

"Friend of the deceased."

He glanced behind him, then leaned toward me. "This is a den of dykes. What kind of friends you hang with?"

"Any kind'll have me. Who're the dicks?"

"Better not use that word here. Might upset the lezbo's."

"Atlas, always the wit."

He said, "Old bird is Kaiser. Kid's name is DiNardi."

"They learn anything?"

"Nah, the lez on the couch is out of it. All she kept saying at first was 'Amy, Amy, Amy' over and over. Now she ain't saying shit." He looked back at Kay for a second, whispered, "It's disgusting, you ask me."

"Did I?"

"I mean it ain't normal."

"Neither are sixty inch biceps."

Kaiser said gently, "Miss Thornberg, there must be a connection. Somebody heaves a brick through your window and a day later your roommate gets gunned down in broad daylight. It's got to be connected." Kay kept staring at the floor. Kaiser said, "Ma'am, we want to solve your friend's murder. I'm sure you want that too. There has to be something you can tell us."

Kay shook her head.

Atlas said, "And on top of that, a private eye just walked into the house." The detectives, who barely glanced my way when I walked in, eyed me with interest now.

I said, "I'm a friend of the family. Met Amy in rehab."

Their faces told me I was insulting their intelligence. Cops get plenty irritated when they suspect you're selling their brains short and these two were irritated to begin with.

Kaiser was paunchy, the little hair he had was gray, and his seamy, sun-splotched face looked like an axe-ravaged dead tree. Fashion was not a high priority in his life. His brown suit looked like it doubled as pajamas. He said, "Name, PI?"

I told him.

Atlas said, "This bird ain't exactly the type of eye advertises in North Shore Magazine, you catch my drift. Strictly a low rent Door Knocker."

Door Knocker is Chicago-speak for a cheap PI who specializes in philandering cases. I said, "Atlas is only half right. I'm cheap, but I specialize in anything anybody'll pay me for."

Kaiser said, "Coincidences are piling up here, Kruger. The brick, the hit, the PI walking in the door right after. How's it all connect?"

"No connection. I told you. I met Amy in the—"

"*Rehab* and you got to be *friends.*"

I said, "Sarcasm doesn't become such a genteel profession, Kaiser."

Kay sobbed into the handkerchief. The dark-haired woman walked quickly over and put her hands on Kay's shoulders, leaned forward to nuzzle her hair. She patted Kay's shoulders. Alan started to cry. The blond woman hugged him tight, whispered in his ear. Atlas said, "Jesus," under his breath.

I said, "Why don't you give Kay time to pull herself together before you grill her?"

DiNardi said, "Nobody's getting grilled here, pal. We're just asking the—*lady* some questions about her—friend."

DiNardi was tall and thin, dark complected, gleaming razor-cut black hair, long eyelashes over doe eyes, handsome features. He wore a pin-striped gray suit, coral shirt, shiny black loafers, pale pink socks. I said, "I think you'd get more information if you gave her time to compose herself first."

DiNardi's face turned red. First I insult his intelligence, then I tell him how to do his job. He said, "And I'm sure you'd like to spend some time alone with her so you can compare notes on whatever the fuck it is you been hired to do. Which you obviously ain't doing too fucking well considering her friend just got her ass blown away at ten o'clock in the fucking morning."

"Detective, there's women here. And a child."

DiNardi said, "And how did they manage *that*?"

I said, "You're a compassionate man, DiNardi." I looked at Kaiser, said, "Bet they'd love to hear some of these comments downtown."

Kaiser made a face. DiNardi was too young or too stupid to realize the line he'd stepped over, but Kaiser knew the score. The two women's faces told him that. And he didn't need a bullshit wrist slap from OPS. Veteran cops hate Mickey Mouse citizen grievances. The hearings eat up their free time and sometimes it costs them dough. He took a deep breath, said, "Maybe you're right, PI." He stood, said to no one in particular, "I apologize for a couple of the comments made here. They in no way reflect my personal views." To Kay he said, "We'll come back to talk at a later time, ma'am."

Kay nodded, still sobbing.

Atlas and the detectives left.

To the two women I said, "I'd like to talk to Kay alone for a minute."

They looked at her. She nodded, put her arms out for Alan. The blonde carried him to her. Kay wrapped herself around him, kissed him. The women left the room taking Alan with them. A door shut quietly within the house.

I sat on the sofa. Said, "I talked to Tricia yesterday."

She swung her face to me. "What did she say?"

"She's okay."

"Tell me what she said."

"Some of it's a bit rough."

"*Tell* me."

"She's convinced you don't need her or care about her. That Amy and Alan were more important to you. She says this group needs her. She feels part of something important again. She doesn't wanna come back. She doesn't even wanna talk about it. Even after I told her you were frantic."

"What else?"

"She said I should ask you why her friends never come over anymore. Also said to ask you what agoraphobia means."

Kay sobbed again. A deep, painful sound. Like her throat and chest might rip open. She said, "Oh, God."

I put my arm around her and squeezed. After some seconds she said, "I suffer from agoraphobia. It means fear of open spaces, crowds, people, situations—fear of everything. You fear every damn thing in the world. Except to go in the backyard, I haven't left this house in three years."

I squeezed her harder.

She said, "Just thinking about leaving it—of walking across the street even—produces a panic attack so severe I feel like I'm going to die. I sweat, I shake, I vomit. My heart pounds so fast I'm afraid it'll explode. You suffer a few terror attacks in public or far from home and you start fearing them so much you'll do anything to prevent one. And staying home prevents them. I'm a prisoner in this house."

I said, "I know about panic attacks. It's one of the reasons I drank so much. One of the hundred or so excuses I got."

Kay said, "Why is Tricia using that as a reason? She always understood."

"I got the impression it's the way you insist other people get help for their problems while dragging your feet on your own. Do as I say, not as I do? Teenagers are death on hypocrisy. Add that to her feeling ignored and abandoned. Then there's the admiration for Shannon Harper. Throw in a substitute family that's involved in a noble cause and makes her feel needed. That's why she wants to be with Friends of the Wild."

Kay lowered her head. I said, "We'll talk more about it later. I just wanted you to know I talked to Tricia and she's fine."

"Fine? They've threatened to kill her if I talk."

"That's why we don't talk. Everything we do or don't do from now on is to keep her alive until I get her back. And I guarantee you they won't harm her as long as we don't talk."

She nodded. There was a long pause. She said, "You want to know what else agoraphobia means?"

"What?"

"Means I won't even be able to attend Amy's funeral."

"I'm sure she'd understand."

"She does—would. God*dammit.*" Her body convulsed as the tears kept coming.

I said, "I know," over and over.

After a minute she stopped. She took a deep breath, said, "Who killed Amy? What's it mean?"

"It means I said some things to Arthur Irwin I wish I had back. He's still in contact with Friends of the Wild and that includes George Kemp. My guess is Kemp killed Amy. Then there's Amanda Truitt. I'm not sure how she fits in. Another thing, the worst thing you and Amy could of done was send me to Shannon Harper threatening cops. That and me popping up all over the place scared her so bad she decided she had to do whatever it took to shut you up."

"Shut us up about what?"

"I wish we knew. It also means even though Tricia went to Shannon on her own, Shannon'll never let her leave on her own. She's not a member anymore, she's a hostage. She doesn't know it, but that's what she is. She's their guarantee you won't talk. And that makes sense because of the agoraphobia. They want to kill Amy and you, but can't get at you very easy. You never leave the house. But killing Amy and threatening to kill Tricia shuts you up just as effectively. It also means they'll be dropping out of sight."

"To that apartment?"

"With their money they might have a lot of those apartments."

"Does Tricia know about this? The murder, the threats?"

"I'm sure she doesn't."

Like it was an afterthought she said, "Are you in danger?"

"Yes."

"I'm sorry. With what's gone on it never occurred to me—"

"Don't be sorry. You've got enough things to carry right now without worrying about me. I'll take care of myself."

"I just feel like I'm responsible."

"We both messed up. You should of been up front about what was going on when you hired me. I should never of given Arthur Irwin a hint we suspected Friends was planning something. But either way, how could you or I know they'd turn so violent?"

She said, "These people are turning their backs on the lives they lived up to now. They can never go back."

"They could except for us. That's why we're in danger. We're the only people who know who they are, who can tell the police who they are. They probably assume we know a lot more than we do about what they've got planned. It's human nature to assume the other fellow knows more about you than he does."

"What should I tell the police when they come back?"

"Nothing. If they find out about Friends of the Wild it'll get out and they'll go so far underground we'll never find them. As it stands now it's a perfect stalemate. Shannon knows you won't talk so long as they have Tricia and we've got to get Tricia back before we talk. Cops'll find out from Doctor Eli about Amy wanting to hire me, but Eli doesn't know any whys or what fors and I'll string the cops along. You don't know what it was about. Amy never said a word to you. You don't know what it was about. Amy never said a word to you. If they ask about Tricia, tell them she ran off, you don't know where. They'll find stuff out, but we gotta make 'em earn it. Play for time."

Neither of us spoke for a bit, then Kay said, "Mr. Kruger? You know what I think about life?" Her voice was as dry as ashes.

"What?"

"No matter what she awards you—riches, fame, love, lovers, any kind of reward—*none* of it adequately compensates you for having to endure the bitch."

I thought that was damn profound.

SEVENTEEN

Kaiser and DiNardi leaned against Atlas's squad car across the street from Kay Thornberg's house. Atlas sat behind the wheel. DiNardi made a motion, called, "Get your ass over here, Kruger."

I slipped my sunglasses on as I crossed the street. Cops read eyes like the blind read braille and I was about to lie my ass off.

Kaiser had only been outside for fifteen minutes but heat and humidity affected him like water affected the wicked witch. Perspiration bubbles big as blisters dotted his forehead and upper lip. His cheeks were flushed salmon pink and his wilted collar was a dingy yellow from sweat. He huffed and puffed for air. He chewed a cold cigar that looked like a bludgeoned rat. In contrast DiNardi looked fresh and cool, like he was ready to be photographed for the cover of *Teenbeat*.

Kaiser eyed me up and down as I approached. He said, "You and Thornberg get your stories straight?"

"No stories to get straight. I offered my condolences."

DiNardi snorted. Said, "How dumb you think we are?"

"Haven't known you long enough to say."

"We ain't so dumb we believe a PI who walks into a house an hour after one of the residents get's bumped off goes there just to say he's sorry."

"Amy and I spent a month together in rehab. You forge close friendships in a place like that."

I almost conned Kaiser. His eyes flickered confusion for a second. But then he shook his head a little as if to jar gullibility away. He said, "Come on, Kruger, what was it? One of these girls bumping and grinding where she shouldn't be? Other one wanted details?"

I said, "Amy Barrow and Kay Thornberg were a happy couple. Amy went all the way to Atlanta so they could have that boy in there. They wanted a family."

DiNardi made the snort again. "Some family. Who plays dear old Dad? What kind of upbringing is that kid gonna have? Raised by dykes, surrounded by dykes. He'll never have a chance."

"Chance at what?"

"Kid's gonna grow up to be a fucking weirdo."

"Lots of kids with hetero parents grow up to be fucking weirdo's, DiNardi."

DiNardi said, "Look punk, this set-up screams jealousy. One of the lez's was getting two-timed, hired you to check it out. Probably Amy Barrow if the two of you were taking a sauce cure together. Who knows what you found out about Kay Thornberg or what other lezzies were involved? Thornberg got wind of it and either she or the new John-Mary took Amy out."

I said, "Why'd they kill her? Kay could of just broke off the relationship. Happens every day of the week. Don't you guys listen to Top Forty radio? Hetero couples, homo couples. Relationship goes bad, you break it off. The one get's dumped mopes around for a few months, then tries again."

DiNardi said, "When emotions like jealousy, betrayal, and rage get tangled together—anything can happen. And there could be money involved. Insurance policies. A will maybe. Could even be some blackmail mixed in. I mean, these *are* dykes we're dealing with."

Kaiser said, "You know how many homicides we investigate happen because somebody decides they wanna break up with their significant other and the significant other has other ideas?"

I said, "I know it happens."

Kaiser said, "And the brick through the window. How's that equate?"

I said, "You equate it. I just called to express my regrets." I laced my fingers behind my neck, moved my head from side to side. Tried to look as innocent as Mary's little lamb.

Atlas said from inside the car. "Maybe the dead dyke got one of them three-hour passes from the rehab, came over here in a jealous rage and threw the brick into the living room because Kruger here reported bad news back to her."

I said, "Atlas, if I was tailing Kay for Amy, why did Kay let me in the house just now like I was a friend?"

Atlas looked perplexed for a second, his face turning red. He said, "Because you're a fucking pervert just like she is."

I said, "Atlas, was it all them steroids made you so smart?"

Without looking into the car Kaiser said, "Nip it, Atlas." He took the cigar out of his mouth, said, "You know, after this stone-walling BS, we link you up with these women, it's gonna be rough for you."

A bridge I'd cross when I got to it.

I said, "How come you're so hot on this jealousy angle?"

"Gotta start somewhere," Kaiser said. "And Kay won't talk. Makes me suspicious."

I said, "Nobody saw who killed Amy Barrow?"

Kaiser said, "We'd have the fuck in jail, anybody did, wouldn't we? The taxi driver was across the street, thirty yards from the victim. Guy's from Guatemala or some goddamn place, knows about fifteen words of English. He wasn't paying attention, just waiting for a fare. He heard a string of shots, he don't know where they came from. He thought it was kids with firecrackers at first, it being so close to the Fourth. Soon's he saw Barrow's chest explode, he hit the seat of the taxi. Didn't hear nothing else, didn't pop back up till he heard police sirens."

DiNardi said, "You hire out for assassinations, PI?"

"CIA's been beggin me to take Castro out for years, but I got such a backlog."

"Don't smart off, wiseguy. It's a logical conclusion you look at this from another angle. Atlas tells us you're a bargain basement PI with severe substance abuse problems. The kind of PI hires out for anything, the price is right. Maybe the dyke across the street hired you to check up on Amy Barrow. Maybe you found Amy Barrow was shaking her booty in the lez bars and when Kay found out she hired you to take Amy Barrow out."

"And maybe that's why I went into rehab? To spy on Amy, see if she was seducing the females in there?"

DiNardi nodded. "Could be."

To Kaiser I said, "I hope you're the brains in this duo. If he is, this is the dumbest partnership since 'Car 54, Where Are You?'"

DiNardi's fist came up. Kaiser put his arm across DiNardi's chest, squeezed his bicep. Kaiser said, "Okay guys, quit. Let's act like adults here. Kruger, look at this from our point of view. We're just casting out what-ifs here. The newspapers are gonna eat us alive on this one. This is the kind of murder scares the shit out of the yuppies. Broad daylight. Nice neighborhood. Middle class white woman minding her own business gets blown away walking to a taxi. We got no clues, we got no witnesses. The two people who could help us won't talk. Help us out, Kruger. You were a cop once, right?"

"Long time ago."

"Where?"

"Ask Atlas."

Kaiser looked in the car. Atlas said, "Area One. We went to academy together."

Kaiser made a face. Area One is on the South Side. Cops, especially white cops, have lots of nicknames for Area One. None of them complimentary.

Kaiser said, "Most Chicago PI's used to be cops. You used to be a cop, you know how much cops depend on civilian assistance."

I didn't answer.

He said, "It help a PI any? Being an ex-cop?"

"Not really. PI's gotta use guile and strategy and psychology to find out what cops learn strong-arming people. A cop gets by bullying people with the tin and gun." I tapped my head. "A PI's gotta have smarts."

"That what we're doing here? Strong-arming?"

I smiled, shrugged.

DiNardi slugged my stomach. I doubled over, took a giant step back. He pulled it, but it was still a sucker punch. It forced all the air out of me.

I wrapped my arms around my belly. As I stared at concrete and sucked oxygen I heard cursing and a scuffle. Kaiser said, "God*damn* it, Leo, why'd you do that?" His voice came from in front of the squad car. The sounds I'd heard were Kaiser pushing DiNardi away from me.

DiNardi, his voice hot, said, "The punk's been laughing at us since he walked through that lezbo's door, Jack. Fuck him! Fuck *all* these fucking weirdo's!"

Kaiser talked in a soft, soothing voice. He said, "He's our link, Leo. Come on, use your head." His voice dropped and he said more that I couldn't hear. Someone walked away, a car door opened and slammed shut.

Then Kaiser stood next to me, his hand on my shoulder. He leaned over so his mouth was by my ear. He said, "You okay, Kruger?"

I couldn't breathe yet and my brain was in the mini-panic that occurs when all your air gets knocked out of you, but I nodded.

He gently rubbed my back shoulder to shoulder, said, "Forgive the kid, eh? He's young and headstrong. He's *Italian* for Chrissakes."

I nodded again.

He said, "No hard feelings?"

I shook my head no.

"Fine. Listen, we're gonna shove off, leave you alone." He rubbed some more, said, "But if we find you been lying to us this morning, as I suspect we will. Well, you just saw the kind of temper Leo DiNardi's got. Cops get lied to so much, sometimes we get *frustrated*, know what I mean? Course you do."

Some air got in. I gasped, "Kaiser, you wouldn't get shit out of me now if you paid me off with Kim Basinger."

Kaiser grunted, walked away. Another door slammed. A car drove off.

I stayed bent over, hands on knees, panting like a sick pooch, staring at straw-colored grass peeking through cracks in gray concrete.

Atlas said, "Hey Kruger, was it all that dope made *you* so smart?" He cackled like a village idiot. Then he drove away too.

EIGHTEEN

Twenty minutes later I sat in the Skylark, rubbing my belly, thinking things over.

I eliminated one course of action. I might as well throw away the addresses Kay had given me. No member of Friends of the Wild would be anywhere near their homes after this morning. They'd be sure Kay wouldn't talk so long as they had Tricia, but they wouldn't take any stupid chances.

And the reason for that was Dan Kruger. The unknown quantity. They had to be uneasy about me after I surprised them at Amanda Truitt's and shot my mouth off to Arthur Irwin. How much did I know; would *I* keep my mouth shut to keep Tricia alive?

I had to get word to them I would. Might keep both of us alive. Keeping quiet about Amy's murder didn't bother me at all under those circumstances. Because if I helped solve Amy Barrow's murder, I'd cause the murder of Tricia Thornberg.

Shannon Harper worried about three people. One was dead, one was a prisoner in her own home, and one, the loose cannon, was me.

I drove to Fremont, rolled past the apartment, checking out parked autos.

I cruised Wilton, then Bradley. I kept an eye out for the black van even though it was absurd to think they'd stake me out in the one vehicle of theirs I knew. I shifted to Park twice, got out of the Skylark to inspect the cabs of jacked up pick-ups.

Then a thought jumped into my head that made me pound the steering wheel. I careened the corner from Sheffield onto Fremont, braked in front of the school, hurried across the street.

I rushed up the porch stairs, breathing fast, heart pounding in my throat. I pushed open the front door, scooted through the living room.

Found Heather sound asleep in the bedroom. Bugs sprawled on his stomach next to her, panting furiously. A half-empty pint of brandy and a dixie cup sat on the nightstand. In the ashtray two crushed roaches lay on top of a mountain of Kool butts. Like most crackfreaks, Heather used pot and hard booze to pillow a crash.

Heather was on her back, arms flung out. A coating of sweat covered her body like liquid Saranwrap, but goosebumps pimpled her arms and legs. I sat on the edge of the bed, felt her wrist for a pulse, winced when I found it. It flickered like a hummingbird. I watched her small breasts rise and fall in time with her rapid, shallow breathing. She moaned. I gently massaged her legs until the goosebumps went away.

I wanted to cry. And not just because of the condition Heather was in. I thought about the future. The hours and days and weeks and months that stretched ahead. Who were Heather and I trying to kid? She'd stayed clean a day and a half outside of rehab. What about me? How long would it be before I drank my breakfast again? Could a person really reverse twenty years of addictive behavior?

And with what was going down, did I want to be sober now?

I looked at the bottle of brandy. I remembered the taste. I remembered the warm kindling in the belly that spreads outward, engulfing the body. Like pulling the covers over your head on a frigid winter morning. I remembered what it felt like to be in the sanctuary of the artificial paradise.

I called Marvin. I said quietly, "I'm scared and confused and in trouble and there's a bottle of brandy a foot away."

"You home?"

"Yes."

He said, "Pick up the bottle, go to the bathroom, pour it down the toilet."

I hesitated.

"Now!" he shouted. "Or next time you show up here your desk'll be in the street."

I said, "But—"

He yelled, "Don't think, do it!"

I did it. Came back, picked up the phone and said, "It's okay, Marv." I held the phone toward the bathroom so he could hear the toilet flushing.

"Sure?"

"For now."

"*She* bring the bottle in the house?"

"Lay off her, Marv."

"You okay?"

"Define okay."

"Don't play games. You okay?"

"I'm sober, I'm alive. Guess I'm okay."

"What's the problem?"

"Nothing a new life couldn't cure."

"Long as you're up, get me one too."

I smiled. Said, "I gotta get to work now and not think. That was good advice."

"Stop by today."

"I'll try."

"Don't try, do it."

I said I would. I said, "Thanks."

I went to the kitchen, ate two Valium, dropped ten more in a sandwich baggy, ziplocked it, stuffed it in my jeans pocket.

I went back in the bedroom, watched Heather some more. I couldn't decide what to do. I whispered, "Any ideas, Bugs? Besides getting shitfaced and hoping it all goes away? We're gonna ignore that option for the time being."

Bugs didn't move. I said, "Sleep on it wabbit, maybe you'll think of something."

I left the house, walked to the Skylark.

A folded page of blue-lined steno paper was under the windshield wiper. On it was written BUT WHAT IF SHE HADN'T BEEN THERE?

I removed the note, walked briskly back to the apartment.

NINETEEN

I dialed Amanda Truitt's number. A woman answered "Yes?" with a subdued, apprehensive voice, like she was expecting bad news.

I said, "George Kemp there?"

A long pause. The voice whispered, "I'm afraid you have the wrong number."

I said, "What about Frank Kelson? Sorrento Gallo?"

No answer.

I said, "Susan or Cornelia?"

"I don't know any people by that name."

"You just wish you didn't."

"What do you want?"

"Why'd you call Kay Thornberg this morning?"

"I never called—who?"

"I'm curious why you let Shannon con you into being an accessory after murder."

Deep breathing on the other end. No talk.

I said, "I wanna tell you some things."

"Who is this?"

"Dan Kruger."

"I don't know a—"

"You don't have to. Just listen up. First off, tell Shannon that Kruger and Kay won't talk so long as she has Tricia. As per your message?"

Silence.

"You got that, Amanda?"

"Yes."

"And then you tell her that promise does not apply if anything, and I mean *anything,* happens to Heather."

"Who?"

"Shannon knows who. Tell her if anything happens to Heather not only will I tell everything I know, but she better watch her ass. Because then it'll be personal. It takes a lot to tee me off, but that would more than do it. Tell her that, will you?"

"Y . . . yes." She sounded like she wanted to cry.

I said, "How involved are you in Amy's murder? Or you just a messenger service?"

Amanda Truitt hung up the phone.

I flicked the a/c in the living room window on, flopped on the couch. The unit made a whooshing racket, drowning out all noise from the street. Not surprising; the thing was almost as old as Heather. One thing that never ceased to amaze me was how many things I owned that were older than Heather. Half my record collection for starters.

I replayed the morning, tried to devise a plan of action. Found I wasn't any better devising action plans sober than I had been drunk. I spent twenty years blaming my faulty thought processes on the liquor and drugs. Maybe I was just stupid. That was a confidence-building thought.

One thing I knew. I couldn't leave Heather alone while she slept. I didn't know how long it would take for my message to get from Amanda Truitt to Shannon Harper, or even if the message would do any good. Harper might have already decided to take us all out and be done with it.

I wasn't sure what to do with Heather when she woke up. Send her back to Johnson City? Cart her with me while I worked? She'd *love* that.

I wondered who wrote the note. Who could've tailed me from Kay's house without me making them? More likely it was someone already watching the apartment. That would explain how they knew about Heather. They saw me dash across the street, knew what had me freaked out, knew what to write to keep me freaked out. And quiet. Was it Kemp or one of the others?

At 1:00 P.M. I turned on the Channel 9 news. Amy Barrow's murder was the second story. The station went live to a reporter in shirtsleeves standing in front of Mercy Mother's. He had a deep tan, permed blond hair.

He intro'd the story by gravely intoning, "Police are baffled at this hour by the brutal murder of a Lincoln Park woman. Amy Barrow, twenty-eight, was gunned down this morning as she left this North Side hospital. Police have no motive, no clues and no suspects."

Switch to videotape. The reported talked details over a long shot of Amy's covered body. He talked some more while a camera behind police lines zoomed in on uniform and plainclothes cops who kneeled by the body and walked around the front lawn of the rehab. There was tape of attendants lifting Amy's shrouded body and sliding it into the back of a Cook County ambulance.

Back to live. Standing next to the reporter was my good friend Detective Jack Kaiser.

Kaiser stared at the ground. He looked more tense than he had outside Kay Thornberg's house. Camera jitters, I suspected.

The reporter said, "I have with me Area Six Violent Crimes Detective Jack Kaiser. Can you tell us anything, Detective Kaiser?"

Kaiser said, "We've just interviewed the head of this institution and we now have what we believe to be a solid lead on this murder." The reporter started to ask about the solid lead, but Kaiser put his hand up and said, "Beyond that I have no comment." He walked out of camera range.

The reporter said, "There you have it, Rick. It appears police have just made an important discovery in this baffling, brutal murder."

Back to the studio. The anchorman said to the camera, "We'll furnish details on this apparent break in the murder of a North Side woman as they are made known." He started talking about a tax hike being debated in City Council.

I said to the TV, "Hey Rick, here's the break. They talked to Eli and now I'm in deep shit. Stop the presses."

I was smoking a Kool, getting my stories straight, when the phone rang at one-thirty.

It was Tricia Thornberg.

She was crying uncontrollably. She said, "I just heard about Amy. On TV."

"Where are you, Tricia?"

"How's my mother? I wanted to call her, but I don't think I can. What would I say?"

"She has friends with her, but she'd rather hear from you. Call her."

"Did you see her this morning?"

"Yes. Tricia, where are you?"

Sobbing, she said, "Is it okay that I called you? I looked you up in the phone book."

"Of course it's okay."

"Who killed Amy? Who would do that?"

"You gotta have a clue."

"How would I know?"

"They treating *you* okay?"

"Of course. I told you these are my friends."

I said, "Tricia, they—"

But before I could say anything more I heard Shannon Harper call, "Tricia, come here," in the background. Tricia said quickly, "I gotta go. If I don't talk to my mother, tell her how sorry I am about Amy. I can't believe she's dead." She hung up.

At two o'clock there was a banging on the front door. I opened it and said to Kaiser and DiNardi, "Ooh, a TV celebrity. At my house."

TWENTY

Kaiser was sweating like he'd just dug a ditch. He said, "You got air in this dump?"

I nodded and they pushed past. The smell of DiNardi's aftershave floated in his wake like poison gas. I said, "Keep it down. A friend is asleep in the bedroom."

DiNardi said in a deliberate, too loud voice, "Sure, we'll keep it down, punk. Anything for an old pal."

I sighed, pointed to the couch. They didn't move toward it, just stood together in the middle of the living room, giving me you-in-a-heap-a-trouble-boy glares.

Kaiser said, "I get so sick of people lying to me."

"Part of your job description."

"I'm sick of it anyway."

"Public expects cops to earn their money, not have stuff handed to them on a silver platter."

"Well then, fuck the public."

"We serve, protect, and fuck. Has a nice ring to it."

"We talked to Dr. William Eli at Mercy Mother's."

"He lied to you too?"

"Why'd you lay the BS on us?"

"I'd never lie to a police officer, police officer."

"You had to know how easy it'd be for us to check out. After we left you, Leo says 'Let's go back to the hospital, let's find out what really went down.' So we drive to the hospital. We aren't there ten minutes we learn Amy Barrow hired you your last day in the joint. Five minutes after that we find witnesses saw the two of you engaged in a prolonged conversation your last night there."

I said, "You learned she *wanted* to hire me."

DiNardi said, "Let's start over, Door-Knocker. Why'd the dyke hire you? Kay Thornberg screwing around on her? Or was it something else? You working for both of 'em?"

"Maybe I didn't take the job."

DiNardi barked a laugh. "Kruger, you couldn't afford to turn down a paper route somebody offered you one." He took a step forward, hands grasping the lapels of his suit coat. "Why'd Amy Barrow hire you?"

"I never said she did."

"And you're a liar."

"Prove it."

"You didn't take the job, why'd you show up at the house an hour after she got whacked?"

"Convey my regrets."

"I got no reservations about hauling a PI's ass in. We can have us a long, leisurely talk about all this. Just the two of us. A private room. No sleeping friends to worry about."

"DiNardi, after that sucker punch this morning you got a better chance reading tomorrow's funny pages without moving your lips than you got getting talk out of me. You try and rough me up in my own house, you're gonna be talking to OPS."

He said, "And you don't cooperate on Amy Barrow you're gonna be sitting in a cell for obstructing justice. Maybe even accessory after the fact."

I shrugged, said, "Whatever."

Kaiser placed his hand on DiNardi's shoulder, gently squeezed it. He said, "C'mon, guy, what's the catch? Who you willing to go to jail for? It can't be Kay Thornberg. She don't care about you. Why you care about her?"

I shrugged again.

They looked at each other, back at me. Kaiser said, "So that's it? You plan to jerk our chain every inch of the journey?"

"I'm jerking nobody's chain."

"You lie to us, we find out you lied to us, then you lie to us again. I call that jerking our chain."

I said, "All Eli heard was Amy Barrow wanted to hire me. He never heard if I took the job or not."

"You think you're tough enough and smart enough you can dig your heels in, make us get everything the hard way?"

I said, "Amy wanted to hire me, my fee was too steep, she let it slide. But we were friends because we rehabbed together so I paid my respects to Kay Thornberg when she died."

Kaiser said, "Kruger, a wino on Lower Wacker could afford you and have enough left over for a bottle of Dog."

I said nothing. Truth hurts sometimes.

He said, "Okay, why'd she *wanna* hire you?"

"Etiquette lessons."

Kaiser smiled without meaning to.

DiNardi's neck and cheeks turned a lovely shade of red. He yelled, "God *damn* you, Kruger."

There was scratchy breathing to my right. The three of us looked that way. Heather stood in the doorway to the bedroom wearing a black *Naked Raygun* T-shirt and a pair of black bikini panties. She pointed the knife at the cops.

I said, "No, hon', not this time. Go back to bed."

Her face was as drawn and haggard as a Dust Bowl refugee's. Her lips looked like solid rust. She licked them and winced. She said, "Who are *these* dirtbags? They tryin' to hurt you?" Her voice was as hoarse as a great-grandmother on her death bed.

DiNardi and Kaiser's reaction to a female skinhead with a knife in her hand was different from Gallo and Fuller's. Kaiser made a bemused smile. DiNardi checked out Heather's long legs, then looked from her to me and smirked. He said, "Kruger, you always hang with the upper crust, don't you? Sugar Rautbord in the kitchen pouring Chardonnay?"

I said, "So long as I don't hang with cops I can look at myself in the mirror in the morning." I said to Heather, "A couple of old friends come to reminisce. Go back to bed."

DiNardi said, "She looks trashed to me. Uppers are like food and drink to skinheads. That it, *ma'am?* You spinning like a top?"

I said, "She's sick. She should be in bed."

Heather stared hatred at DiNardi, but there were roaches in the bedroom ashtray and God only knew how much speed she'd stashed around the house. She said, "I heard angry voices and I wanted to make sure you were okay."

I said, "I'm fine."

She went back into the bedroom.

DiNardi said, "Jesus Christ."

Kaiser said, "What'd you mean 'Not this time'?"

"Didn't mean nothin'."

Kaiser said, "That's nice. That she wants to protect you like that."

I said, "She's tougher than I am."

DiNardi said, "How about we toss the crib, Jack?" He grinned a toothy grin at me, said, "This dump stand a stop?"

"We just say no to drugs in this house."

Kaiser shook his head. He said, "Kruger, part of me admires you, but another part of me thinks you're the cheapest, stupidest son-of-a-bitch on the planet."

"Somebody has to be, right?"

"We'll be seeing you."

I said, "Don't be strangers. If anything pertinent comes up, you two'll be the first I call."

DiNardi made fists, bounced them against his thighs. Staring at me he said, "You see, Jack. This *fuck* breaks our balls every chance he gets, you keep letting him get away with it."

Kaiser said, "Come on, Leo, let Mr. Kruger attend to his sick friend." DiNardi got an astounded look on his face, but followed Kaiser out of the room. As he opened the door, Kaiser turned and said, "Don't think you got a good cop-bad cop on your hands here. I'm just more patient than Leo is."

They were gone a minute when there was a knock on the door. Kaiser was by himself when I opened it. Lines of sweat rolled down his face. He said, "Listen, I don't know what they are, but obviously you got your reasons. I come back later without the dago, you wanna talk?"

I said, "Maybe. I got to talk to somebody first."

He wiped the back of his hand across his forehead.

I said, "Why'd they partner you with that hothead anyway? Talk about nice house, nobody home."

He shrugged, said, "Leo's a decent cop."

I said, "He might be if you stuffed a handful of Valium down his throat before he hit the street."

Kaiser cocked his head, looked thoughtful. He said, "Now that's a thought."

TWENTY-ONE

Heather lay on her back on the bed, knees in the air, her left arm covering her eyes. Under the T-shirt, her right hand massaged her stomach.

I said, "How you feel?"

"Where's the brandy?"

"Lake Michigan."

"You poured it *out?*"

"Had to."

"Asshole."

"Seems to be the consensus."

"I *need* it. I feel sick."

"You look dead. And I don't appreciate you bringing booze in the house. Pills and pot are one thing, but—"

Bugs moved away from her toward me. The slight motion intensified her sickness. She moaned, clamped her arm harder on her eyes. I reached down, lifted Bugs, stroked his back. I said, "Want some Valium?"

She didn't answer.

I said, "How much speed you got stashed?"

"Jesus Christ, I had any speed laying around I'd let myself get this sick? Call Maria Leary."

"No way. You aren't either."

"You're a bastard, you know that? I hate you."

"You'll get over it."

I didn't take the anger personally. Speed crashes bring out a person inside you you never knew existed. An evil, venomous twin who experiences only hate and rage and depression.

After some seconds, she rasped, "Why were cops here?"

"They think I'm holding out on them."

"Are you?"

"Yes."

"You in trouble with the law?"

"I'm in trouble with everybody."

She moved her arm up to her forehead, squinted up at me. "Like the two yups who showed the other day?"

"There's some people in that group a little rougher than those two."

She put her arm back on her eyes. "Screw all of 'em," she said.

"I'm worried about you, Heather."

"I've done speed runs before."

"Not the speed. These people have something big planned and they don't mean to be stopped. They've killed one person already."

"Who?"

"Amy Barrow."

She grunted.

I said, "They threatened my life, they threatened to harm you. Here." I removed the windshield note from my pants pocket, held it to her.

She looked at it. Said, "Low rent slimeballs. I'll kill every one of these shits they mess with me."

The speed crash twin lost it completely. She ranted in detail what she'd do to low rent slimeball shits who messed with her. This was how she'd started the night she trashed the cafeteria at Mercy Mother's. I petted Bugs, quieting him as she raved. When she finally stopped I said, "Heather, they're not gonna come at you one on one. Amy got shot walking to a taxi."

She lit a Kool from a pack on the nightstand, inhaled deeply, started to gag. She ran to the bathroom. I listened to her dry heave. I felt sorry for her, but some of me was saying, "*Damn you, Heather. You're gonna mess up my sobriety.*" Hostile baggage, Eli would have called it. Well, screw you too, Eli.

When Heather came back she plopped face down on the bed, her arms cradled under her stomach. The bed jiggled like it was a water mattress.

I said, "I think you should go back to Johnson City till this is over."

"I'd rather get killed than go back to Johnson City."

"Just for now. You can come back."

"No! Leave me alone."

"They won't let me do that."

"I'm sick."

"I can't imagine why."

"Don't give me any sanctimonious crap, Dan. That's the last thing I need from you: Sanctimonious crap. You're a fine one to talk. I've seen you puking your guts out on a public street, don't forget that. I've seen you go through three bottles of brandy and a case of beer in one weekend—"

"And now you're seeing me sober. I don't need to hear about 'used to's'. So shut up."

"Fuck you," she screamed.

A long silence. I said, "Maybe we should reassess this relationship, Heather. All things considered, it doesn't look real promising right now."

"That's fine with me, Mr. White Knight. Mr. Sanctimonious, Holier Than Thou asshole—"

I left the room, closed the door. There was no reason to continue the conversation.

I phoned Kay Thornberg. A woman who wasn't her answered. I said, "Can I speak to Kay?"

"She can't come to the phone right now. I'll take a message."

"This is Dan Kruger. I'm—"

"I know who you are. I was here this morning. Kay told us about you. Some of it anyway."

I liked the way she said it. Her tone implied she wasn't prying for information, just informing me she didn't know what was going on. I said, "You the blonde or the brunette?"

"I have blond hair." Her voice was harsh.

I said, "Sorry. Sexist, right? Referring to women by the color of their hair."

"At least you know what to apologize for." Her tone softened. "My name's Hedy. I've known Kay a long time. She says you're a friend. Amy trusted you."

"For all the good it did her."

"Don't blame yourself. From what I hear you've helped as much as you could."

"How's Kay?"

"Not good, but she's with friends. We won't leave her."

I said, "What about Alan?"

"He says Amy's name a lot."

I said, "Did Tricia call there?"

"No."

"Tell Kay she called me. She's distraught about Amy. Also ask Kay if a friend of mine can stay there awhile. She's in trouble because of me and she has nothing to do with this."

"Who's the friend?"

"My girlfriend. I think. The same people killed Amy threatened her."

"They threaten you?"

"From the start."

"Hold on."

Hedy came back a minute later. "Kay says of course your friend can stay here. And she wants to hear every word Tricia said."

"When I get there."

I hung up, went to the sugar jar in the kitchen, back to the bedroom. I said, "Come on, Heather, I got a place you can stay. There's boards on the windows, lots of people. It's like a fort."

She still lay face down. She made a muffled noise into the pillow. It took a bit before I realized she was crying. I sat next to her, massaged up and down her spine. She said, "You didn't mean what you said, did you? About splitting up?"

"Of course not."

"Because I didn't mean what I said. Dan, I just feel so Godawful."

"I know that. Here." I held out two Valiums and a dixie cup of water.

She turned around, sat up. Her jittery hands spilled most of the water out of the cup as she raised it to her mouth. She gagged, but got the chill pills down. I took some of her clothes from the closet, tossed them on the bed. She stood and pulled up a pair of tattered black jeans, stepped into the boots. She shrugged into her leather jacket, said, "What about Bugs?"

I said, "Bugs'll be okay. These people might kill us, but they'd never harm Bugs."

As I said it I realized I liked them a little for that.

TWENTY-TWO

George Kemp leaned against the side of the Skylark. His massive arms were crossed against his chest. He stared at the street. He wore a white polo shirt tucked into pleated jeans, no socks, black canvas espadrilles.

Heather and I walked to the car. Her right hand slipped into the pocket of her leather jacket for the butterfly knife she carries there. She said, "Dan?"

I said, "No. Get in the car." She walked around the front and got in the passenger seat, didn't shut the door.

I stopped a few feet from Kemp. He didn't look up. Like he was addressing an ant he said, "I just watched two policemen leave your house."

"How'd you know they were cops?"

He didn't answer.

I said, "They didn't learn anything."

He nodded. "You told a friend of mine you'd keep quiet."

His voice was too polite, formal almost. Like his idea of normal conversation was two diplomats discussing war.

I said, "What's going on? What's Shannon got planned?" You don't ask, you don't get.

"Shannon Harper is a great woman. Maybe one of the greatest women who ever lived."

I said, "Sure she is. Mother Theresa, Joan of Arc, and Shannon Harper."

"I don't think history will laugh at her, friend."

"She's so great, why'd she kidnap Tricia Thornberg? Why'd she have Amy Barrow killed?"

"Tricia Lynn is with us because she wants to be with us."

"Amy's dead because she wanted to be dead?"

He didn't answer.

I said, "Why you here?"

"Wanna talk about Kay."

I said, "She's worried sick about Tricia. We don't know what you're up to, but tell Shannon nobody'll talk if she sends Tricia home."

"That's not an option. Tricia Lynn wants to stay with us."

"She'll change her mind soon enough."

A long pause. He said, "You ever wonder why you're here?" I shook my head. He said, "Why you do the things you do?"

"I don't, but the Temptations did."

He kept going like I hadn't talked. "I used to ask myself why I was so good at buying and selling foreign money. At guessing right time after time about futures and fluctuations, downswings and upswings. I made a decision, made eye contact, put my hand in the air. That's what I did. The money I made doing that? Obscene. I used to spend hours staring at the wall wondering what the point of all this was. What, I asked myself is the *fucking point?*"

"The wall ever give you an answer?"

He ignored me. "Shannon Harper is a woman with a vision. You probably have no idea what I'm talking about. Or even understand the concept of a person having a vision. You impress me, friend, as a person who slogs along day to day, never questioning things, never asking what the point of it all is. But some people aren't like that. They're special. Touched by God, maybe. They see how things should be instead of how they are."

"Tell me about Shannon Harper's vision, George."

"Kruger, you ever studied Eastern philosophy, their religions?"

"Never have."

"I started after I met Shannon. Those people have an enlightened view of life. A mystical approach. Makes us Westerners look primitive as cavemen. Reincarnation, karma, dharma, fate, koan—these are advanced ideas. They believe each of us has a duty to perform. That's why we're here. To perform that duty, that *assignment*. It's like a play where we all have lines. We rehearse and then the play starts and we wait in the wings until we hear our cue. Then we walk on stage, speak the lines, and get off. Some of us just have bigger lines or parts."

"That's not Buddha, George, it's Shakespeare."

He said, "Friend, I know *my* duty was to accumulate money for when I met Shannon Harper. So I could help her do her work. Complete her vision. *That's* the point, friend. It was all preordained."

"You'd think Shannon Harper had enough money to do her work."

"Things aren't always as they seem. I was put here and guided so I could arrive at a specific point in time in a position to assist Shannon Harper. It's time for me to read my lines. Complete my assignment."

I checked out George Kemp's enormous biceps. Like they were tires and his words air, they seemed to swell and stiffen as he talked, although now his voice was as gentle as a Quaker's. I said, "What are you telling me, George? I mean I love animals too, but—"

"I'm telling you, should you decide to cross us. You should know you won't cross just us, you'll be crossing fate. Interfering with God's plan. That's a heavy load to take on, friend. Me *and* God."

He looked at me again. Like at the bus stop, he didn't pose tough. His face was devoid of expression. Except for his eyes. His eyes were lit, insane.

I said, "You're right, George, it is a heavy load. Too heavy for me."

He turned, looked inside the car. He made a short bow to Heather and politely said, "Good day, ma'am. I hope I didn't unduly alarm you." He walked down the middle of the street, turned right on Addison, never looking back.

I stared after him. When he disappeared from sight I suddenly smelled cut grass and hot rubber, heard buzzing insects. I hadn't noticed any of these things while we talked.

I got in the car, turned the key. Heather said, "That the dude who wrote the note?"

I nodded.

"God, he's big."

I said, "I wish that's all he was."

TWENTY-THREE

Driving to Kay Thornberg's house I told Heather the situation there. She was scrunched down, head resting against the door panel, eyes shut. She grunted. She felt comfortable in any segment of society so long as it wasn't the mainstream.

She said, "You gonna tell me why all this is happening?"

"Later maybe."

She said, "God, my body is cashed."

"I'll tell Kay you're sick and need to sleep. The V's helping?"
"Little bit."

More women were at the house now. Six sat in the living room. They spoke in hushed voices. They looked at Heather and me with curiosity but no hostility and kept talking. Hedy led us down a hall, knocked on a door and pushed it open.

A bedroom. Kay sat in a chair by an open window. She stared into the back yard of the house next door. Sheer white curtains framing the window shifted slightly with a faint breeze. Alan sat in her lap, his thumb in his mouth. He stared with wide eyes as we entered the room.

A woman about the same age as Kay sat on the bed. She stood and left the room when she saw us. She smiled sadly as she passed me.

I said, "Heather needs to sleep. She's sick."

Kay looked at Heather. There was no change in her expression when she saw a girl with no hair wearing a motorcycle jacket and shredded black jeans. She said, "She can have Tricia's room. The next door down. I'll make sure she's not disturbed."

I sat where the other woman had been. Heather stayed by the door, her hands shoved into jacket pockets.

Kay said, "Hedy told me Tricia phoned you today."
"She feels she can't call you."
"I don't understand why."

I said, "I think I do. It's like people who ridicule religion and ignore God all their lives, and then when they find they got cancer or something they feel it'd take real gall to expect God to answer their prayers. I think Tricia feels it'd take a lot of gall to call you now."

Kay shook her head slowly. She said, "Or maybe *I* have to make the first step. I've thought a lot the last few days. Looking at things from another perspective besides my own for a change. Maybe it *was* me. Amy and I were so in love and so 'into' our new family and Animal Sanctuary. It's obvious to me Tricia couldn't help but feel excluded. It should have been obvious before."

"That's something you two'll have to work out."
"If we ever get the chance."

I said, "You'll get the chance. Before she called today I

wouldn't of said that. Ninety percent of all families in the country have problems like this. When kids hit a certain age things go haywire. Almost always it gets worked out."

"But how often doesn't it?"

I looked back at Heather, thought "Sometimes," but didn't say it.

Kay said, "Why couldn't I see it?"

"Don't beat yourself up about the past. One thing I learned in rehab. Learn from it, but don't drub yourself over it."

Kay said, "Her hostility, the obsessive friendship with Shannon, the silence, the pouting, the sulking, the rebellion. All of it a cry for help. For attention. Her way of telling me she felt ignored. And probably more."

"More?"

She was quiet for some seconds, then said, "She said to ask why didn't her friends ever come by anymore?"

"Yes."

"I always made sure her friends knew I was gay. I'm proud of it and that makes me—militant sometimes."

"You said you detested closets."

"Yes, but now I wonder if that contributed to the way she felt. When she was younger, she never even questioned it, but when she became sexually mature everything changed. I should of realized that. Just because it was healthy for me to be so open, doesn't mean—" She caressed Alan's cheek.

I said, "You two talk about it?"

"I always told her I didn't care if she chose hetero or gay, got married, stayed single, or decided to be asexual—whatever she wanted. There's lots of options. All I wanted was she should be comfortable with her sexuality. But what does a teenager know about comfortable sexuality? Teenagers have enough problems coming to grips with their sexual identity without having to deal with a situation they don't understand and none of their friends accept."

"Her friends talk?"

"I told her once if a friend ridiculed or ostracized her because of me, they weren't really a friend. But that's a difficult thing to lay on a teenage girl. And easy for me to say. I know the most important thing for teenagers is to be accepted and approved by their peers. I never gave it much thought until you mentioned it the other day and then heard her comment."

"Tricia ever say she was getting harassed?"

"No, but that doesn't mean she wasn't."

"She's distraught about Amy."

"Does she know who killed her?"

"She says no, but she has to suspect it's someone in Friends. She knows they've got plans. She knows you hired me to find her. She knows how Shannon feels about you and Amy. She's smart enough to put two and two together."

"That's all she said?"

"We didn't talk long."

"Does she know they plan to keep her by force?"

"I didn't get to tell her. I don't think she'd believe it anyway. She still admires Shannon Harper, although there's got to be cracks in the reverence now. I told her Shannon had threatened us, and now that Amy's dead—."

Heather said weakly, "Mrs. Thornberg?"

Kay looked at her, eyebrows raised. Heather said, "For what it's worth, you sound a lot more compassionate and understanding than most people. I hope you and your daughter get a chance to work things out."

Kay said to me, "How do we start?"

"Next time I talk to her, I wanna tell her you'll leave this house, meet her somewhere."

Kay let out a long breath. "You have no idea what you're asking."

"You're right, I don't, but you said you had to make the first move. Prove to her how far you'll go."

Another wait, then Kay said, "Mr. Kruger, do you know I've sometimes thought of killing myself just to get out of the house? And that is not a joke. If you don't suffer from it you can't imagine the terror. The randomness of that terror. The fear of that terror. I can't tell you how many mornings I've lain awake at three A.M. telling myself that today was the day I started to kick this. That today was the day I called a therapy group or a hospital. I didn't because I could live with it during the day. Family and friends were here and life was okay and they took care of me and I accepted what I was. We didn't even talk about it. It was a given. Like I had one leg or something. But at three A.M. you dwell on the demons who have a hold on you."

I said quietly, "You do indeed."

She nodded. "But then I'd get up and the closer the time came to *doing* it, the more panic-stricken I'd get until when I got to the front door or put my hand on the phone the terror would have me helpless. It's been a year since I even pretended. I told Amy if she kicked the alcohol, my problem was next. But deep inside I don't know if I really can. People suffer from this all their lives. Sometimes it takes years to make the most minute progress."

"And sometimes it's cured, right?"

"Sometimes."

"Focus on that. Because now Amy's dead and Tricia is a prisoner. You've got to try. Let me tell Tricia you'll try for her."

She said, "I don't know," looked out the window again.

I waited a minute. I looked back at Heather. She shrugged. She didn't know what we were talking about. I said, "I talked to Amanda Truitt and George Kemp this morning."

Kay nodded to show she was listening.

"Amanda is the woman who called you about Amy. I told her we wouldn't say a word so long as Tricia's with them. George Kemp came by to tell me the message got relayed to the group. I'm not sure he believes us though."

Kay swung her head toward me. Fear riding her voice, she said, "Would they kill Tricia? I mean, if we don't talk."

I was reasonably certain they wouldn't as long as Tricia wanted to stay with them. But if she tried to leave, or I snatched her, all bets were off. I said, "No, they won't."

I stood to leave. As I opened the door Kay said, "Mr. Kruger? Tell Tricia I'll meet with her outside the house. But set it up close by, okay? As close as possible?"

"I'll make it next door if I can."

As I walked back to the Skylark, Kaiser and DiNardi passed in their unmarked Ford, headed toward Kay's house. I gave them a cheery wave, whispered, "Keep the lip zipped, Kay."

TWENTY-FOUR

I took Lake Shore Drive north. Got off at Hollywood. I drove down Devon, past the blocks of Indian and Pakistani shops and restaurants that dominate that street west of Western Avenue, watched groups of women in multi-colored sari's float in and out of the stores. I turned around, drove back to Broadway. I pulled into a parking lot between a jewelry store and a bagel shop, smoked a Kool.

By the time I stubbed it out I was confident no one had tailed me. I drove to Cyprus Street.

I knew their names, their addresses, their friends. I knew they had something major planned. I knew they'd killed Amy Barrow. I knew they threatened to kill Tricia Thornberg. They knew I knew those things. The apartment on Cyprus was the only lead I had Friends of the Wild didn't know about.

I hoped.

I backed into a service alley at the side of another apartment building half a block east, stopping when I was twenty yards beyond the sidewalk.

A row of tall bushes protected me from sight. Gaps in the hedge provided me a partial view of the curb in front of their building. I removed my binoculars from the glove compartment, set them next to me.

I smoked and reviewed the case. As time passed profound pessimism set in, pessimism being the cornerstone of my philosophy of life.

I didn't even know what the apartment was for. There was a chance no Friend would show for hours or days. Even if they did, what did I do if they walked in and didn't come out? Sit here all night? Knock on the door and ask to chat? And a worse case scenario: The Rasta Kid might've narced on me, causing them to abandon this place altogether. I said out loud, "Dan, you got no choice 'cause this is all the lead you got."

It took awhile, but I got lucky. At 6:00 P.M. the black van passed the service alley and parked in front of the courtyard apartment building. I raised the binocs. Watched Sorrento Gallo and Boyd Fuller climb down from the van, walk out of sight toward the building.

Twenty minutes later they came back. Gallo pushed the back end and Fuller pulled the front end of a large baggage cart. Suitcases, metal boxes, and long cartons wrapped in clear plastic were strapped to the cart. They went to the slide door side of the van, again passing from sight. I trained the binoculars on the back window of the van. Saw shadows moving inside.

It took fifteen minutes to load up. Then the two men rolled the empty cart back toward the apartment building, returned five minutes later without it. They climbed into the van, went west, Gallo driving.

I pulled onto Cyprus and followed.

The van got on Touhy Avenue, took the northbound ramp onto I-94. As I merged with traffic I got an idea where we were headed. I was glad the tank was full. I'd botched a tail once early on when the Skylark had to make a pit stop. Now I top off the tank every morning just in case.

It was early evening. The sun was a blazing orange ball slanted almost even with the window of the car, but it was still sticky hot. Sweat felt like grease on my neck and back. I pulled my shirt up, worked it off. I silently cursed the people in the van. The brand new van with the windows rolled up and the a/c no doubt on max.

I-94 was jammed, turning into a huge parking lot when we got to the tollbooth plaza after it becomes the Tri-State. But tailing a van is a breeze even in heavy traffic.

I smoked my Kools, mopped my brow and neck with the Wash 'n' Dris I carry in the glove compartment, listened to the Red Sox wax Melido Perez for six runs in the first inning. Historically, Melido's games should start in the second inning. I'm positive he considers the opponent's first time up batting practice. Or maybe he just likes a challenge. In the old days I'd have been screaming, "Get his ass out of there," with each hit. Or worse. I once put a quart bottle of Strohs through a TV set when Salome

Barojas gave up a three-run ninth inning home to lose a game to the Yankees. But the last few seasons White Sox ineptitude hadn't seemed to bother me as much. Must be I'm mellowing in my old age. Besides, the Cubs were wretched again this season and that always makes me so happy I can't get too upset if the Sox only stink.

I could have used a drink. It wasn't a craving, the nerves weren't screaming for it like during detox week or when Heather's brandy bottle was crooking its finger, but there was definitely desire. I knew why. Long drives bore me and I always attacked boredom with booze. Of course I attacked worry, fear, anxiety, depression, and every other negative emotion with booze, but boredom was a biggie. I said out loud, "Not today, Dan. Maybe tomorrow." My nerves said, okay we can deal with one more day. I ripped open a new pack of Wash 'n' Dris with my teeth and inhaled the vinegary smell.

We continued north, past Great America amusement park and numerous exits I knew we wouldn't use. We entered Wisconsin. I grinned at billboards that said WISCONSIN VIGOROUSLY ENFORCES ITS DRUNK DRIVING LAWS and similar messages. These signs are prominently posted because legal in Wisconsin used to be eighteen as opposed to twenty-one in Illinois, which meant every weekend the Dairy State would get invaded by throngs of thirsty teenagers.

It was dusk when we got to Milwaukee. The Sox game started to fade, which was fine by me as it was 8–1 and Melido was long gone. I found a classic rock station.

The highway became the North South Freeway and I was sorely puzzled, Freeway being such a unique concept to a resident of Illinois. Anything down there with more than four lanes they stick a tollbooth every hundred yards or so. The radio station was on a roll—lots of '60's British Invasion, Motown, Atlantic and Stax. Each new song I boosted the volume a little. When Aretha's "Respect" intro'd I couldn't turn it right any further. The dash rattled like a Saturn rocket lifting off.

At 8:45 P.M. the van exited at the Grafton exit. So did I.

It went west on a sparsely trafficked two-lane highway. Insects splattered against the windshield and nipped my face. It smelled like—country. I'm a city boy. I couldn't get any more specific. I turned down the volume and dropped back, kept my eyes on the van's tail lights. After ten minutes the van turned right onto a blacktopped country road.

After two miles a long, four-story, multi-colored brick and dark glass building loomed on our left. There was a huge parking lot on the near side with maybe fifteen cars clustered together next to the building. Not many lights were on inside the building, but rows of closely bunched, high-powered floodlights illuminated the outside. A chainlink fence ran around the entire complex. At the entrance to the parking lot a large sign said HARPER COSMETICS—AUTHORIZED PERSONNEL ONLY! Two men were inside a brightly lit guard house. Three dock doors facing the parking lot and a pair of double glass doors in the middle of the building at the end of a sidewalk running from the parking lot were the only entrances I saw.

The van, which hadn't slowed as it passed the building, stayed on the blacktop until it came to a four-lane highway. It turned left. After a couple of minutes a Holiday Inn appeared on the right. The van turned in, stopped outside the motel office, which had *Holiday Inn* scripted in purple neon.

I drove past the motel, pulled into the gravel parking lot of Sam's Steak House, which was fifty yards beyond the Holiday Inn office. Sam's windows were black, but awash with neon beer signs. His lot was almost full too. Overfed middle-aged couples in polyester licked their lips and patted their stomachs as they waddled to their cars.

Boyd Fuller exited the van, went inside the office, returned a minute later. He said something into the window of the van, started walking down a long, two-story wing of hotel rooms, looking at his hand, then at door numbers. The van turned around, coasted alongside him.

At the end of the wing the van pulled into a parking space. Boyd Fuller went up a flight of stairs. He opened a door at the top of the stairs. He went to the next door, unlocked and pushed it open too.

I got out of the car, hunkered down, balanced my elbows on my knees, trained the binoculars on the van.

I watched Frank Kelson, Susan Chapman, and Cornelia Haas

follow Gallo and Fuller up the stairs to the rooms. Each carried an overnight bag.

I got back in the Skylark, waited half an hour. Sorrento Gallo came out once. He went to an ice machine, filled a bucket, returned to his room.

I now knew the something big concerned Harper Cosmetics. But Tricia wasn't with these people and Tricia was all I cared about. I could tell the local police about these people and their van full of whatever it was full of. I could tell them what I suspected these people were up to.

But that would harm Tricia. And as I thought about it—and I'd been thinking about it a lot since my second talk with Kay Thornberg—if rabbits were getting poison dripped into their eyes back in that building, to my mind the people who owned that building deserved a little hell.

I went into Sam's, ordered a steak sandwich and large Diet Pepsi to go, received directions to Milwaukee.

I gassed up at an Amoco station, headed south.

TWENTY-FIVE

It was 11:30 P.M. when I got back to the Cyprus Street apartment. I removed the five-way hand lantern from the trunk. A young Asian couple on their way out held the front door open for me. They both smiled, the man made a tiny bow. I returned it.

I heard a rumbling noise in the distance when I turned onto the fourth floor hallway. As I got closer the rumble took on a reggae beat. Outside the Rasta Kid's apartment the floor and walls shook. Now I knew what the "high explosion" was.

I knocked hard on the Friends apartment door. Waited, knocked again. I was certain the apartment was empty, but better safe than sorry. I've been sorry enough times in my life. I pounded one more time. Used the skeleton key to open it.

The baggage cart stood in the middle of the first room. I walked through the place, tossing the flashlight beam back and forth like a blind man using a cane. Everything was gone. Including the cat. I went into the second room, trained the light on the wall where the writing had been. Nothing. I rotated the light around the room. All four walls were painted brown. The smell of paint was strong.

I pointed the light into the fridge, cupboards, and closets, knowing I'd find nothing. The entire time the one-three reggae beat thundered through the kitchen wall.

When I left I stopped next door. The earthquake inside continued for three minutes. "What Is Life?" by Black Uhuru. My favorite reggae band. But they probably weren't this loud in concert. Soon as the song started to fade I commenced pounding on the door, hoping someone would hear it before the next track started.

The Rasta Kid did. He wore shades and a toothy smile as he peeked his head around the open door. He shouted, "Hello neighbor, enter." The smile died when he saw it was me.

I yelled, "Remember me? The asshole?" I pronounced it like he had: Ahhs-ole.

He shouted, "I remembering too well."

"Your neighbors don't complain about this?"

He opened the door wider so I could see inside the room. Six black men with dreadlocks as thick as his and ten women, white and black, sat on the floor, crosslegged, leaning against furniture. The room was mostly dark. Smoke drifted like fog. Nobody was frowning.

The Kid pointed at one of the men and said, "My downstairs neighbor." He pointed at one of the women. She had trim cut blond hair and wore a navy blue suit. He said, "My upstairs neighbor." The woman looked like an investment banker. Except she started giggling when he pointed at her. I don't think investment bankers know how to giggle.

With the door open I could see the Kid was wearing exactly what he had the first time I'd been here. One pair of baggy white terrycloth shorts.

I said, "This is the last time you'll have to talk to me."

"No, you wrong, mon. Last time was the last time I had to talk to you." He laughed so hard he had to bend over. He looked back at the people inside to see if they thought he was as funny as he did. They couldn't have heard a hydrogen bomb go off in the courtyard, let alone a conversation in the hallway, but they laughed anyway.

"A few questions, that's all."

"Or you gonna be sending lawman here, right?" He laughed again. The prospect of lawmen seemed funny tonight. The condition he was in, brain cancer would seem funny.

"No lawmen. Just wanna know more about the new next door people."

"You still looking for the teenage girl?"

"Still am."

"You not exactly Charlie Chan, know that?"

"She been here?"

"Charlie, he'd of snapped that little girl right up by now. Laid some profound proverbs on the peoples while he was at it. Confucius say, 'You are one inept mofo, you know that?'"

"Been told that by more people than Confucius. You see the next door people bringing boxes in and out?"

He took a long toke off the spliff in his hand. Holding the smoke in he said, "What dose people, mon? They like Natty Dread?"

Natty Dread was the Jamaican Jesse James. I said, "Why you ask that?"

"Dem people carrying guns around."

"What kind?"

"Fucking machine gun guns." He put his hands like he carried a sub-machine gun and went "Ack-ack-ack-ack," exhaling the smoke in a rush while pretending to spray bullets.

"They carried guns out in the open?"

"No mon, not slung on they backs, but I know what dem guns in cases look like. And two were out of cases underneath some other things in a cart they lugged about. Uzi carbines? Colt AR-15s? Street Sweeper-Striker 12s? I seen plenty in my time. In dey case and out."

Drug trade guns. I imagined he had.

"They had those?"

He nodded, looked smug.

He said, "Yesterday I offer to help one of the short-haired women. She lugging a big ol' heavy suitcase, sliding it along the floor. She snipped 'No, thanks' at me quick as a lick. I say, 'Okay, suitcase yourself.'" He laughed again, bending over, the spliff in his hand sending a stream of pungent smoke to the ceiling.

"When was the last time you saw the new next door people?"

"I see all dem last night. I waiting for the elevator, they coming up the stairs. They looking solemn, dem people."

"The girl with them?"

He nodded. Toked again.

"What'd she look like?"

"Like a foxy young thing."

"I mean her face. What was her facial expression?"

"Like the rest. Very grim."

I said, "You say anything to them?"

"I say, 'Hello, neighbors.'"

"What'd they say?"

"None of dem say a word. One guy—short, built like a bull? He give me one badass stare. I smile back. That guy a muscle-bound freak. I mess him up big time he decides to get rude."

I took my wallet out, handed the Kid two five dollar bills. Said, "For munchies, mon. You won't be seeing the new next door people or me again. I hope."

The Kid smiled wide. He stuck the two Abes inside the front of his shorts and said, "Okay, maybe you not such a asshole. You want to party? We got plenty of ganja, extra wimmen."

I said, "I'll take a raincheck. Confucius say I got to find the girl."

He said, "Don't know what we gonna do with the extra wimmen." He bobbed his head, made the peace sign, closed the door.

As I walked down the hallway I felt a little buzz from the reggae noise and the second-hand ganja. It was not a horrible feeling.

Damn it.

TWENTY-SIX

I drove to Fremont, mulling over the night's events. Friends of the Wild didn't need Uzi's and Street Sweepers to rescue rabbits and gerbils from research labs. I thought about some of the things Kay had said. Did they really have a guerrilla war planned against animal torturers? Putting their own lives on the line? Were they *that* fanatical?

And where was Shannon Harper, George Kemp, and Tricia Thornberg?

That bothered me because the more I learned, the more I doubted George Kemp was going to let me and Kay walk. He almost had to kill us sooner or later. Kay and I were the only two people who knew names. And if bodies started piling up they had to assume we'd name those names. Especially me. Tricia wasn't my daughter.

And if they killed Kay they'd kill Tricia. They couldn't expect her to accept the murder of her own mother as "Sorry, we had no choice," no matter how estranged the relationship.

I concluded sleeping alone was not a healthy idea. I decided I'd retreat to Fort Thornberg too. I didn't know why, but I thought of her house as a refuge. A Kruger Sanctuary. Maybe it was the women staying there. Safety in numbers. Somebody would be awake every hour.

But I wasn't going there right away.

Kaiser sat on the top step of the stairs to my apartment. The cigar was lit, glowing bright orange in the dark. A bottle in a brown paper bag sat next to him. The top of the bag was rolled tight around the lip of the bottle. He didn't wear his coat. His shirt collar was unbuttoned, his tie stuffed in the shirt pocket, the end of it spilling out like a huge forked tongue.

As I walked up he said, "You've kept me up way past my

bedtime, but it's important so I don't mind." His tone implied he minded very much.

"The wife gonna be sore?"

He snorted. "How many cops my age you know still got a wife? Least the wife they started out with?"

"That a problem?"

"You'd be surprised how few things are a problem to me. Things I considered of utmost importance when I was twenty-one, I couldn't give a fuck about now. Like having a wife waiting for me when I get home. Got two cats though. Bet they're pissed."

"I probably got a PO'd rabbit inside."

"A rabbit?"

"Bugs."

He made a face I couldn't decipher. He spread his fingers in front of him like he was inspecting his manicure. He said, "You wanna hear something interesting? It's been four years since I slept with a woman."

"That is interesting," I said. I assumed the bottle was almost empty if he was volunteering information like that.

"That's not the interesting part. The interesting part is I don't care. To me it ain't worth the hassle anymore. Tell the truth, I don't care if I ever do it again. When I was twenty-one if I went four *days* without getting laid I thought the world was gonna stop. So you see what I'm saying?"

"Sure," I lied. "Where's Dreamboat?"

"Probably frolicking in some sweet young thing's boudoir. He's quite the stud is young Leo. Just ask him. Calls himself Studman."

"Young Leo is also quite the prick."

"Exactly what the sweet young things find out after they know him a week or two. He doesn't hold females in very high regard except in one area. He loves to relate details next day, especially if the women humiliate themselves."

"Leo's a class act."

He said, "I wonder if Leo'll call himself Studman when he gets to be my age? What do you think?"

"Leo strikes me as the type who'll always think being Studman is as good as it gets."

Kaiser chuckled and said, "Probably." He took a healthy sip from the bottle, sucked on the cigar. He said, "So I've told you there's things most people care about that I don't. But one thing I do still care about is murder. I have this *need* to put murderers behind bars. I wish I could impress on you how important this need is to me."

"I think I understand."

"I mean life in the big city dictates people have to occasionally donate their wheels and their jewelry and their entertainment centers to the city's poor once in a while. They might have to endure smash and grabs, muggings, bullshit racist attacks, but—" Kaiser put his index finger in the air—"no human being should have to die because he or she chooses to live in Chicago. Murder is where I draw a line, make my stand."

"We all have to draw a line, Kaiser."

"Don't mock me."

"I'm not, believe me."

"Tell me about the Barrow murder."

"Can't do it."

"Can't or won't?"

"You I can't, your partner I won't."

He said, "Listen PI, I been sitting here three hours. I'm tired, I'm sweating like a fat whore in a two dollar hotel room. I got 'rhoids and this wooden stair ain't gonna help 'em any."

"I got reasons."

"I *know* you got reasons, but this is murder. I can't let you keep flipping me off if you know something about a murder."

I said, "I'm not doing it out of spite, Kaiser."

"You said you had to talk to somebody first. Did you?"

"No."

"Liar." No malice or anger behind the word, just resignation.

"What do you expect from a low rent door knocker? Truth, honesty, and the American way?"

He sipped again. Said, "We got the same runaround from Kay Thornberg. She says she has no idea why Amy hired you. We go round and round and eventually Leo accuses her of two-timing Amy. Asks if that's the reason Amy hired you. He says, 'You licking the wrong bush, Thornberg?'"

"I apologize to all the pricks in the world for calling DiNardi one."

"Crude, I know. Plus he could of picked a better time than the night of the murder to throw it at her."

"How'd she react?"

"Not too well. She starts screaming, 'Get out of my house!' Buncha' other women come storming into the room looking like they plan to tar and feather us. From the size of some of 'em they probably could of done it too. Then the girl from your house comes running into the room."

I winced, said nothing.

"Wearing black panties and a black motorcycle jacket. That's it. Didn't have the knife though."

I stayed quiet.

He said, "What's with the leather jacket in July?"

"She calls it her Leather, capital L. Says all weather is Leather weather."

"She wear it to bed?"

"If I ask her to."

"If you ask her to?"

"Just a joke."

He said, "I ask her why is *she* here. She says you and her had a fight, she came here to stay. I'm looking at her and all these other women standing around, glaring at us, and I'm thinking, what is this, some kind of fucking lesbian-weirdo dormitory? I ask her why does she come *here* after you guys fight. She says she knows Kay from way back. Girl's a bigger liar than you are. Plus I get vibes from her she's one of those people hate cops on sight."

"She hates lots of people on sight."

"I imagine the feeling is often mutual."

I took my Kools from my shirt pocket, shook one out and lit up. Said nothing.

Kaiser said, "Another sorry link in the chain of a pretty sad story."

"Kaiser, I told you, I'm not holding out to be difficult. Sometimes I have to draw a line too."

"Meaning?"

"My personal code might not be noticeable but I have one."

"Do you?"

"Kaiser, if I talk, somebody gets dead."

He took a taste of cigar, turning it around in his mouth. He said, "You know who killed Amy Barrow?"

"No," I said. The only light shining on us was from a street lamp across the street, so he couldn't read my face. He was too high anyway.

He said, "What's going on?"

"I only know a little and that's the truth."

"Who gets dead if you talk?"

"A teenage girl. I won't let that happen."

"Somebody's holding this teenage girl?"

"That's all I'm saying. And I'll deny I said that to anybody else."

Kaiser was silent a long time. He removed the cigar from his mouth, appraised it. He said, "I suppose if you just got out of rehab you wouldn't want a snort of Yukon Jack."

"Before I went into rehab I wouldn't of wanted a snort of Yukon Jack."

Kaiser smiled, still looking at the cigar. "What's it like in rehab?"

"You go to meetings, you talk to shrinks, you piss into bottles."

"It work?"

"Ask me on my deathbed."

He drank again, said, "Okay Kruger, I'll buy. Just so long as you know you're gonna have to talk sometime. I got a teenage daughter. Don't see her hardly at all, but—" His voice trailed off. He scratched his chin. Said, "And like I said, nobody should have to die because they choose to live in Chicago."

I said, "No, they shouldn't."

"But in a perfect world, blah, blah, blah, right?" He made a sardonic laugh.

I said, "Right."

"Think we'll ever see a perfect world? Not you and me, the human race I mean."

"Isn't this?"

He grinned, stood and started to walk away, carrying the bottle in the crook of his elbow like a football. He swayed a little as he walked. He went twenty feet, stopped and turned to me. Said, "Kruger, if this conversation ever comes up, *I'll* deny it took place. And you realize Leo and me keep working on our own."

I said, "When the time comes to talk, I talk to you, Kaiser. You give me a break, I return the favor. I don't want DiNardi anywhere around. I wouldn't piss on that bum if he was on fire."

He said, "You got it. We fuck Studman." He tottered across the street into the pool of light from the street lamp, laughing softly to himself.

TWENTY-SEVEN

I went inside, fed Heather's fish, scooted a drowsy Bugs inside his cage, threw bunny paraphernalia in a grocery bag. I drove to Lincoln Park.

Hedy opened Kay's door.

I said, "Can a man crash this party?"

She smiled, said, "Only if he doesn't act like one."

Three women slept in sleeping bags on the living room floor. Two more watched TV, faces close to the screen because the sound was down to a whisper. A black-and-white Katharine Hepburn movie. The TV was the only light in the room. It coated the people and furniture a ghostly blue-gray.

White light bled from under Kay's bedroom door. I knocked softly. Kay said, "Come in." She sat in the chair by the window. Heather sat on the edge of the bed, a paperback book in her lap. Both held long-stemmed glasses of white wine.

I said, "Can you handle two more boarders?" I lifted Bugs's cage.

Kay said, "It's that bad out there?"

"Getting worse all the time."

Heather said, "Those two cops came here. You wouldn't believe what that one slimeball said to Kay."

"I heard about it. You should've stayed out of sight."

"Kay was upset."

"Commendable compassion but faulty judgment."

Heather said, "Screw 'em. They asked me a ton of questions,
but I blew 'em off. The slimeball got mega upset. I kept saying,
'Take me downtown, you don't believe me.' I knew they
wouldn't. The old guy with the splotchy face said I was a bigger
liar than you. I told him you taught me everything I know."

I smiled in spite of myself.

Kay said, "Tell me what you learned."

"The plan must be a monster. Guy lives next to the apartment
on Cyprus says they got Uzi's and Street Sweepers. I watched
five members load the van with the suitcases I told you about
and what I assume were guns. I followed them to Milwaukee.
They're staying at a Holiday Inn a couple miles from the Harper
building. Tricia, Shannon Harper, and George Kemp are the
three that didn't go. You told me you raided Harper once,
right?"

"Yes."

"The research lab is in the building?"

"The basement. Research, production, quality, customer
service, everything's in that building."

"How'd you get in?"

"Broke a first floor window in back."

"You had to scale the fence?"

"They put the fence up after we raided. Added the guard
house by the parking lot. Three security guards patrol the building at night now too."

"Why are they in Milwaukee if the mansion is down here?"

"Harper Cosmetics used to be in Chicago, but it was spread
out all over the place. Offices in the Loop, production in Park
Ridge, more offices in La Grange. When they built the new
building, they wanted to consolidate the operation. They got
some kind of sweetheart deal from Wisconsin to build there. Tax
breaks, utility incentives."

"Shannon ever talk about her family to you? Besides the animal research stuff."

"Not really. I know she doesn't speak to her mother or father, but it went way back, long before she joined us."

"So the animal stuff was more like the final straw?"

Kay said, "I suppose so. What about the apartment?"

"Empty. They don't need it anymore. They painted over the name and slogans. Nobody stayed in it, it was never a hideout. It was an out of the way place to meet and consolidate supplies. That building, that area, they could of walked a herd of elephants in and out and nobody would of said a thing."

"But we still don't know what the 'plan' is, right?"

"Except that it involves Harper Cosmetics, no we don't. But that's a start."

Kay said, "I told Heather everything. If she's in danger, she should know why."

Heather looked sheepish. Said, "I asked."

I said, "It's okay. You knew a lot of it anyway."

Heather lifted the book in her lap, said, "I wanna know more, Kay." Kay smiled.

Heather, Bugs, and I went to Tricia's room. I set Bugs's cage on the floor. Heather and I lay on the bed on top of the covers. She snuggled close, rested her head on my shoulder.

I said, "How you feel?"

"Not good, but light years better than this morning. I slept a little and the wine helped. You're not mad about it are you? Me drinking?"

"Just don't bring any more bottles home."

"I'd rather have smoke, but I didn't think it'd be a good idea to twist a stick and blow it around a bunch of middle-aged women. They seem pretty cool, but you never know."

"Best to be prudent in these matters."

She said, "I like Kay."

I said, "Me too. I feel for her. She's been through a lot."

"She told me about Tricia. She's really beating herself up about it. She talked about how she's a prisoner in her own house. You know about that?"

"Yeah."

"She ever tell you how it started?"

"No. How?"

"A lover broke up with her, the one before Amy? Left her for someone else. Kay was a total, stressed-out wreck. Couldn't eat, couldn't sleep. The Saturday before Christmas she went shopping at Marshall Fields. She was on the elevator going to the top floor and it was packed so tight with people you couldn't move or breathe and she was smothering in this heavy overcoat and all of a sudden everything got real weird. She had a panic attack so severe she started shaking and crying. Everybody started staring at her and pointing. She felt totally humiliated. And scared to death because she didn't know what was happening. She thought she was having a heart attack, was gonna die right there. Her head was swirling and her chest hurt, her stomach was churning, sweat gushed down her face. She said her heart kept exploding in her throat. She doesn't remember what happened right after that. She thinks she totally freaked and like thrashed her way off the elevator. Next she knew she was crying hysterically in the back seat of a taxi and then she was home. Soon as she walked through the front door it all went away. She felt fine. For two weeks after that every time she went out the attacks happened. Not right away, but sooner or later. And it got to be sooner and sooner. Then it got so she knew they'd happen. She waited for them. She said her safe boundary shrank from City to North Side to Lincoln Park to block to house. You ever heard of that before?"

"Read about it."

"She said lots of people suffer from it. Some people are housebound like all their adult lives."

"I know."

"She told me lots of stuff. It was like she couldn't stop talking. Her friends'd come in, she'd say we were fine, she wanted to talk to me. I kept asking her would she rather be alone, she kept sayin', 'Please stay.'"

"She needed to talk tonight. And she likes young people. She used to teach at a college."

"Roosevelt. She told me."

"What else did you talk about?"

"Like I said, the animal rights stuff. The torture and stuff? I'm gonna look into that. It's sick, you stop and think about it, eating corpses and blood and wearing something else's skin."

"She makes you look at it from a different perspective."

"She gave me a book. *Animal Liberation* by Peter Singer?"

"I saw it on your lap."

"She says it's like a primer. She kept talking about how we exploit other life forms. She says, 'Animals are not ours to eat, wear, or experiment on.'"

"They have lots of snappy slogans."

"I never *thought* about stuff like that. Never questioned it. Leg-hold traps, factory farming, Draize and LD 50 tests. I never knew about that stuff."

"What about your Leather and Doc Martens?"

There was a pause. "Not yet."

I chuckled.

She said, "She told me what it's like being lesbian."

I smiled in the dark. "You ask her?"

"Kind of."

"Kind of?"

"Well, I admire people who catch shit from straights."

"I'm forever finding out new things about you."

"What do you think about it?"

"About what?"

"Gays."

"It's their life and you only get one."

"You know we're 'hets'?"

"Breeders, I think they call us too."

She giggled. Said, "She told about when she used to be able to travel. If she went with a lover, they'd get a hotel room with a double bed, sleep in one, then in the morning they'd jump up and down on the other one to make it look like one of 'em had slept in it. But some of it's sad. Her friend before Amy—the one gave her agoraphobia—used to break up with her every time the holidays came around."

"Why?"

"Because it was tradition this woman's entire family show up at the parent's house somewhere in Michigan for Christmas. This woman's parents didn't know she was gay so she wouldn't take Kay with her. The friend didn't know how to deal with just telling Kay she couldn't go, so every year she'd start all these fights around Thanksgiving, end up leaving. Then she'd call right after New Year's, wanna get back together. That's sad, isn't it?"

I agreed it was.

Heather started to yawn. She hadn't gotten much sleep the last forty-eight hours and she had the wine buzz. In a minute she snored. I could smell the alcohol on her breath. It smelled sour and distasteful and didn't inspire any cravings.

I shut my eyes, knew right away I wouldn't sleep. Insomnia is perhaps my oldest companion. One of the reasons I started drinking. I got out of bed, headed down the hallway. The light still peeked under Kay's door. I knocked softly.

She still sat in the chair by the window. A photo album lay open on her lap. More were stacked on the floor next to the chair. A full glass of wine stood on top of the albums. She said, "You want to look at pictures of Amy?" Pictures came out "pishers."

I said sure, and that's what we did. Sitting side by side on her bed we looked at pictures. All were taken in the house or the backyard. Tricia was in some, looking sullen and withdrawn. Some were group shots of what must have been Animal Sanctuary. The people in Friends of the Wild were in those. Arthur Irwin was in one.

In ninety percent of the photos, Amy had a highball glass or a can of beer in her hand and in many shots she was obviously half in the bag. This Amy had a lopsided, animated face; she looked nothing like Amy in rehab. Instead of making Kay sad, looking at memories seemed to comfort her somehow. She smiled often.

Around four A.M. I told Kay I was sleepy. She said, "I might actually get some sleep tonight myself. Now." She held up the glass of wine, said, "Three bottles of Chardonnay later." A look came over her face as she realized. She said, "I'm sorry."

I said, "Don't be. Wine was invented for times like this. Just don't start thinking every waking moment is a time like this."

She said, "I like Heather. She's different, but—"

I said, "I hadn't noticed that."

We both smiled.

I stood, said, "She likes you too. And believe me, she don't 'like' easy."

She said, "Mr. Kruger?"

"Yes?"

"A favor?"

"If I can."

"Please don't keep the rabbit in that cage all night."

"Bugs gnaws things, leaves pellets all over."

"It's okay if he does that. I just can't stand thinking of him caged up all night."

I went back to Tricia's room, opened the cage. Bugs was asleep and didn't move. Just before I fell asleep I realized that despite seeing them in so many photos, Kay and I hadn't mentioned Friends of the Wild the whole time I was in her room.

TWENTY-EIGHT

When I woke up I bolted upright in a panic. Whipped my head side to side. Saw stuffed Garfield cats, Bon Jovi and Tom Cruise posters, blue frilly throw pillows, a huge fuzzy green alligator like you win at parking lot carnivals. Where the hell was I?

Then it all flooded back to me. Friends of the Wild. Uzi's. Equal Punishment. Amy Barrow. Tricia Thornberg. The girl I was supposed to bring home. The girl whose room I was in. The girl who was in even bigger trouble than me.

And didn't know it.

Heather had her back to me, curled in the fetal position. She snored like a chainsaw. I got out of bed. A digital clock on the dresser said it was just after ten. I fed Bugs, still happy in his cage, kneeling beside him as he ate, whispering what a good rabbit he was.

Kay, Hedy, and two other women sat at the kitchen table. Alan fidgeted on Hedy's lap. Kay propped her head with both hands, stared at the table top. She didn't look up when I entered the room. A mug of coffee and a *Sun-Times* were in front of her. I went to the stove and poured coffee into a white styrofoam cup, sat across from Kay.

Hedy said, "There's more bad news."

I said, "The only way to start a day."

Kay pushed the paper toward me. It was open to page five, the Metro Briefs. I scanned headlines like CHEMICAL CLEANUP and NU GETS GIFT. My eyes stopped at STREET SLAYING. The story under the headline said Arthur Irwin had been shot to death shortly before midnight as he walked from his "late-model sports car" to his "rented townhouse." He was thirty-four. There were no witnesses, no clues, no suspects. A Violent Crimes detective named Bachrach said all avenues of investigation would be pursued. I was sure Arthur Irwin would appreciate that.

I said, "Anybody call here?"

Hedy nodded. "I took it. Kay was still asleep."

"A woman?"

"Yes."

"What'd she say?"

"She said, 'Show Kay Thornberg page five of the sports final *Sun-Times.*' Said to show it to you, too."

"She sound scared?"

"Very scared."

"She say show it to me, like she knew I was here?"

"I couldn't tell, but she mentioned you by name."

Terrific.

Kay said, "Hedy, you guys have to leave. I can't expect anyone to stay with me now. I can't subject my friends to this."

Hedy said, "Don't be absurd, Kay. We'd never abandon you."

I'd wondered why I hadn't spotted George Kemp last night. I thought when I saw Kaiser on my front steps that was the reason. But now I knew why. Thanks to me Arthur Irwin knew something was up too. And he had no reason not to talk. I felt sorry for Irwin, smug upscale bastard that he was. I go to his house where he's minding his own business. I tell him Friends of the Wild is up to no good. He calls his buddies to fill them in. And for being such a nice guy, what's his prize, Don Pardo? One bullet to the brainpan.

So far the people they'd killed were ex-comrades. People who *agreed* with them. I started to wonder if this had *anything* to do with animals. I muttered, "Better you should've kept your big mouth shut, Arthur."

Kay looked up. A spider web of lines around her eyes looked carved by awls. Her cheeks seemed to be covered with a waxy lacquer. She moved her mouth twice before any words came out. She croaked, "What are we doing to these people?"

"Not us, Kay," I said.

"I feel responsible for this. Amy and Arthur both. I brought these people together."

I said, "People who introduce married couples aren't responsible for the divorce. Shannon made a conscious decision to commit murder. You weren't part of that decision."

Kay shook her head. She said, "Mr. Kruger, you've got to get Tricia away from those people."

I nodded.

I phoned Marvin at the office. Asked if anybody had called for me. He said no. I asked if any bodybuilder types had been in the office. He said no. Had he seen any walking around out front? Up and down Lincoln Ave.? Sitting in cars? He said no, no, and no.

Which didn't reassure me one bit. Because of course Marvin hadn't been looking for any bodybuilder types.

I left Kay's house by the back door, walked briskly to the alley behind the garage. The alleys that bisect virtually every residential block in town are one of Chicago's most unique and lovely features. I say lovely because Chicago alleys have saved my bacon on at least two occasions in the past.

The Skylark was three blocks south. I stayed in the alley the whole way, swiveling my head like a paranoid owl.

The car didn't blow up when I turned the key, so I drove toward the Gold Coast. Found a parking spot at the end of Lincoln just off Clark. Made the long, sweaty walk south on Clark, east on North, south on Astor. All I could think of to do was beard the lioness in her lair. Surely the one place they wouldn't kill me was on the front porch of the mansion.

I pressed the bell and waited. I looked up and down the beautiful rich bitch street. Words floated through my mind. Words like money, power, safety, money, security, freedom, money. I said out loud, "Why, God? Why these people and not me?"

The door opened. I turned and faced Shannon Harper.

Her jaw dropped like a rock off a cliff. The color in her cheeks drained away. I didn't like this reaction. The fact I was alive seemed to shock hell out of her.

She hissed, "What are you doing here? What do you want?"

"Tricia Thornberg."

Color flooded back to her face. She said, "How many times do you have to be told something? She came here of her own free will, she wants to stay, she's staying."

"Like you'd let her leave if she wanted."

"Get off my property."

"So George can blow me away? Like Amy Barrow and Arthur Irwin? Like you threatened to do to Tricia?" I said all this very loud in case Tricia stood nearby.

She said, "If you aren't gone in ten seconds, I call the police." She glanced behind her, curled a lock of hair and tugged on it.

"Shannon, Shannon," I said, shaking my head. "Were I you I wouldn't even think a threat like that, let alone speak it. What if I call your bluff? Situation you're in—"

"What situation is that?"

I couldn't let her know I was hip to Wisconsin or the apartment on Cyprus or the automatic guns they were packing. It gave me a little edge. Damn little, but still. I said, "Let me talk to Tricia."

"She's not here." She glanced behind her again.

I stretched to see behind her, wanting to know what she kept looking at. I saw more black suitcases lined against the wall but that was all. I said, "Where is she?"

"It's none of your concern. You talked to her once. She told you she wanted to stay with me. Give it up for Godsakes. Tell Kay this is the way it is."

"Couldn't give it up if I wanted to. That muscle-bound lunatic won't let me."

"We tried to tell you. I *warned* you. You never should of gotten involved in this, Kruger."

"I just wanna see a mother and child reunion. It's a job, I need the work."

She flushed redder. Said very slow and hard, "She doesn't want to go back, got it?" Another glance behind her. "You are going to regret you didn't listen to me. You had to keep poking, didn't you? You couldn't just back off for a week—"

"What was Amy's crime? She couldn't do much poking locked up in rehab. What's your excuse for murdering her?"

Shannon yelled, "Look in a mirror, you wanna see who killed Amy Barrow." She slammed the door in my face.

I walked to the Historical Society building eight blocks away, trying to think things through.

Five-eighths of the group and all the supplies were in Wisconsin, which meant the curtain was about to rise. Yet Shannon sat in the family manse, routinely answering the front door like a housewife in Palatine.

I thought about "You couldn't just back off for a week, could you?" I thought about the suitcases on the floor behind her. I thought about something George Kemp had said, then something Kay said. I thought about the case from a fresh angle. A different starting point.

And wore a severely puzzled expression when I walked through the door of the museum. Because what I was thinking just didn't add up. I turned right, walked down the corridor toward the Society Cafe. I stopped at the public phone across from the museum gift store, dialed Amanda Truitt's number.

The way she said "Hello, who is it?" I knew I had a chance. She was scared spitless.

I said, "You plan to call Kay about a murder every morning, Amanda? Not a nice way to start the woman's day."

She didn't answer.

I said, "This is Kruger. You mentioned my name this morning."

"I know who you are." Her voice was as soft as Downy, but a terrified waver ran through it. I got a mental picture of her cringing into herself.

"You plan to call her about me tomorrow?"

Again, no answer.

"You sound sick."

She sobbed. "I am. I don't know why this. . . I've been Shannon's friend since grade school. She shouldn't take advantage of me like this." The sobbing got louder. "This isn't right."

"No shit it isn't right," I said. "I just talked to Shannon."

"So?"

"The trap's about to slam shut."

"What do you mean?"

"You got any idea what Shannon's up to?"

"No! She won't tell me what she's doing. She made me phone the rehab and talk to Amy. Find out when was she getting released. She made me phone Kay. She can make me do anything. She makes me do things I'm embarrassed about. Things I'm so ashamed of I wouldn't tell anybody. Ever since we were little." She stopped to get her breath back. "But this time I'm not embarrassed, I'm scared. Shannon's changed. It's like I don't know her anymore. She orders me around like I'm a slave instead of her friend. And this George Kemp person is— He needs a lot of therapy I think."

I said, "Therapy? George Kemp needs a daily dose of thorazine."

She snuffled noisily into the phone.

I said, "I have to talk to you."

"I can't—"

"I'm at the Historical Society. You can walk here in ten minutes. Meet me upstairs."

She said, "If Shannon ever found out—"

I said, "Do it, Amanda. They'll kill anybody who can link them to whatever it is they cooked up. That means me, it means you, it means Tricia. Maybe you can give me the key to stop them."

She said, "Would she really hurt Tricia?" I liked Amanda Truitt at that moment. She sounded more concerned for Tricia than herself. In my experience this is a quality so rare as to be unheard of. Or maybe it only illustrated Amanda Truitt's lack of self-esteem. Why Shannon Harper could talk her into doing anything, including things that made her ashamed.

I said, "You know Shannon better than I do. What do you think?"

"I don't know what I think. But Tricia's a sweet girl. She looks up to Shannon. She's naïve and trusting. Why would they kill her?"

"They have their reasons and, believe me, they couldn't care less about sweet, naïve and trusting. Meet me here. I'll ask some questions, then you go home. Nobody'll ever know we met."

After a long silence she said, "I'll be there in half an hour. Is that okay?"

Hell yes it was okay.

TWENTY-NINE

I knew Amanda Truitt soon as she walked through the door. She looked just like I'd pictured her. Small, timid and scared to death. She stopped inside the turnstile, glanced around uneasily like an Arkansas farm girl stepping off a Greyhound bus at State and Madison.

I waited on a landing halfway up the marble staircase that's straight ahead of the main doors. Our eyes met and I nodded. She kept her eyes locked on mine the entire time she walked up the stairs.

Amanda Truitt was maybe five-two. Looked anorectic. Gaunt face. Paste-colored, almost translucent skin. More like a skull than a face. Her close-set dark eyes were full of worry. She had short, spiky black hair. The gel she used on it sparkled in the summer sun that washed the stairwell from the skylight. She wore a green and blue checked sun dress and white sandals. A canvas tote bag hung from her right shoulder.

I took her hand, which was meatless and moist as a damp sponge, and led her to the second floor.

We walked into an American history exhibit. The Road to Revolution. Two rooms of glass cabinets containing muskets and powder horns, faded flags, yellowing letters, treaties and books. The corners were roped off exhibits of Federalist furniture. On the walls hung paintings of our earliest heroes. Lots of other stuff, but very few people. Perfect.

Off a hallway between the third room of Revolutionary War history and the start of a new exhibit was an alcove containing two backless sofas. Cylinder track lights bathed the alcove a soft blue.

I sat on one sofa, motioned Amanda to face me. She sat on the edge. I noticed her feet were skin and bone and very small.

She licked her lips, stared at the floor. She said, "If Shannon finds out I'm doing this—"

"Stop worrying about it."

She smoothed her dress, then folded her hands like a child in church. "I knew Shannon was capable of almost anything, but I never thought she'd be involved in murder."

"You thought she was incapable of murder?"

"I thought she was too smart."

"Isn't she worried you'll go to the police, knowing what you know?"

"She knows I'd never do that."

"Why not?"

"We've been through too much. She's closer to me than any sister could ever be. And what she'd do—"

"How long have you known her?"

"Since grade school. Fifth grade." Her voice rose like it was a question.

"What school?"

"Francis Parker. I went to public school until fifth grade."

Yale's probably cheaper than Francis Parker.

Amanda read my mind. "My parents had to scrimp and save to send me there. My father was an electrician, my mother didn't work. I never felt like I belonged there. Nobody'd talk to me. I hated the place until I met Shannon. I still remember the first time she asked me if I wanted to go to her house after school."

"Why?"

"I was just flattered someone that rich and smart noticed me. My parents felt like that too. My mother kept saying, 'See, see why we're sending you there, Amanda? You're going to meet lots of important friends.'"

"Did you?"

"No, just Shannon. I don't make friends easily."

"But you and Shannon became good friends?"

"Best friends. Then."

"Did she have lots of friends?"

"Not then. I know it's hard to believe now, but she was shy too. She, like, blossomed when she got older, opened up more? I never have been able to do that. I try, but—"

"What was it like at the Harper mansion?"

"Very formal."

"How so?"

"The atmosphere was formal. Cold and stuffy. Nobody talked. You never heard conversations. There were butlers and maids all over the place. The "help" Shannon called them. The family mostly communicated through the help. And the help whispered to you and each other. Like they'd get fired if they spoke in a normal tone of voice. It was spooky. We spent all our time in her room or in the old stable house in back. You know in all the years I've known her I heard her father speak one time. He'd nod to me sometimes, but usually he just walked past like I wasn't there. He did that to Shannon too, especially if he was mad at her."

"So you felt uncomfortable there?"

"Very. I was always made to feel the difference in social status. Even the help made sure I knew. Looks, the mocking way they said, '*Miss* Truitt.' Things like that. It never changed over the years. When I was sixteen I got treated the same as when I was ten. I felt sorry for Shannon. Living in an atmosphere like that. I mean, they were rich, but—"

"She ever visit your house?"

"Sometimes. But in a different way she was just as uncomfortable. My mother treated Shannon like she was royalty. Fawned all over her. It was embarrassing. To Shannon and me."

"What did her father say the time you heard him talk?"

"Shannon had these Shelby collies? One day somebody left a side door open. One of the dogs got inside and made a mess on a Persian rug. Mr. Harper, like, *kicked* the door to Shannon's room open and stormed in. He picked her off the floor so they were face to face. His face was beet red and he was shaking her."

"What did you do?"

"I couldn't move. I sat on the floor, terrified. Mr. Harper said, 'If it ever happens again, I won't punish you, I'll have the dog put to sleep.' He turned around and left the room, slammed the door. We didn't even know what he was talking about until later. Shannon started crying and couldn't stop. I was so scared I told her I had to go home. I didn't know what to say or do. I was only twelve or something."

I said, "He ever do that? Kill any of her pets?"

"No, but he would have if he wanted to, believe me."

I said, "Is he why you think Shannon is capable of anything?"

"Maybe. In high school, when she was fifteen, she went from wallflower to extrovert like overnight. Her entire outlook on life changed. She got this new philosophy, a new personal code."

"What was it?"

"That nothing is wrong. Or right. Know what I mean?"

"I'm not sure."

"Most of us have a basic concept of right and wrong or good and bad, you know? But to Shannon it's like all actions are the same. Everything is relative? Giving money to the Salvation Army is no better or worse than shoplifting a coat. They're just things you *do*. She has no ethics, no principles."

"She's amoral?"

She blushed, looked at me, then quickly away. "That's it. Amoral. I'm not a prude or a goody two shoes. Not by any stretch. But the things Shannon can do without thinking twice, the things she's talked me into doing—" Amanda blushed redder. Quietly said, "And worse, she can do it over and over." She nervously smoothed her dress again.

I said, "I keep hearing what a mesmerizing personality this woman has, how people follow her like lemmings. Personally I don't see it. I've talked to her three times, all she's been is irate and unpleasant."

"That's part of the hold she has. Her temper. It can be very scary. If she's ever been mad at you, you'll do anything to keep it from happening again. But sometimes she's like the most warm and giving person in the world. You have to know her over time to appreciate Shannon. The disparate parts of her personality are another reason she's so fascinating."

"Explain."

"Most people don't have that degree of extremes in their makeup, you know? Angel and devil?

I said, "There's good and bad in everybody."

"I know, but Shannon is really *out there* both ways. And the way she talks you into doing what you don't want to do. Would never do on your own. She's so enthusiastic about things. And it's contagious. She can make a thing sound like the funniest or most noble or most interesting thing in the world. Sometimes she talks you into good things, sometimes bad things. But never boring things."

"You involved in animal rights, Amanda?"

"No."

"Why not?"

She shrugged. "I mean, I understand some of it, but it just seems like there's more important things. Homeless people, violence against women and children, drugs, crack babies. You know?"

"I know. Is Shannon's involvement genuine?"

"She's loved animals since I've known her. More than people I think. I've seen her get hysterical because a pet was sick or dying, but one time we saw an old man get hit by a car. I mean really smashed. Like, flying through the air? The man was lying in the street screaming and blood was gushing out his nose and ears. People were yelling and running to help." Amanda shuddered and was quiet for some seconds. Said quieter, "It was horrible. I went totally to pieces, but Shannon was almost nonchalant about it. Like, too bad, you know?"

"She try to get you involved in animal rights?"

"Always. She lectured me all the time about leather and fur. She told me if she ever saw any Harper cosmetics in my house, she'd never speak to me again."

"It change things between you two. Since she got so radical about this?"

Amanda nodded. "I don't feel close to her anymore. It's like she's floating away. Something's inside her I can't get at or through. She's different somehow—a different person. Our friendship has deteriorated."

"That bother you?"

She stared at the floor for some seconds, then said, "Yes, very much," in a hushed voice.

I said, "I'd heard Shannon and her parents didn't speak. Your story helps me see why."

Amanda made a sickly smile.

"How's she feel about the rest of her family? She sad they don't talk?"

"Obviously she detests her father. I don't think she has feelings at all for her mother or sisters. I'm not sure what all went on in her childhood. The things I saw were bad enough and I'm sure it was worse when I wasn't around. It had to be traumatic to foster the hatred she has for her father."

"But she put up with it until she was fifteen?"

"Right. Then she did the total rebellion thing. She like exploded. She'd do anything to anger or embarrass her father. She was in trouble with the police all through high school."

"What kind of trouble?"

"Vandalism, petty theft. Shoplifting. She got busted so many times at Marshall Field's I'm surprised they didn't have her picture at every counter. The family lawyer probably put a kid through college on Shannon."

I said, "Sounds like she craved attention and decided that was the only way she could get it." Sigmund Kruger.

Amanda shrugged.

"Where's the rest of the family now?"

"Five years ago, right after the new building was finished in Wisconsin?"

"I've seen it."

"About then her father semi-retired and her parents moved to Florida. Miami Beach. By then Shannon'd caused so much turmoil Mr. Harper disowned her."

"She's out of the will?"

Amanda nodded. "She gets to stay in the house on Astor—forever if she wants—and she receives two grand a month allowance for life, but that's it. Other than that, she doesn't get a thing. To get that she had to sign a bunch of papers. Her father told her the family wants nothing more to do with her."

"How'd she react to that?"

"She would of killed her father that weekend if she could've gotten to him. She—" Amanda stopped, shuddered again. I could only imagine how Shannon had acted that weekend.

Amanda said, "She kept saying 'I'll fix his ass if it takes a lifetime!'"

Bingo. This was the part that hadn't fit. All my theories had been based on the assumption Shannon Harper was rich, would one day be richer. I said, "Anybody else in the family try to remain in touch with her?"

"To them she doesn't exist."

I said, "Were you friendly with her sisters?"

"Lorraine and Ashley? You kidding? I told you, the whole house let me know where I stood. Those two treated me worse than the help did." She sighed. "They were lots older anyway. Ten, fifteen years. We were just these little kids to them."

"Where are they now?"

"New York, I think. One in Manhattan, one upstate. They married men richer than they are. They're into the Newport 400 thing or whatever it is. I saw a picture of Lorraine in the back of *Vanity Fair* once. At one of those society parties?"

"And they never speak to Shannon?"

"They didn't speak to her when they lived in the same house. It's like she was never on the same page as the rest of the family and they had to make her pay for it."

"What about her mother?"

"All her mother cared about was lunches, benefits, committees—stuff like that. And tennis. She was addicted to tennis. Always at this club downtown playing tennis. I can't remember the name of it. She spent time with Lorraine and Ashley because they were like her, but she pretty much shut Shannon out of her life. Especially after Shannon went wild."

I put a Kool in my mouth, didn't light it. I was almost thinking of Shannon Harper in sympathetic terms. I said, "Her father and mother always in Florida?"

"They go back and forth, especially in summer."

"Where do they stay when they're up here?"

"An estate on a lake in Wisconsin a half-hour drive from the Harper building." She made a face. "They call it The Cabin, but it's about the size of a shopping mall. Has fifteen rooms, two huge heated swimming pools—one indoors. A yacht."

"You been there?"

"Once, a long time ago."

"Her parents there now?"

"I don't know."

"Who runs Harper Cosmetics now her father is retired?"

"Shannon's uncle is executive vice-president or something. It's been in the family for like ninety years. Her great-grandfather started it. There's always a male Harper around to take over when one retires."

"Never a female?"

"No way. Harper women do lunches, play tennis, and shop. They don't do business. That's another thing used to make Shannon nuts."

I said, "How many times did Shannon's friends meet at your place?"

"Twice."

"How'd she ask?"

"She said she needed to talk to some friends, they lived all over town, could she talk to them in my den?"

"You know any of these people?"

"Two."

"Who?"

"Sorrento Gallo. I like him. He used to be nice to me. And Frank Kelson. He's been totally obsessed with Shannon for a year. I think he's creepy, but Shannon says he's really okay. The rest I didn't know."

"Did you mind they came over?"

"Not at first, but they were so secretive and—tense. I got nervous. These people did not say hello, did not smile, did not make eye contact with me, nothing like that. Even Sorrento ignored me. And then Shannon told me to make that call to Kay Thornberg the day after I'd called and asked Amy when she was getting out. I've been a wreck since then. I feel responsible for Amy's death."

Everybody felt responsible for these murders except the people responsible.

Amanda said, "Shannon shouldn't have done that to me. I'm her oldest friend."

"You have no idea what they're up to?"

"No."

"She didn't even give an excuse why she brought these people to your house?"

"Just that it wasn't safe to meet at their houses. They needed a neutral sight she called it."

"Didn't that sound suspicious to you?"

"Yes, but I'm her friend. I asked her what it was all about. She said, 'Amanda, shut the fuck up,' in this ice cold voice. In my own house, in front of those—strangers. Like all of a sudden I'm dirt. These people are more important to her than I am."

"Did you hear her say *anything* to these people?"

"Last time they were there George Kemp left early. When he was leaving he held the den door open and asked her something I didn't hear. Shannon shouted 'We're operating under a time budget here, George, remember?' and she sounded totally exasperated. He said, "Does that mean no?" and she said real loud, 'Whether it gets done or not, I go through with it.'"

I said, "Is she sleeping with George Kemp?"

Amanda blushed again. She said, "I assume she is. She sleeps with everybody she knows almost. It's like her favorite game. To see if she can seduce everybody she meets. Funny thing is, I don't think she even enjoys sex."

"Kemp in love with her?"

"Probably."

"You said George scared you?"

"They all acted strange, but he's—" She stopped and thought a bit. "He's never said a word to me, okay? So I have no real reason to feel like this. Nothing I can put my finger on. He just has this look that gives me goosebumps. He's like a robot. He looks at you and through you at the same time, and it's like he knows what you're thinking. It's hard to describe. But Shannon has him wrapped around her little finger. Like most people."

"If she's sleeping with Kelson and maybe the rest for all we know, isn't Kemp upset about that?"

"Maybe he'll put up with anything to stay close to her."

I studied Amanda's sad face. Thought, "Like most people."

Amanda said, voice cracking, "Why would she *do* this to me?"

"Because you're an old friend she can get to do anything knowing she doesn't have to worry about consequences. She wanted a voice Kay and Amy didn't know to make those phone calls. And any future ones. Kay knows everybody else in that group. And as long as she was coming over to get you to do that, she figured she'd kill two birds and rally the troops."

She lowered her head. Whispered, "But we go back fifteen years. We were confidantes. More than that even. She just met these people."

I said, "Would you talk to the police about any of this? I mean, later if something major happens?"

She shook her head violently. "No. I'm scared and she humiliated me, but I'm only telling you these things because you want to help Tricia and you said you wouldn't talk to the police. You won't, will you?"

"Not as long as they have Tricia."

Amanda made a face I couldn't read. Half relief, half annoyance. I was confused for a second, then flashed on what the deal was.

Amanda Truitt was torn apart inside. The emotions coursing through her were those of a lover scorned. She was distraught over the way Shannon was treating her, hated her for it. But there were fifteen years of intense loyalty, love and devotion to Shannon that she couldn't toss aside. She wanted to see Shannon punished. Not for murder, but for the shabby way she was treating her oldest friend. Except Amanda couldn't let herself be directly responsible for causing the punishment. I had to do the dirty work. Maybe she couldn't admit to herself that's what she wanted, but that's why she was here talking to me.

I said, "You ever see Tricia?"

"A few times. She was the only one who talked to me. Acted nice? She knew I was upset."

"Will you help Tricia?"

"If I can."

"Go to the mansion, get her alone." I handed her my card. "Tell her she has to call me. I'll be waiting."

"You know what they're up to, don't you?"

"I don't think anyone knows what they're really up to except Shannon. What's Shannon's father's name?"

"Mr. Harper." Amanda looked confused. Like it never occurred to her to call him anything else.

"His first name. He's got a first name, right?"

She thought for a long second. "Blair. Blair Alexander Harper."

THIRTY

I drove to the low-slung one-story plate glass and cinderblock building on North Lincoln. The building that houses Angelo's 24-Hour Pizza Parlor, the Gold Harvest health food store and the Midwestern Insurance Group office of Marvin Torkelson, one-quarter of which contains Dan Kruger, Private Investigations.

I hunched my back as I made the quick walk from car to door. Like tensed muscles would stop a bullet.

Marvin's shoulder pinned his phone to his ear. His tasseled loafers rested on the edge of his desk. He made a gesture he wanted to talk to me when he was done.

I sat behind my desk, put my feet up. Filthy, untied Nikes instead of burnished tasseled loafers. Lit a Kool.

I dropped my eaves on Marvin. He was using phrases like "conversion option," "insured claimant," "limitation of liability," "annuity schedule."

He said words like that into the phone all the time, but I didn't know what any of it meant because I couldn't afford even his cheapest policies. It was a running joke. Not a *funny* joke, but a joke.

I started to ponder life's little jokes. Recent events had put me in a pondering mood. Astor Streets versus Freemont Streets. Vacation "cabins" the size of Rhode Island versus apartments the size of a steamer trunk.

As Marvin kept talking insurance jargon my thoughts moved quickly to the subject of free choice as opposed to fate. How and why did we arrive at our various stations in life? Why did Marvin get to use phrases like "conversion option" to make a living and

I had to use "hideouts," "kidnapping," and "dead meat" to make mine? Why was Marvin's ride a fully loaded spanking new Caddy while I schlepped around town in a Skylark that rolled off the line when Nixon was president? Why would Marvin retire early, his diversified investment portfolio assuring him financial security if he lived to be a hundred and fifty, while I'd be peeping through keyholes till I keeled over? An event which probably would occur in some flophouse while I heated a can of Alpo for dinner. When was the last time Marvin tiptoed down an alley to evade some deranged maniac? When was the last time I pocketed a couple grand chatting on the phone with my heels on my desk?

I sucked deep on the Kool, shook my head. What joker wrote this script anyway? And what did he have against me?

I thought about Kemp's theory of fatalism. It soothed me. Interesting concept: fate deciding everything. What happens is meant to happen. Can't be changed. I liked that. It absolved me of having to wonder why at every critical juncture of my life I made the worst decision possible. It was my destiny, my kismet to live stupid and die poor. I never had a chance. I started humming "Que Sera, Sera."

When Marvin cradled the phone he grinned like a little boy touching Michael Jordan. I said, "Sell another poor sap three times the coverage he needs on a policy he didn't want in the first place?"

He shrugged, still grinning. "It's a jungle out there. A man has to protect his family." The grin faded. "You never came by yesterday."

"I was busy."

"All day?"

"All day."

"Busy doing what?"

"Working."

"Just working?"

"Just working."

His look indicated he wasn't so sure about that. Couldn't blame him. I crossed my heart, said, "Hope to die."

He stared some more, then said, "Man phoned for you right after you called this morning."

"Give a name?"

"No. Said he was at your house, you weren't there. Claimed he needed to talk to you. It was important, it had to be today."

"Say why?"

"I asked him. He hemmed and hawed, then said it was about a job, but he blurted it out like it just occurred to him. Seemed odd to me. I mean, if the man wanted to hire you it wouldn't take him ten seconds to remember why he was looking for you, would it?"

"What'd you tell him?"

"You split town for the weekend, I'd take a message."

"He buy it?"

"I dunno. He was quiet for a bit, then said, 'Okay, thanks. No message,' and hung up."

"He ask where I went?"

"No."

I said, "What'd the guy sound like?"

"That was another thing. It sounded like he was reading everything he said off a cue card."

"That's my man."

"He involved in the case you talked about?"

"Yes."

"How bad is it?"

"I'm about to find out."

"You got any ideas?"

"Some. But I can't talk about it because someone gets killed if I do."

"You?"

"Besides me."

Marvin shook his head. "Christ, Dan, why don't you get a decent job?"

"Like selling insurance? Now that's a thought. Make big bucks screwing working stiffs out of their life savings by scaring 'em half to death."

Marvin flipped me off, went back to his paper shuffling.

I needed to call Harper Cosmetics, but couldn't tie up my phone because I wanted to talk to Tricia Thornberg more. I didn't know if Amanda Truitt would get into the mansion. Even if she got in and did what I asked, there was no guarantee Tricia would call. But I had to wait and hope she would.

I reached over, picked the new *Esquire* magazine off Marvin's desk. Started an article about the current state of American fiction. Two paragraphs in I felt like a Russian peasant reading a French menu. I couldn't figure out what the hell the guy was saying. Something about a lack of vital vision and social intimations. I tossed the magazine back, rummaged through my desk until I found an old copy of *Playboy*. At least I understood why vital vision was needed here.

At 2:30 I asked Marvin could I use his phone. He said, "What's that on your desk?"

"I'm expecting an important call. Capital I."

"Ma Bell's got this option, Call Waiting? Only been available about a decade."

"I happen to believe call waiting is rude, Marvin. You know I always hang up when people put me on hold when they get another call. It's like saying, 'Whoever this is, they're more important than you are.'"

He said, "Make it short. I got working folks to fleece."

I called Milwaukee 411, got a number for the Harper Cosmetics corporate office. I asked the switchboard lady could I speak to Blair Harper. The woman, who talked with a German accent, asked who I was. I was ready for that, being the brainy, well-prepared PI that I am. I said I was Mr. Herschel Abramowitz, attorney for daughter Ashley. I figured family would be the best way to get to Blair Harper in a hurry. The woman hesitated a bit, said, "You know, don't you Mr. Abramowitz, that Mr. Blair has been retired from the daily operations of Harper Cosmetics for quite some time?" I said sure, I knew that, but Mr. Blair wasn't at his residences. Somebody at one of them said to try here. Could she see if he'd be in later? She put me on hold, I listened to an elevator music version of "Satisfaction." Felt like beating the phone against the wall. Things like Muzak renditions of landmark rock 'n' roll songs totally invalidate my philosophy of life. Well, cheapen it anyway.

Ms. Switchboard came back a minute later. Said, "Mr. Abramowitz, Mr. Blair is due in this afternoon for a board meeting scheduled at four o'clock. Would you like to call back then or shall I take a message?"

I said, "He won't be able to reach me. I'll call back."

I set the phone down. Without looking up Marvin muttered, "And you question the ethics of my profession, Mr. Abramowitz?"

This time I flipped him off.

Back to my desk. There was indeed a deadline. Sometime after four P.M., the proverbial fan would be clobbered by feces. I was starting to get a handle on this thing. And if I was right I probably didn't have to worry about George Kemp anymore. Odds were he was at the Harper mansion, and would be staying there.

My phone rang at 3:45.

Tricia Thornberg said, "Mr. Kruger?"

I slid the chair to the desk, hunched over the phone. I said, "Tricia, get out of that house."

"Is *that* what was so important? We've been through this. I'm not leaving."

"Your mother wants to talk to you. Anywhere you say, she'll go there."

"Yeah, right."

"She told me she'll make the effort."

"I've heard it before."

"Tricia, Shannon says she'll kill you if your mother and I talk."

"Come on. Talk about what?"

I said, "Didn't Amanda tell you?"

"Amanda said to call you, it was important. She acted so weirded out I thought it *was* important."

"Amanda's weirded out because she's scared to death."

"Why?"

"Why do you think?"

Silence. Obviously Tricia had been giving things some thought and she wasn't liking all she came up with, regardless of what she said to me. She said, "I feel sorry for Amanda."

I said, "Me too."

"She tries so hard to be friends with Shannon. She told me

they're best friends, but Shannon barely tolerates her, she has nothing but contempt for her. Amanda's kind of pathetic. It reminds me of—"

"Of what?"

"Never mind."

I said, "Shannon has contempt for most people"

"That's not true."

Again I said, "Leave the house."

"I can't."

"You can't?"

"I mean I won't. We have work to do."

"This afternoon, right?"

No answer.

"Involving Shannon's father?"

"Her *father*? They don't even speak."

"Someone's speaking to Shannon. She knows her father'll be at the Harper Cosmetics building in Milwaukee at four o'clock this afternoon."

Tricia said, "What do you know about Harper Cosmetics?"

"More than you know about Shannon Harper."

"That's a lie! I'm closer to her than anyone else on earth."

"Amanda Truitt thinks the same thing. George Kemp, Frank Kelson, Sorrento Gallo. They all think she's in love with them. She's using all of you."

"Stop it."

I said, "Tricia, listen to me, get out of that house. Meet me and your mother. You don't have to go back and live with her. You can stay anywhere else you want. My place, a hotel, the Y. Just leave Shannon. Today. Now."

"I can't do that. Not *now*." For the first time Tricia sounded a little scared.

"You can't do it because she won't let you. We set up a meeting with your mother and I'd be there, but you wouldn't because Shannon won't let you out of her sight."

"I can leave any time I want. I don't want to, that's all."

I said, "Things've changed there, haven't they? The way Shannon treats you, the way George is behaving?"

"No."

"They killed Amy, they killed Arthur Irwin, they'll kill you if things break down. Trust me. Please, Tricia."

She breathed heavily into the phone, but didn't answer.

I said, "Amy didn't—"

Very fast, Tricia said, "Shannon swore to me none of us killed Amy."

"You asked her? You aren't as sure about her as you want me to think."

"I believe her."

I said, "Who else would want Amy dead?"

"Why would we?"

"To shut us up."

She said, "Shut you up about what?"

Her tone of voice told me she *didn't* know. Not the real deal. I said, "Your mother will go *anywhere* to meet you—" and then the line went dead. I looked at the receiver, shaking my head. Muttered, "*Damn*it!"

Marvin was staring at me when I finally laid the phone down and pushed back from the desk. He doesn't hear me plead very often. He said, "Whatever it is, Dan, I hope it works out," in a sincere voice.

I slumped in the chair, stared out the window. I said, "Not looking good at this point."

THIRTY-ONE

I drove to Kay's because if I didn't I'd drive to a liquor store. I'd buy the biggest bottle of Christian Brothers they had and me and the bottle would spend the afternoon on the couch. I'd pull the covers over my head. Visit the artificial paradise where reality is forbidden and life is like it should be instead of like it is. Where I could be anything I wanted, accomplish whatever I desired. And feel warm and secure doing it.

But visiting that world and dreaming those dreams would not

get Tricia Thornberg home. I wasn't sure what would, but that definitely wouldn't.

As I drove the narrow Lincoln Park streets I thought about Shannon Harper. I was sure I had it nailed now. And if she hadn't ordered the murders or made the threats I would have left it alone. Let her go for it. She had her reasons, she saw her opportunity, she was taking her chance.

I got to Kay's at 4:45 P.M. Atlas sat in a blue-and-white parked half on the curb in front of the house. He wore mirror sunglasses. Grinned when he saw me like a cat spotting a one-winged tweetie-pie. He said through his passenger window, "Couple men inside gonna be very happy to see you, Dannyboy."

I said, "What the men need you for?"

"Lincoln Park's my beat. See, you stick on the job, eventually you get to work the high class neighborhoods. You don't get stuck in Area One forever. Something's up inside. DiNardi wants I should monitor the lezbo's house. Your name got mentioned more than once."

Terrific.

Kay sat between DiNardi and Kaiser on the couch again. Heather and Hedy sat in chairs. The TV was on, sound low. The early news.

Kay and Hedy looked scared to death, their faces slack, cheeks flushed, eyes popped with fear. Heather slouched, legs crossed at the knees, staring hatred at DiNardi. Bugs dozed in her lap.

Kaiser glanced at me, then at the floor. He wore the rumpled brown suit. He looked to be in immense pain. Yukon Jack flu no doubt.

DiNardi smiled, said, "Been waiting for you to show up." He wore a gray two-button jacket with a hint of violet in it, black worsted slacks, pale pink shirt, dark tie, black loafers. Hair gleamed like patent leather.

I said, "Did you go to school to learn how to dress good, DiNardi, or it a gift?"

DiNardi picked up a photograph that lay on the table in front of Kay. He said, "Come here, got something I want you to look at."

"I said, "You dress better than Ricardo Montalban.""

He ignored me, said, "Come on, look at this."

I stepped forward, took the photo from his hand. I bent into the light from the reading lamp on the table to look at the picture. The photo had been taken in Kay and Amy's living room. There were fifteen people in the photo. Including Arthur Irwin, Amy Barrow and every member of Friends of the Wild.

I said, "Kay and Amy with some friends. So what?"

DiNardi said, "This morning I get a call from a detective named Bachrach who's investigating the homicide of an Arthur Irwin. Name ring a bell?"

"Bachrach or Irwin?"

"Always the wiseguy."

"Never heard of either."

"Irwin got blown away in Old Town last night. You read about it maybe?"

I shook my head.

"A hit like Amy Barrow. Somebody waited in a car for Irwin to show, pumped him full of bullets, drove away." He nodded at the TV screen. "He got twenty-five seconds on the news little while ago."

"Didn't see it."

"Don't matter. He'll get more soon as they learn about this photo. Bachrach tells me on the phone there's similarities between this homicide and ours. So Jack and I head over to Irwin's apartment to check it out."

I said, "Course you would."

"We're looking the place over and I start leafing through a photo album on the coffee table, just browsing, looking at faces, when whoa Nelly, look what I find."

"This photo?"

"That photo."

"It significant?"

He said, "Arthur Irwin is the skinny, dopey looking guy sitting on the floor. The floor of the same room we're in right now. See the couch and the big window behind everybody? Of course the window is boarded up now because somebody threw a brick through it the other day. And see who else is in it? Amy Barrow. The same Amy Barrow who hired you your last day in rehab."

"Who *wanted* to hire me."

"Right, right. *Wanted* to hire you. The same Amy Barrow who used to live here and got murdered the same day, in the same way as Arthur Irwin. I'm gonna climb way out on a limb and predict Ballistics will tell me with the same gun. Sitting next to Amy Barrow we got Kay Thornberg who originally told us— before I whipped this photo on her—that she never heard of any Arthur Irwin. And see the dude with the sneer and the Johnny Cash clothes? Standing next to the redhead babe? Name's Frank Kelson. You knew that, right?"

"I know Kay, I knew Amy. Why would I know the rest of these people?"

"Kelson's big brother is affiliated with a North Side gang. Reggie Kelson?"

"I'm supposed to know him too?"

"The White Square Riders. You hearda *them*, right?"

"Never have."

"You don't know much, do you?"

"No, but I don't have to."

"Reggie Kelson lives in Joliet these days. Stateville. Reggie used to exchange guns for cocaine and heroin with the colored gangs on the South Side. Had himself a gun connection in Miami. Purchased Uzis down there, traded 'em up here to the Superfly's for nose candy. But Reggie Kelson got pinched dealing the stuff last year. Frank Kelson was his big brother's gofer."

And must have inherited his Miami connection. I said, "What's it all mean?"

"Means you and Kay been bullshitting us big time."

"We've been through this, DiNardi."

"Well, here's where it stops, because the BS is so deep now we need hip waders to get through it. Every day it gets easier to see something's going on here. Something you two could tell us all about."

I looked at Kaiser. He looked away. I said, "That the only photo?"

"Only one."

I said, "Too bad Irwin didn't write down names and a date."

"Too bad for us."

"That's what I meant."

DiNardi said, "I know what you meant." He stared up at me, made a sarcastic chuckle. "I pulled your police file."

"So?"

"I wanted to know why it was you didn't last but eighteen months as a cop. Found it was cause you couldn't handle winging the colored kid. Quinton Aaron Pryor. You and Quint ever get together these days, reminisce about the good ole days over a beer?"

I knew what had happened to Quintin Pryor, but I said, "I doubt he'd wanna talk to me."

"I punched his name into the computer. Punk is dead, man. Killed in '82 while holding up a liquor store on Cottage Grove. Before that he was in and out of Cook County and Joliet like you and I go in and out of the supermarket. So actually you woulda rid society of a future lowlife, you'd been a better shot. I read the shrink's reports said how bad you were traumatized, how the post-incident stress was too much for you. How you had some kind of breakdown, became unglued. Then resigned."

I said, "Pryor was an innocent bystander who started running down an alley when he saw two cops running toward him. We were chasing someone else, but Quint and his buddy started running anyway cause black teenagers don't take chances when they see Chicago cops running at 'em. With shit like I pulled I can't imagine why."

"Your marksmanship any better these days?"

"Haven't fired a gun since."

"Turned you into a regular bleeding heart, didn't it? Kid didn't die, he was probably a gangbanger—who cared?"

"I wasn't cop material in the first place."

"Why you a PI then? That's close."

"When I grow up, maybe I'll figure out what I wanna do. Cut the crap. Why bring up the ancient history?"

"I bring it up because I think it means if we drag you downtown and work it right, you'll crack like an egg."

"Don't bet the farm, DiNardi."

He said, "Tell me the names of the other people in the photo."

I said, "Am I in it?"

He raised his eyebrows.

I said, "I'm not in it, am I? If I'm not in it how should I know who these people are? I know Kay, I knew Amy. How does it follow I know all their friends? Where's the logic, DiNardi?"

"Can't even ID Tricia Thornberg? The skinny girl on the couch with the mile long legs? Her picture is all over this house. Kay never even told us she had a daughter, let alone that she ran off."

Kay whispered, "Please. It isn't relevant."

DiNardi turned. In a low, hostile voice he said, "Tell us what's going on and *we'll* decide what's relevant, *ma'am*. You get a rock through your window one day. Next day two people in this photo are murdered in the same way. One of the two hired this low rent PI two days before *that*, and you sit here and tell me shit ain't *relevant*? You're gonna in*sult* my intelligence like that? There's two murder victims and a runaway in this photo, sitting in front of a window had a brick thrown through it. What's the connection?"

"It was a party."

"Look at these faces. These people look like they're *partying*?"

Kaiser said in a soft voice, "She the one, Kruger?"

I nodded.

DiNardi swung his head from me to Kaiser. Said, "She the one what? The fuck is goin' on here?"

Kaiser didn't answer. He closed his eyes, rubbed the bridge of his nose with his thumb and index finger.

DiNardi said, "Jack, you been talking to this clown behind my back?"

Kaiser opened his eyes, said quietly, "Back off, Leo."

Kaiser looked at Kay for a long time. Knowing now it was her daughter who'd get killed. Thinking about his own daughter. Thinking what he'd do if his daughter was in that kind of a jam. Knowing the answer was "anything." Including lying to police.

Kaiser stood and said, "Come on, Leo. These people don't know anything. So what if Irwin and Barrow knew each other? Lots of people get murdered who know each other."

DiNardi's eyes flashed rage at Kaiser. He said, "You can't be serious, Jack. I bet this punk knows the name, the motive—the whole works. Why you let him keep busting our balls?"

Kaiser walked to the door, hands in his pockets. His back to the room he said, "Come *on*, Leo. We got work to do."

DiNardi grabbed the photo from my hand, stomped to the door, shaking his head violently.

Kaiser stood for a second, looking at the floor. He said, "How much time, Kruger? I can't give you much."

I said, "Twenty-four, maybe forty-eight hours. I got it nailed, I think it starts soon. You'll get your man. What's a little time?"

"You guarantee I get my man?"

"I guarantee it."

He left.

Heather said, "That was great, Dan. That scumbag went berserk.

Kay sagged back on the couch. Hedy went and sat next to her, put both arms around her. Kay said, "They threatened to take me downtown. Can they do that?"

"No, but most people don't know that and go."

"I got sick. I ran to the bathroom to vomit." She shuddered. Said, "Why did Kaiser give us the break?"

"Old cops know you don't always go strictly by the book. Last night I told him the situation. He knows Tricia is in danger. I didn't name her, didn't tell him she was yours, but he figured it out. He has a teenage daughter too. Even so, DiNardi is gonna talk to a superior about this or work overtime on his own. Soon as he ID's the people in that photo, and I'm sure some of Irwin's neighbors know a name or two, he's off and running. He gets the names, he gets enough to screw everything up. He does that, Tricia's just as dead as if we spilled our guts."

The three women looked at me. Like I had some kind of plan.

At 5:10 P.M. the TV talking hairdo, Charles Chambers—"The Man on Top of Chicago's News"—said they were switching to their sister station in Milwaukee for a just breaking story about a hostage situation. Charles Chambers, the talking hairdo, looked into his monitor.

THIRTY-TWO

I moved fast to the TV, upped the volume, kneeled on one knee in front of the set.

A Connie Chung lookalike, impeccably dressed in cream and navy, appeared on the screen. Behind her a row of squad cars were lined against a wire fence. Their light racks whirlybirded red, then blue. A heavyset woman with short blond hair and scared eyes, wearing a snug white blouse and rimless glasses, stood next to her. In the distance, beyond the squad cars, was the Harper Cosmetic building.

The reporter said, "I'm standing outside the Harper Cosmetic complex fifteen miles north of Milwaukee, the scene of what appears to be a multiple hostage situation. Details are sketchy right now."

Shouts sounded off camera. The camera panned away from the reporter, zoomed in on the front of the building. Gallo and Fuller's black van was parked sideways in front of the glass doors, the slide-open side facing the building.

Off-camera, the reporter said, "What we know now is this. At approximately four-fifteen this afternoon an unidentified number of people in the black van you're looking at right now stopped at the guardhouse at the entrance to the employees' parking lot. A hooded man got out of the van and sprayed bullets into the guardhouse, wounding the two security guards on duty. The hooded man then entered the guardhouse and released the gate." The camera came back to the reporter. She said, "Though wounded, one of the two security personnel was able to call state police. Both men were removed from the scene by ambulance just moments ago. We have no word on their condition. The van then drove through the lot, across the front lawn, coming to a stop directly in front of the main entrance, blocking it from our view."

More shouts. The reporter stopped talking and looked behind her. The camera panned back to the van, zoomed in shakily.

Two people walked around the back of the van, one in front of the other. The man in front wore a dark suit and had both hands in the air. The one in back wore a black aviator style jumpsuit and a white hood with eye and mouth holes. From his size and the way he walked I was sure the man wearing the hood was Sorrento Gallo. So was Kay. She gasped. Said, "Oh, my God."

Gallo cradled what looked like an AK assault rifle. He tilted it up toward the back of the first man's head. The muzzle of the rifle was attached to the first man by a length of cord wrapped around his neck and the gun barrel.

Someone close to a microphone shrieked, "My God, it's Mr. Leavell."

Gallo yelled something the microphone didn't pick up, then turned the man in the business suit around with the gun and they went behind the van and out of sight.

The reporter, still off-camera, said, "The hooded man said they're holding fifteen hostages and they'll be contacting authorities shortly."

The camera came back to her. She said, "I have with me a Miss Henrietta Marks, who witnessed what happened after the van parked outside the building.

Henrietta Marks was losing it. She spluttered, "Mother God, that was Mr. Leavell with a gun tied to his head. Mother God, poor Mr. Leavell." The reporter put her free hand on Henrietta's shoulder. Henrietta lifted her glasses, wiped her eyes with her fingers. She said, voice shaky, "I don't know all that happened. Just before quitting time we heard screams by the reception area and next thing we knew two men with hoods over their faces burst into the office, shooting bullets into the ceiling and screaming at us to put our hands in the air. One said the men had to go to the front door to unload boxes from a van parked out front."

"Did the men with guns say why they were doing this?"

"No, they didn't."

"What happened next, Henrietta?"

"Five workers left the office with one of the hooded men. The other stayed with us."

"Did that man say anything?"

"Not a word."

"Did any of you say anything to him?"

"No, we were too—" Henrietta Marks started to lose it again.

"You were in shock?"

Henrietta Marks nodded vigorously.

"What was going through your mind right then, Henrietta?"

In a small voice she said, "That I was going to die." Tears slid down her cheeks.

The reporter said, "What happened then?"

Henrietta took a deep breath, said, "Few minutes later, the other hooded man came back and said we were all to leave single file out the front door."

"Did you see anything when you left?"

"I saw suitcases and boxes stacked inside the reception area."

"Did you see any more hooded men?"

"Just the one who stood with us in the office. But I heard shooting and screaming in other parts of the building, upstairs and downstairs."

"What then?"

"We all ran to the parking lot and stood there. Other parts of the plant came out at intervals and then the police started arriving." She started blubbering again. Said, "My God, poor Mr. Leavell."

The reporter said, "And who is Mr. Leavell, Henrietta?"

"My boss," she sobbed. "I can't imagine why anybody'd want to harm him."

The reporter said, "Do you know how many hooded men there are inside the building?"

Henrietta Marks said, "In the parking lot one of the receptionists said four."

Somebody was still at the Holiday Inn. I *did* have it nailed.

The reporter nodded, said, "Thank you, Henrietta Marks for that eyewitness account. You're very brave."

The reporter looked behind her to see if anything else was going on, then turned to the camera. You could tell by her face the very brave Henrietta Marks was already a vague memory. She said, "And that's all we have at the moment. We believe four armed, hooded men hold approximately fifteen hostages inside the Harper Cosmetic building. We don't, at this time, know who the hostages are or why they're being held. But we'll stay here and keep you up to date as long as this story unfolds."

The picture of the reporter telescoped into the corner of the screen and Charles Chambers came back on. Charles looked sterner than a hanging judge. He said, "Lynn, does anyone at the scene have any idea what's behind this incredible event?"

The reporter said, "Authorities have told us nothing, Charles. We did learn there was a sizeable layoff of personnel recently, but whether that is linked in any way to this situation we just don't know."

Charles said thank you and Lynn blipped off the screen. The station went to a dog food commercial which was almost funny.

I turned, looked at Kay Thornberg. She said, "What are they doing?"

I said, "I have a theory. Doesn't mean it's right, but everything fits. It all starts with the fact Shannon Harper isn't an heiress. Her father disowned her five years ago. She can live in the mansion, but the only money she receives is two thousand a month. Kemp's been bankrolling Friends of the Wild. He hinted as much when I talked to him the other day. Shannon hates her father for the disowning and a lot of other things. She's consumed with revenge. She plans to not just avenge animals, she plans to avenge herself. She's got seven people so dedicated to a cause—and her—they'll do anything she tells them to as long as they think it's promoting that cause."

Kay said, "But what's the plan?"

I said, "Friends of the Wild is kidnapping her father. She's getting her inheritance one way or the other. The four people in the building will hold those hostages long enough to make sure the money gets to her. They've been told the money will finance the group's future. Let them conduct raids, purchase more arms and supplies. But once she gets the ransom I bet the house Shannon's blowing the country."

Kay said, "Christ, where's Tricia in all of this?"

"At the mansion with Shannon and George Kemp."

Heather asked "What will they do to her?"

I said, "Nothing for now. She's their guarantee we keep quiet."

Kay said, "I can't believe she'd do this. I can't believe it."

"It's the only way it adds up. It's her shot at the family money, and her way of getting back at a man who abused her throughout her childhood."

"What kind of abuse?"

"Mental, emotional, physical."

"Sexual?"

"Her behavior indicates it's possible."

Kay said, "Oh, God," and shut her eyes. I knew she was thinking only of Tricia now.

Heather said, "Can she get away with this?"

"If she gets the money and gets somewhere before anyone ties her into it she's home free. Right now nobody knows she's involved except us and we can't talk because of Tricia."

"Where does she have to get?"

"Anywhere doesn't have an extradition treaty with us. Lots of countries don't. Or even a country that does, if it's corrupt enough. There's lots of places you can live on the lam like a king if you grease the right palms."

Kay said, "My God, there has to be something we can do. To get Tricia." Her voice was getting hysterical again.

I said, "Kay, remember Tricia is safe as she can be for right now. If we try something stupid she won't be. We're going to get her, so relax." I wished someone would say that to me so I could.

"Will Shannon take Tricia with her where she's going?"

"She might, to assure you and I don't talk until she gets there."

"Will she kill her? After her usefulness is done?"

The jackpot question.

I knew I had to get help and I knew who it had to be.

THIRTY-THREE

We sat through stories about the economy, local politics, national politics, a failed coup d'état somewhere in Southeast Asia. Sports. Sox won big, Cubs got clobbered. For once I couldn't have cared less. Weather. Tomorrow would be hot and humid. The dork pointing at the weather map probably pulled down a hundred grand a year to tell me it was going to be hot and humid in July.

They went back to Milwaukee half an hour later. The lady reporter was farther from the scene. The cop cars were fifty yards behind her now. The light racks were turned off. She had to be in the field on the other side of the blacktop road.

She said nothing had changed. Four armed men were holding fifteen hostages. Nobody knew why. She interviewed a beefy state trooper who appeared to be more interested in looking down the front of her blouse than in anything going on behind him. He implied he knew things. He gave the impression he might tell her those things if she'd slip away with him somewhere. He flirted shamelessly on live TV.

On the six o'clock national news it was the second story. The lady reporter came back on. She told the rest of the USA what she'd told Milwaukee and Chicago.

Heather said, "This is too weird. The entire country is hearing this, but the only people who know what's going on are in this room."

I said, "Except for one other person."

And one other person deserved to know. Now that I had a half-assed plan.

I went to the kitchen, dialed 744-8261. Area Six Violent Crimes. I got bounced around, eventually talked to a sergeant I knew. He gave me Kaiser's home phone number. I left a message on his machine. I leaned against the door jamb between the two rooms and stared at the TV, oblivious to what was on it.

Kaiser called at 6:45 P.M.

I said, "You off duty?"

"I'm home, ain't I?"

"Sober?"

"For awhile."

"Studman's not around?"

"It's not like we associate off the job. Maybe not on the job after today. He requested a new partner. He's out right now carting that photo door to door."

I said, "Let's drive to Milwaukee."

"Why in hell do I wanna drive to Milwaukee?"

"Be very beneficial to you."

"I get my killer?"

"You hear the story, you get your killer."

"On my way."

He picked me up in a green and white Cutlass at 7:15 P.M. He wore the baggy brown pants and an unbuttoned white short-sleeve shirt. A holstered .38 lay on the seat next to him. He toked on the cigar. The a/c was running full blast, so he cracked the window when I got in. Stogie smoke streamed toward the sliver of air between glass and metal.

I said, "You hear about the hostage thing in Milwaukee?"

"Something on the radio on the way over. It tie in with us?"

As we drove west and north to the Tri-State I told him the story so far, advanced my theory. He nodded several times, tugged occasionally on the skin below his chin. When I was done he said, "It all adds up. So we gotta get Tricia back, apprehend this George Kemp and Shannon Harper before they fly the coop with the dough."

"That's it."

"So why aren't we staking out the Harper mansion? The girl you want and the two people I want are down there."

"Kemp and Harper aren't gonna let Tricia out of their sight. Probably haven't since I poked my nose into this. They won't leave the mansion till it's time to pick up the cash. When they do, if they make us, it's bye bye Tricia."

"Makes sense."

"We'll let the bag man lead us to the people we want."

"What about the rest of 'em?"

"Wisconsin's headache."

"Gonna be a mess. Kelson's guns from Miami, the two murders in Chicago, the shootings and kidnapping in Wisconsin, planned in Chicago."

"Not my worry."

"Mine though. How they gonna get the money to Shannon Harper?"

"Five people went north, four are at the building. The one who isn't is the key. The money gets delivered to him or her. The four inside the building tell the authorities they're the whole corps, you gotta negotiate with us. They'll drag it out long as it takes. They have Blair Harper call the family on the q.t. He says, 'I got a gun taped to my head. You don't deliver the dough to whoever, wherever, they're gonna blow my head off.' Long as the family says zilch to the police and you gotta assume they won't talk until they get Blair Harper back, the money has all the time it needs to get down here."

"How'd she manage to talk them into this?"

"Wasn't hard. These are fanatics with a capital F. They think the whole thing is about animals. I'm sure Shannon worked out a plan convinced 'em they'll get out of the building alive."

He said, "Oh, they'll get out alive if they have fifteen hostages including Blair Harper. Wisconsin police aren't gonna start blasting away when the van leaves if there's fifteen innocent people inside, especially when one of 'em's the richest bird in the state."

I said, "As to how they plan to get away with the thing scot free, I'm sure Shannon sold them a plan for that too. Maybe even one that'll work."

"Can't see that. They'll get out of the building all right, but get away scot free?" He shook his head. "I don't know."

"Maybe they wanna be martyrs. Trade five, six years of their lives to glorify the cause."

"Hard to believe."

"These people are *intense.*"

We drove in silence for a few miles. He said, "Imagine, you kidnap your father and you're not even a suspect."

"It *is* kind of ingenious. Getting seven people to do your dirty work for you. You get rich, they go to jail. She pulls it off she's gonna laugh for a long time."

"We gotta see she don't pull it off."

We crossed the state line at dusk. Kaiser puffed on the cigar, lost in thought. Suddenly he said, "Apart from the kidnapping and murder, what do you think about these animal rights people?"

I gave him a glance. He kept his eyes on the road. I couldn't read his expression, but he'd used the word "people," he lived with two cats, and he made a point of saying "aside from the kidnapping and murder." I said, "Never thought about 'em until this week. Seems there's stuff to be upset about."

He said, "Kay Thornberg doesn't strike me as a crackpot."

I said, "I gotta admit someone tried to drip poison in Bugs's eye so some crone on Lake Shore Drive can have red lips, there'd be hell to pay."

He said, "You ever heard of Jainism?"

"No."

"Hindu sect founded by Lord Mahavir. Not a lot of followers even in India. Like maybe two percent of eight hundred million people." He looked at me, maybe expecting a laugh, but I nodded. He said, "Jainists embrace non-violence and the philosophy of complete and total reverence of life in every form. Down to insects and bacteria."

"Bacteria?"

"So they're a little extreme. I read about it somewhere, been checking into it. They got a temple out in Bartlett. I been there a couple times."

"You pulling my leg, Kaiser?"

"Why you say that?"

"This doesn't exactly fit the stereotype. A crusty old homicide cop interested in stuff like that."

"Hey, I didn't say I was gonna *join*. It just intrigues me and why shouldn't it? Every morning I walk through the door at 2452 West Belmont I get rapes, murders, armed robberies, beatings handed to me. Solve this, solve that. I see stuff, hear stuff make a normal man puke. Inspect corpses look like road kill. I talk to women so traumatized by sexual attacks you know they'll never be normal again. People who've filled their pants, don't even realize it they're so out of it from fear and shock. Kids been abused so bad you wanna execute the offender right on the spot. I arrest punks so mean and twisted they're like devils walking around in human bodies. You're always asking yourself how can people treat each other like this? There's got to be something, some *people* out there help you deal with shit like that. Why shouldn't I get interested in a philosophy that promotes peace and love? Why wouldn't I want to retreat to that? Get away from the cesspool I wallow around in all day?"

"It's true, cops *don't* see man at his best."

"Since I was a kid I loved animals. I got my two cats right after my wife left me, took Susan with her. My ex hated pets, we couldn't have any in the house. I wish Susan still lived with me, but I'll take the cats over my wife any day of the week."

"Cat's names?"

"Clark and Audrey."

"Male and female?"

"Generic now. You live with animals you learn they have personalities too. You start to think maybe a life form is a life form. I'm not saying equal, but my job teaches me the human life form maybe ain't so special as we like to think."

I said, "I came to that conclusion long before I was a cop."

He said, "Tell you the truth, I admire groups like Friends of the Wild."

"Until they start murdering people."

"I told you that's my line. But if what you say is true I almost don't hold the people inside that building accountable for the murders. They think they're rescuing animals."

"Almost?"

"After you deal with humpty dump scumbags for humpty dump years you know some people got it coming. Animals never do. They're perfect innocents. I got eighteen months to pension time. Then me, Clark and Audrey are outta here. I'm getting a small farm in the middle of nowhere, I'm tending animals and reading great books."

"And drinking Yukon Jack."

Kaiser smiled. Said, "In moderation."

"Right. You ever talk about this with DiNardi?"

"DiNardi? Hell, I don't talk about this with *anybody,* least of all DiNardi." We were silent for ten seconds. In a sheepish voice he said, "Hey, Kruger, I'd appreciate it, you never told anybody about this. I shoulda never opened my mouth. I sound like a fucking flake. It's just because of that girlfriend of yours and the rabbit and after what Leo and I read in your file—"

"You took me for a fucking flake too, right? Relax, I'm glad you told me. But I gotta ask you something now I know you a little better."

"What's that?"

"If this is the real you, how in hell do you put up with a neanderthal like DiNardi?"

He chuckled low in his throat. Said, "It hasn't been easy, guy, it sure hasn't been easy." He looked over at me. "So, what about you? You got a philosophy or religion or anything?"

"Oh, I got a motto I try to remember when things get tough."

"Let's hear it."

"Life is a series of incidents that seem important at the time."

Kaiser thought a bit. Said, "Keeps things in perspective. That's good. I like it. Where'd you read that?"

"A comic strip."

"Appropriate a place as any to get your philosophy."

"More appropriate than most."

THIRTY-FOUR

Kaiser's tin got us past the roadblock set up on the blacktop road just off the highway. We drove the two miles to the Harper building slowly.

The building was lit up like a shopping mall on opening night. A flat bed truck with two high power floodlights was parked on the lawn on the other side of the wire fence. One light pointed at the black van, the other played the length of the building back and forth. A floodlight in the parking lot was trained on the loading dock doors. A curve of brightness rose over the top of the building from the rear and far side. They had floods there, too.

County and state squad cars were lined along the outside of the fence, facing both ways, depending on which end of the blacktop they'd entered. Groups of cops huddled and talked it over.

The media had been pushed across the road into the field, behind a line of saw horses and rope. Three vans with TV station logos on the side and two station wagons with radio call letters on the doors sat off to the side. A small crowd of reporters and men carrying mini-cams on their shoulders stood against the barrier. Lights and a small satellite dish were set up behind the reporters, the lights much smaller and dimmer than the floodlights.

We parked behind the last squad car. Walked back on the blacktop. Kaiser waggled the leather flap with his badge in the air as we went. A pimply-faced state cop told us a suit named Rosenthal was in charge.

Finding Rosenthal was easy. Everybody was looking at four plainclothes men standing next to a slate-colored Chrysler with all four doors open directly across the lawn from the black van. Three of those men looked at the fourth.

Rosenthal wore tan slacks and a navy blazer. He stood tall, was gray at the temples, had prominent bug-eyes. He looked totally stressed out. He gripped a 7-Eleven cup of coffee with one hand. His other cradled a hand talkie.

Kaiser showed him the badge, said, "Jack Kaiser. Chicago Violent Crimes." I nodded, said "Kruger." I set my face in grave "real cop" mode, but the Guns 'n' Roses T-shirt and ripped jeans maybe clued him I wasn't.

Rosenthal said, "What brings you north, Detective?" More than a little animosity in the voice.

Kaiser said, "Like to be where the action is."

"This ain't your action."

Kaiser said, "You got a handle on it yet?"

"Why the interest?"

"Because if it's an animal right's group involved there's a

couple in Chicago we been keeping an eye on capable of a stunt like this."

Rosenthal stared at Kaiser. He said, "What makes you think this is animal rights?"

"The research lab here got raided once before. The company's position on animal research is well known. The movement is growing, getting bolder. Only a matter of time before something like this happens."

Rosenthal looked from Kaiser to me, back to Kaiser, then said, "That's what it looks like." He set the coffee and the talkie on the roof of the Chrysler, pulled aside the lapel of his coat, removed a folded sheet of paper from his shirt pocket. He handed it to Kaiser.

There was enough bleed off from the floods to see faces, but not words on paper. Kaiser took a pen size flashlight from his pants pocket, trained it on words typed in capital letters. He ran the light slowly left to right, line by line. I leaned in to read too. It said:

WHEREAS 100 MILLION ANIMAL LIVES ARE SACRIFICED EVERY YEAR IN LABORATORIES ACROSS THE NATION AND WHEREAS HARPER COSMETIC COMPANY CONTRIBUTES ITS SHARE TO THAT TOTAL AND WHEREAS IT HAS STEADFASTLY REFUSED TO QUIT TORTURING ANIMALS AS PART OF THE RESEARCH OF ITS PRODUCTS EVEN AFTER REPEATED REQUESTS AND WARNINGS AND WHEREAS THE CONTINUED TORTURE OF THESE ANIMALS HAS BEEN WELL-DOCUMENTED AND WHEREAS THIS TORTURE HAS BEEN AIDED, ABETTED, AND ENCOURAGED BY HIGH-RANKING EMPLOYEES OF HARPER COSMETIC COMPANY, UP TO AND INCLUDING BLAIR ALEXANDER HARPER AND HIS BROTHER DAVID CABOT HARPER WE THE UNDERSIGNED HAVE DECLARED WAR ON HARPER COSMETIC COMPANY AND ALL THOSE WHO TORTURE ANIMALS. THE FIRST CASUALTIES OF THIS WAR WILL BE THE AFOREMENTIONED HARPERS AND THE SADISTIC MENGELES IN THEIR RESEARCH DEPARTMENT. BUT MAKE NO MISTAKE. THIS IS BUT THE FIRST BATTLE. OUR OBJECTIVE IS THE TOTAL AND COMPLETE ERADICATION OF THE ANIMAL INDUSTRY.

WHEN THIS MESSAGE IS TURNED OVER TO THE MEDIA, AND MADE PUBLIC, INSTRUCTIONS WILL BE ISSUED.

FRIENDS OF THE WILD.

EQUAL RIGHTS, EQUAL TREATMENT, EQUAL CONSIDERATION, EQUAL PUNISHMENT.

Kaiser and I looked at each other. He said, "War? Casualties?"

I said, "Whereas, a time to worry." To Rosenthal I said, "How'd you get this?"

"They released a hostage an hour ago. Sent it out with him."

"What's going on inside?"

"Sounds grim. They removed all the animals from the research lab in the basement, wired it with explosives. We figure that's rubble no matter what happens. They divided the hostages into four groups, put each group in a different room, gagged 'em, tied 'em to chairs. *Those* rooms are wired with explosives. He says they won't even let these people use the toilet and as you can imagine, these people *need* to use the toilet. We cut the power, but he says they got plenty of kerosene lamps and flashlights. There's a cafeteria in the basement too, so these clowns can stay there indefinitely. Guy says he was in a room with both Harpers and two white smocks. Says all four were getting knocked around pretty good. Also says he thinks two of these loons are women. They keep hoods on, but two sound like women."

I said, "You phone in?"

Rosenthal pointed at the cellular phone in the Chrysler. "Every five, ten minutes. Somebody picks up, soon as we ID ourselves, click."

Kaiser handed the paper back to Rosenthal. Said, "Gonna release this to the press?"

Rosenthal sipped coffee. His eyes popped out a little more. He said, "Christ, I guess. What choice do we have? I have to wait for a man who's flying in from New York. Charles Larsen. He's an expert on this shit." He looked at the building for a bit, then turned back to us. Something inside him exploded. He heaved the cup against the side of the Chrysler. Coffee splattered two men standing behind the car. Rosenthal said, "Lunatic fringe terrorist bastards! Four nut cases and look at this—"

He waved his arm at the cars and the floodlights and the press. "We got a circus on our hands. Nationwide. And they start killing people in there, blowing the place apart, we're gonna look like first class chumps. All because of four nut cases worried about rodents."

Kaiser said, "Maybe they're afraid when they get to heaven they'll find God is shaped like a rodent. They're covering their ass."

Rosenthal made a disgusted face.

Kaiser said, "Never heard of Friends of the Wild, but might be an old group with a new name. Mind if we stick around after we get a bite to eat?"

Rosenthal almost shouted, "Just stay out of the way."

We walked back to the car. I said, "We can't stick around here."

"What was I supposed to say? We're gonna shove off now so we can stake out the guy receiving the ransom from this kidnapping? That you don't even know *is* a kidnapping."

I said, "Those hostages would rest a lot easier if they knew a rock like Rosenthal is in charge."

Kaiser chuckled.

We drove the five miles to the highway on the other end of the blacktop. Kaiser said, "You pegged it, Dan. The hooded people inside are gonna dazzle 'em with bullshit, drag this thing out, turn it into a PR wet dream until they get word the money is safe and sound."

"Wonder what they plan to do then?"

"Here's hoping we never find out."

As we passed the roadblock on this end another television satellite truck turned onto the blacktop. Kaiser said, "TV eats shit like this *up*."

We found the Holiday Inn, turned into the lot. I showed him the two rooms the five people had rented the night before. Both rooms were dark. Kaiser said, "Think the fifth man's still here?"

"Better be. We got no other place to look." We cruised toward the motel's office. I turned my head to face front, said "Damn!"

Boyd Fuller was ten feet from the passenger side of the car, head down, walking briskly toward the rooms. He carried a white sack.

In one motion I unsnapped the seat belt, slid below window level.

Kaiser stomped the brake, said, "What the hell?" My knees slammed against the glove compartment.

I said, "Keep going. The blond guy next to us, that's the fifth man."

Kaiser pulled under the brightly-lit, brick-ceilinged office area, through more parking lot and into the lot of Sam's Steak House.

I sat up, looked behind. Fuller climbed the stairs to the rooms. I said, "He see me?"

"Nah. He looked up when I hit the brake, but since he don't know me, he didn't even change expression. Just looked at the car, looked away, kept walking."

Kaiser turned the Cutlass around so it faced the Holiday Inn, shifted to Park.

I said, "You got binoculars?"

"In the glove."

I removed a pair of lightweight 7 × 35s with extra wide angle. Handed them to Kaiser, then scrunched down. Said, "Stakeout time. You got first watch."

Kaiser said, "Yassuh, boss." After a second he said, "A stake-out at a steak house. Cute."

THIRTY-FIVE

Sitting and waiting for somebody to do something is easy work. More boring than watching a faucet drip, but easy.

And it's easier when you have company. I've taken Bugs on stakeouts, but our conversations tend to be one-sided. I was glad I was with Kaiser. Especially now that I liked the guy.

I tuned in a Milwaukee all-news station, kept it on low volume so we could keep abreast of events at the hostage site. They played it like it was the prelude to Armageddon. The studio anchor referred to it every three or four stories and they switched back to Harper's for ten-minute updates so their man on the scene could tell us in a loud excited voice that nothing had changed.

An hour went by. More people were leaving Sam's than arriving. Kaiser moved the Cutlass every fifteen minutes, from one part of the lot to another, once into a space in the Holiday Inn lot.

I knew what he was doing, but after the fourth time we moved I said, "I could stand a nap, but I can't sleep if you keep starting and moving the car."

"That's a motel right there you wanna sleep so bad."

I said, "How long you think it'll be before Fuller hooks up with the money?"

Kaiser said, "Maybe soon, maybe not so soon."

I said, "My thoughts exactly. That's why I wouldn't mind a nap. Case it's closer to not so soon."

He said, "This way nobody notices us like they would if we stay parked in the same place. Somebody goes past us on the way in, comes back out and sees us in the same spot, it ain't gonna look good. You wanna explain what we're doing here to Wisconsin law? Why we didn't let them in on it?"

"It's just a theory, Jack. We got no proof. Really, how long you think it'll take?"

Kaiser said, "I'm sure they had Blair Harper call in the ransom demand before all the employees were out of the building. I'm sure lawyers and various Harpers are at the company's bank right now arranging to borrow the cash, everybody sworn to secrecy, but it probably depends on how much she asked for as to how long it'll take."

"You worked a kidnapping before?"

"Couple of parent snatches. Custody cases. You?"

"One," I said. "No ransom involved. Just a guy ran off with a girl, taking advantage of the fact she was scared to death. I ran them down, was taking her home. She got murdered outside a restaurant we stopped at."

"How old was she?"

"Fifteen."

"Tricia's age."

I didn't say anything.

He said, "Why you'd go to jail before you'd talk to us and risk getting her killed."

I nodded.

"Blame yourself? About her murder?"

"Pretty much."

"You didn't pull the trigger."

"I didn't think either. I should of never let her out of my sight."

"Rough."

"I didn't draw a sober breath for two months."

"I got the impression you never did anyway."

"I was usually buzzed. This was two months of total oblivion."

"You felt like when you shot the black kid?"

"Worse. I got to know the girl."

"Your motto didn't help much I bet."

"Not even a little."

"Cynical philosophies usually don't help much come crunch time."

"It definitely wasn't a trivial incident."

We didn't talk for a while. I remembered Asia Dawson. I thought of her a lot even now. She was a good kid. Amazing considering her home life. I wished she could've grown up. I had to see to it that Tricia would.

At 10:30 P.M. the field reporter read Friends of the Wild's Declaration of War. Kaiser said, "Larsen must've finally showed. Told Rosenthal what to do."

The reporter said, "No one knows what this means precisely, except it doesn't bode well for those held inside."

We both laughed.

Kaiser said, "Now that's an astute observation."

"Man has a firm grasp of the obvious."

Then the reporter read the names of the people held hostage. The two Harpers, five high level management personnel, seven research lab workers. The first seven people had been in a board meeting at 4:15 P.M. The released hostage had also been in that meeting. Police still wouldn't allow that man to speak to the press.

Kaiser said, "What's worse, you think? A board meeting or being held hostage by armed fanatics?"

"Too close to call. I wouldn't wanna be one of those lab workers."

"They don't all work with animals do they?"

"Probably very few do, and I imagine even they don't on a regular basis, but that ain't gonna cut 'em any slack with this crew."

At eleven o'clock the field reporter said a second hostage had been released with another "announcement" the "terrorists" demanded be made public. This announcement described the Draize and LD 50 tests, then told in detail the condition of the animals they'd rescued. It didn't sound pretty.

Kaiser said, "I hope they knock those white smock bastards around good."

"You can book that."

Suddenly the reporter's voice got high and shrill. He said, "We've just heard a burst of weapons fire from inside the building." Excited voices chattered in the background. Then the reporter said, "There again. A longer burst this time. Lasting at least ten seconds. One of the terrorists is shooting at something or someone."

I said, "Probably Frank Kelson writing his name on the wall."

Kaiser said, "More fun than pissing in snow. How'd Kelson hook up with these guys anyway? He probably pulled wings off of butterflies when he was a kid."

"Hots for teacher."

"Huh?"

"In love with Shannon Harper. If Shannon said sex was evil he'd cut off his Johnson. Just so happens she loves animals."

The reporter babbled away about more shots. Kaiser said, "You think they'll kill anybody?"

"I think Blair Harper is history. I don't know about the rest. Hard to say when you're dealing with such irrational minds. And Shannon set this up. She's the most irrational of the bunch. And she's got her reasons."

Kaiser said, "Scariest words I know. Everybody has their reasons."

Three long hours passed. Nothing new here or there.

At 1:00 A.M. we moved into a space in the Holiday Inn lot six doors down and across from Fuller's room. We were nestled between a Chevy truck and a Camaro in a dead spot where there was no light from the parking lot light poles.

At 2:00 A.M. a new anchor came on. Had a voice to cure acute insomnia. The hostages were still the headline story, but this guy droned that the police now believed nothing would happen until morning. Also, repeated attempts to reach members of the Harper family for comment had been futile.

Sitting here we saw that every ten minutes Fuller pulled the drapes of his room's window aside and peered into the lot.

At three o'clock we watched a drunken couple try to pull each other up the stairs below Fuller's room. The woman looked young and Hispanic. She had "heavy" hair; puffed high in front and long down the back. She wore a white blouse and a denim miniskirt half-pulled up over her wide butt.

Kaiser said, "She wearing underwear?" In the darkness I couldn't tell. He raised the binocs. Said, "Damn, she isn't." I grabbed them away. Said, "Verification is a very important part of police work."

"Essential," he said.

The woman couldn't stop laughing. The man, short and fat and wearing a hideous lime green Hawaiian shirt and peach shorts, had his arm draped around her neck, his hand down her blouse. He was so busy feeling her up he tripped on every other step, each time falling to his knees, dragging her down too. Each time she hooted louder as they rolled around getting to their feet.

I said, "Young love. Ain't it grand?"

Kaiser said, "They should of demanded a ground floor room."

"Rate they're going, they may say hell with it and do it on the landing."

"If they make the landing."

But the couple made it up the stairs and into a room. We both clapped softly. Kaiser said, "*Bravo.*"

At 3:30 A.M. I was dozing when Kaiser shoved me, motioned me down. We slid to eye level.

A black Lincoln inched past us, pulled into a spot next to a pale blue Civic directly below Fuller's room.

Two people were inside the Lincoln. They didn't get out. When Boyd Fuller next looked out the window, he immediately exited the room, hurried down the stairs. He went to the passenger side of the Lincoln. He bent over, talked to the people inside.

My window was down. I pressed my back against the door panel, craned my neck so my ear was almost outside, but I could barely make out the soft murmur of voices, no words.

The driver got out of the Lincoln, opened the trunk. Fuller joined him. The driver was tall, slim, silver-haired. Had a politician's haircut, wore an expensive dark suit. Looked like a corporation lawyer, which no doubt is what he was.

Fuller opened the trunk of the Civic. The guy in the swell suit removed five leather briefcases, one after the other, from the Lincoln's trunk. He handed them to Fuller who tossed them into the trunk of the Civic.

I whispered, "Too bad you're so intrigued by Jainism."

"Why?"

"The non-violence." I pointed at the gun between us. "We shot three people right now we'd be millionaires."

Kaiser looked at me. Said, "Greed is very negative energy."

When the drop was completed the Lincoln left. Fuller didn't go back to his room. He waited until the lights of the Lincoln disappeared, then got behind the wheel of the Civic, backed out of the parking spot. We lay on the seat while he passed us. Popped up to watch him pull onto the highway.

Kaiser and I got out and peed on the concrete. Kaiser said over the top of the car, "I'm writing my name over here."

I said, "I'm *printing* mine."

When we got back inside, we pulled onto the highway too.

THIRTY-SIX

The sky started to clear on our left as we pursued Fuller south, turning from black to purple to navy to a deep, dark orange.

My eyes felt sandy from no sleep, my stomach queasy from too many Kools. I worked the baggy of Valium from my pants, swallowed two. Asked Kaiser if he wanted one. He said, "Five's or ten's?" I said five's. He said he wanted two too. He threw them back in his throat, gulped. Said, "Why didn't you tell me you had these earlier?" He sounded peeved.

"We'd of zonked."

"What'd they say about Vs in rehab?"

"They don't want you taking aspirin in rehab, but if they think I endure life without some kind of shock absorber, they're nuts."

"Amen."

"I just wanted off the sauce."

With dawn coming on Kaiser gave Fuller plenty of room. Fuller had no reason to expect a tail, but he might remember the Cutlass from Kaiser braking it in the hotel parking lot. And of course, if he saw my face, we'd be playing "Rockford Files" all the way home.

We pounded through a sleeping Milwaukee. High in the air on the freeway. Saturday morning. Very few cars. Kaiser drove slumped against the door panel, his right wrist draped over the top of the steering wheel. His left hand tugged his ear or made nervous swipes around his mouth. His teeth clenched a new cigar he'd asked me to get from the glove compartment. He hadn't lit it yet. His stomach was probably cashed too.

I said, "Don't fall asleep."

"Don't worry about me. You're the one yawning his ass off."

"I'm not driving the car. I fall asleep we don't die."

The all-news station recapped the hostage story at quarter to five. Still nothing new. They switched to the reporter at the scene. He sounded half asleep and bored now. He said authorities expected the terrorists to contact them soon.

I said, "Wait till Kemp calls and tells them Shannon split with the dough. Terrorists'll be contacting the authorities in a goddamn hurry."

Kaiser said, "How you think she's got it worked out?"

"I think soon as she gets the money, she gets to O'Hare and gets gone."

"What about Kemp and Tricia?"

"I been thinking about that too. I'm of two minds. One says she don't take 'em with her because she's only one knows she's doing this for herself, not the group. She'll trick them somehow."

"What's your other mind say?"

"My other mind isn't too clear on the relationship she has with Tricia or Kemp. She love them? Using them? It confuses me because she happened to keep those two with her and sent the others to Milwaukee. Obviously they're dispensable. Tricia and Kemp aren't."

"Plus those two are intensely loyal."

"They're all intensely loyal."

"Good point."

"I mean she needs to keep Tricia with her to keep us silent, but I'm wondering if there's more there than that, if there has been all along."

"From what you've told me about Shannon Harper, there's good reason to wonder."

I lit another Kool. Wondered about Shannon and Tricia some more.

Kaiser said, "Where would you head if you had a ton of cash?"

"And had to worry about getting sent back?"

"No. Say you hit the Lotto. Could go anywhere on earth."

I thought for a bit. "South America I think. No, wait. England. I always think of London like it was in 1966. Swinging, you know? The Stones, Beatles, miniskirts, Emma Peel, John Steed."

Kaiser looked at me on the last two, eyebrows raised.

I said, *"The Avengers.* You never watched *The Avengers?"*

"Keep it down. Nobody knows I never watched *The Avengers."*

"Greatest TV show ever. What about you? Where would you go?"

"India. No question about it."

"I should of guessed that."

On an empty stomach Vs kick in right away. I felt myself nodding. I shook awake when Kaiser pushed me and said, "Got any idea where they're gonna pass the cash?"

"Maybe. Why?"

"I lost the son of a bitch."

"You what?" I sat up fast. "How could you lose him on a straight stretch of four lane highway?"

Kaiser slapped the steering wheel, laughed like hell. "Thought that'd get you awake. He's still up there, bout a mile or so. Other side of the ETMF semi-trailer."

"You got a twisted sense of humor."

"Most cops do. I've noticed yours isn't exactly Leave It to Beaver. Deal is, I have to stay awake, so do you."

We were silent for a bit, then he said, "I got to admit, Kruger, this night was a lot more enjoyable than if I'd worked it with Leo. I worked with Leo twelve hours straight by now I'd be hearing for the fifteenth time how some ditzy broad with watermelon tits got on her knees and begged him for more bump and grind. Then I'd have to hear about the bump and grind part."

"Not much of a compliment, but thanks. I gotta admit you've been better company than Bugs ever was."

"So it's settled. I'd rather work with you than a no class sexist pig, you consider me a step up from a rabbit."

I said, "Louis, I thing this is the beginning of a beautiful friendship."

Fuller exited at Touhy. I said, "I know where the drop is. The apartment on Cyprus I told you about where they stashed everything? They never knew I made it. It's out of the way and they think it's safe."

The sun was up now, an intense fireball that glared straight at us as we headed east. Kaiser lowered the sun flap, muttered,

"Damn!" I knew what he meant. I didn't have my shades and I was sunblind.

Fuller pulled into a 7-Eleven. We parked just off the street in the lot of a 24-hour Walgreens three buildings down. Fuller hurried to one of the public phones bolted to the front wall of the 7-Eleven, fumbled for change, dialed a number.

Fuller was off the phone in less than a minute. He drove the mile and a half to Cyprus. We let him stay three blocks ahead, not caring if we lost him. When he turned, I said, "That's Cyprus. Go down a couple and circle back. I know a good spot to wait."

At 6:20 P.M. we stopped next to the dumpsters in the service alley where I'd waited Thursday night. We'd seen the Civic parked at the other end of the block when we turned on Cyprus from our end, but couldn't see it from where we were now. I got out, walked to the hedge, kneeled, peered through parted branches. I said, "I can see him from here."

"Then stay there. He leaving the car?"

"No."

I stayed on my knees, lit a Kool. My body was totally drained, but my nerves burned with electric pulses. I knew when I had to move the electricity would jump start the body. A strange feeling. I said so to Kaiser.

He was half turned in the seat, so he could see me and the street behind him. He said, "Me too. Exhausted, but pumped for action."

I said, "Reminds me of going two days with no sleep and then eating a Dexie. Body stays fried, heart and nerves go haywire."

"Naturally it would remind you of something like that."

At seven o'clock a red Corolla drove past us toward the apartment building and the Civic. Shannon Harper drove. Tricia was in the passenger seat. George Kemp sat in back.

I said, "They're here," like the little girl in *Poltergeist*. I stood and said, "We do whatever we have to to keep Tricia alive." I knew Kaiser agreed. I just needed to say it out loud.

Kaiser got out of the car, came around to my side. He stuffed the .38 into the waistband of his trousers. Said, "We stay out of sight best we can till we get to the cars. Surprise is our only advantage."

We started down the alley toward the street. Kaiser said, "Dammit!" I stopped and stared, dumbfounded.

Leo DiNardi drove the unmarked Ford past the front of the alley.

THIRTY-SEVEN

We broke into a run as we turned from the alley onto the sidewalk. I said, "How in the hell?"

Kaiser said, "Dammit," over and over, louder each time.

I said, "He's gonna get Tricia killed."

Our only advantage was totally blown to hell now. DiNardi would handle this with an iron glove. And I knew what Shannon would do soon as she saw me and cops. Soon as she saw she wasn't getting her money. Saw I was responsible. Shannon's revenge-obsessed mind would compute: "I don't get my money because of you; you don't get Tricia because of me."

Fuller opened the Civic's trunk. The Civic was on our side of the street, facing east. The Corolla faced west directly across from it.

Shannon and Tricia exited the Corolla, walked toward Fuller. Both wore shorts and oversized T-shirts. A canvas bag hung from Shannon's left shoulder. George Kemp stood next to the Corolla's passenger side, watching the other three.

DiNardi braked the Ford behind the Corolla. He stepped out, flashed his badge. Shouted something. His back was to us, I couldn't hear what he said. He started toward Fuller, Shannon, and Tricia, his hands in the pockets of his black windbreaker.

Kaiser and I cut between two parked cars, ran in the street. Kaiser's arms chugged back and forth like a locomotive connecting rod. His feet slid along the concrete like he was gliding on ice. He huffed and puffed, groaned. I though how silly the guy looked until I realized he was in front of me.

The animal people froze as DiNardi moved toward them. The

last thing they expected was a man with a badge.

As for DiNardi, he was here to talk about murder; he had no idea he was walking toward a trunk full of kidnap money.

The animal people looked behind DiNardi, saw us—me— running full tilt at them. DiNardi turned and saw us too. I shouted, "Tricia, run! Get away from there!"

George Kemp reacted first. He reached inside the Corolla, came out with a Mac 10 automatic pistol. He raised it above the roof of the Corolla. Pointed it at me. The man he wanted to kill yesterday. He didn't think to kill the closest man first, then gun for the two further away. Easy was too complex for him. He'd wanted me so it was Kruger first, then the other two.

Leo DiNardi was between the Corolla and the Civic. Kemp had clicked the clip of the Mac 10 against the roof of the Corolla as he brought it up. The sound made DiNardi look fast at Kemp.

Before Kemp could aim, before my brain screamed, "Hit the street," DiNardi's right hand came out of the windbreaker, extended toward Kemp. A revolver was in his hand. DiNardi pulled the trigger soon as his arm was straight. The top of Kemp's head disintegrated. He feel backwards. He was gone, really gone.

Everyone moved now. I kept my eyes on Tricia. She folded in half, screaming, trying to back away from what she'd just seen. Shannon grabbed her arm, dragged her to the open front door of the Civic, pushed her inside.

DiNardi pivoted so he faced the Civic. He yelled, "Freeze!" He pointed the gun at Shannon. Shannon turned, yelled to Fuller, "Use it, goddammit!"

Kaiser and I got to the cars. Shannon turned back to face us. I smashed into her. She sprawled along the side of the Civic. DiNardi cursed.

The collision sent me to one knee. I stood, coiled to ram Shannon again. She leaned against the side of the Civic by the rear wheel. She put her right arm inside the bag on her shoulder, pulled out a gun. She pointed the gun at me. It looked like a cannon. I dove inside the Civic. I pushed Tricia toward the passenger door, keeping her head down with my right hand, shielding her body with mine. I fumbled for the lock with my left hand.

Kaiser and DiNardi yelled, one slightly after the other, "Freeze, police officers."

What Shannon wanted Fuller to use must have been a gun stashed in the Civic's trunk. A shot sounded from there. An answering shot came from the side of the car. Boyd Fuller screamed. Something heavy clunked on the street. Fuller yelled, "Okay, okay, okay," hysterically.

Tricia thrashed in panic. I couldn't get at the lock knob to pull it up so I could push her out of the car.

Shannon screamed, "Stop it, Kruger!"

I stopped it, turned to face her.

Shannon stood outside the driver's door. The cannon was a .45 and it stared at my face. If she pulled the trigger I wouldn't have a face. Shannon looked fast from me to Kaiser, back and forth. Kaiser lowered his gun when he saw the deal going down. I couldn't see DiNardi.

My body went ice cold. I shifted to cover Tricia as best I could.

Shannon hesitated a second. Things had happened too fast. She couldn't decide what to do. She couldn't see DiNardi and she needed to know where DiNardi was. She wanted him to know she'd kill me and Tricia if they didn't let her leave. She started to turn toward the back of the Civic.

Another shot. The side of Shannon's face splattered apart in a reddish spray. Her head snapped forward like it had been lassoed and yanked taut. She collapsed hard to the street.

Tricia screamed in my ear. A long, shrill, steady sound like an air raid whistle. I hunched to my knees on the car seat, looked behind me.

DiNardi stood just behind the Civic, arm outstretched, his gun pointing where Shannon had been.

In the space of thirty seconds Leo DiNardi had saved my life twice.

THIRTY-EIGHT

For three hours, at various sites, I talked to cops, morgue attendants, doctors and reporters.

The Rasta Kid showed just before we left Cyprus. Wearing his shades and white terry cloth shorts he jostled to the front of the crowd that fringed the crime scene. I put my palms up at my side, shrugged to say 'So, I was wrong.' He shook his head sadly, flashed the peace sign. Mouthed, "You find your girl?" I nodded.

At Mt. Sinai North, we questioned Boyd Fuller after he received treatment for the shoulder wound Kaiser gave him.

Any doubts I had concerning my theory about Shannon vanished when we listened to what he had to say. He said he knew something was wrong when he saw me running down the street. Shannon had told the five people in Milwaukee that Kay and I were dead. It would be in the papers the next day. With us dead nobody on earth knew who was in Friends of the Wild.

Shannon had said she'd drive the Civic. She'd be alone with the money in case the plan fell through, in case her family suspected her involvement and voiced their suspicions to the police. If she got picked up she should be alone because after all she was the ringleader, the one who should take the heat. Of course she'd never name a name.

Friends of the Wild, including the four people at the Harper building, were to rendezvous at a farm of sympathizers in southern Indiana. Shannon had drawn maps so they could get there. Fuller showed us his.

The escape plan she'd devised for the four people in the Harper building was nothing special. On Wednesday night the Wisconsin five had driven cars to Milwaukee, parking four of them in different residential neighborhoods, driving the fifth one back to Chicago. After the four people inside heard the money had changed hands they were to wait until dark, leave with all hostages. They would drive to Milwaukee, break off into four groups and drive the cars to Indiana. Each driver could release their hostages when they saw fit. She assured them that as long as they held hostages and promised to kill them if pursued, they wouldn't be pursued. That threat and darkness would get them to Milwaukee. Switching from the van to the cars would get them to Indiana.

These were intelligent, successful people except when they listened to Shannon Harper.

When the group was together again they'd drive to Bedford, Massachusetts. Shannon had linked together an underground network of animal rights activists across the country. People as committed as they were. People who'd provide shelter and support. Friends of the Wild would launch a guerrilla war against animal torturers. Random violence against labs, furriers, farmers, butchers, hunters. Nobody would be safe. They would use terror to bring the animal industry to its knees. Between the money extorted from her family and the refuge network she'd set up, they could carry out a nationwide terrorist war for years. Future generations would consider them heroes of liberation on a par with John Brown and Gandhi and Martin Luther King. How she was able to compare a terrorist group to the last two people made sense to none of us, but it must have seemed logical to Friends of the Wild.

Later, at Area Six on West Belmont, Kaiser and I talked to DiNardi. He leaned against a plastered wall in a narrow, under-lit hallway in the basement. We had to wait for a bit while he talked to a *Tribune* reporter. DiNardi looked as smug as a fox exiting an empty henhouse. When the reporter left, first thing he said was, "Saved your amateur ass, PI, didn't I?" Kaiser told him to lay off and asked how he got to Cyprus.

He told us he ID'd someone in the photo around eight o'clock the night before. The someone wouldn't talk, but a friend of the someone ID'd Shannon Harper. Told him she was a member of the Harper Cosmetic family, gave him the mansion address. The Harper Cosmetic hostage thing was all over the news. Shannon was connected to two murder victims and now her father, uncle, and thirteen other people were being held hostage. Like most cops, DiNardi didn't believe in coincidence. He didn't know what, but something was going down and Shannon Harper was in the middle of it.

He went to the mansion. Lights were on, he was positive people were inside, but nobody answered the door.

He went home, lay awake thinking things over. Tried to call Kaiser, got the machine. Tried again. And again. He figured if Kaiser wasn't home by 1:00 A.M. Kaiser knew what the something was. He called both my numbers, got no answer.

He became irate, thinking about Kaiser working with a PI instead of his partner.

So at six o'clock he drove to the Gold Coast, was about to turn onto Astor as Shannon and the Corolla turned onto North from State. "Better to be lucky than good," he smirked. "But best to be both. Too bad you're neither, PI."

I ignored that. There was a lot I wanted to say, but I swallowed hard and said, "I was afraid your lucky would cost a girl her life. But you ended up saving hers and mine. I'm glad you were there."

DiNardi looked me up and down for a second, then said, "You *were* willing to take a bullet for the kid." He looked away. That was as good as I'd get out of him.

Still looking at the other wall he said, "And by the way, you wanna dress better I suggest you spend more time reading *GQ* and less time looking at *Rolling Stone*."

He said to Kaiser, "I still want a new partner."

Kaiser said, "That'd be for the best, Leo."

They didn't smile but they shook hands. DiNardi strutted away down the hall.

At two o'clock Kaiser and I drove Tricia home. She'd been given a sedative at Mt. Sinai, then questioned by detectives at Area Six. After that a therapist talked to her for two hours. The therapist would see her every day for a while.

Tricia and I sat in the back seat. She said, "All that stuff Shannon told us. The nationwide network, the safe houses, the guerrilla war. It was all made up?"

"All of it. She didn't talk to anybody about anything. She was driving the Civic to O'Hare to fly away with the money. If you guys followed those maps to Indiana, you'd of probably ended up in the middle of a cornfield."

"I can't believe this." Her speech was slow and slurred from the downers.

"I know you admired her and feel betrayed, but she had her reasons for betraying you."

"But I can't believe it. I can't believe she'd do this to me—to us."

"She joined Animal Sanctuary because she believed what you believe. This thing wasn't even a vague idea. But somewhere along the way it flashed on her this group of people would do anything she said. She had one bona fide psycho in the group who'd bankroll any scheme she came up with, kill anybody she told him to. Kemp was so screwed up he thought the only reason he'd been put on earth was so Shannon Harper could command him."

"George killed Amy?"

"Yes."

"But Shannon was so involved. What about her principles?"

"Sad to say, greed almost always wins out over principles. And she could of continued to support animal groups and with a lot more money. That was one rationalization. In the end, she couldn't resist the setup. She vowed revenge against her father after he disowned her. You guys were like God set the opportunity to do that in her lap. She was five days away from getting it done when Amy and your mother hired me to get you back. She'd been blowing them off, figured she could do that for another five days and after that she couldn't care less what they said. She'd be half a world away. But then they bring in this outsider who talks cops. She never thought they'd do that. It freaked her out so bad she had Kemp gun down the people who could mess her plan up. Only thing saved your mother and me was we told her we wouldn't talk so long as she had you. Even with that Kemp would of offed me yesterday if I'd gone home instead of your house. Just to be sure. I imagine she was good and paranoid the day the plan went down."

"She really would have killed me?"

I said, "You, your mother, me—anybody."

Tricia started to cry. She said, "But she said she loved me." I patted her shoulder like I'd patted her mother's a few days be-fore. I said, "Your mother loves you, Shannon needed to use you."

Kaiser parked two doors down and across the street from her house. Tricia said in a small, pain-husky voice, "I can't go in, Dan."

I was ready for that. I said, "I'll talk to your mother."

Inside, I told Kay, Hedy and Heather what had happened. Said to Kay, "Your daughter is in Kaiser's car outside. She's in shock. Says she can't come in."

Kay's face transformed. She looked like a woman suddenly confronted with both heaven and hell. She whispered, "I know. I *have* to make the first step. For me and her."

She opened the door, started across the porch. Heather, Hedy and I moved to the doorway to watch. Kay stepped on the top stair.

She stopped on each step. Both hands had a death grip on the railing. Her breathing grew so labored she sounded like a boiler about to explode.

At the bottom of the steps she halted for almost a minute. Her sides heaved. The back of her shirt was transparent with sweat. Every nerve in her body was telling her to turn and run back inside, but she didn't. She could see the car now. She waved at Tricia. Tricia watched.

Kay started across the lawn. There was nothing to grab onto here. She walked tiny steps, her arms outstretched and quiver-ing like the ground was a water bed and she needed to do that to keep her balance. Suddenly she bent over, wrapped her arms around her stomach, dryheaved. She crouched, butt on heels, looked at the grass. Dryheaved again.

Heather said in a low voice, "Godammit, what does Tricia *want?*"

Kay stayed down for another minute, then stood, lurched for-ward. Slowly made it across the lawn, the sidewalk, got to the curb.

When she stepped onto the street, Tricia burst from the Cut-lass. She ran to her mother. They hugged and cried. I said to Heather, "That's what Tricia wanted. One step on the street.

She knows what that took. And she knows Kay did it for her."

Heather said softly, "I'm going to stay here a while. About the animal stuff—there's lots of things Kay can teach me. She said it was okay with her if it was okay with you."

I said, "You don't need my permission to do anything, I've told you that. You come home whenever you want."

An hour later Bugs and I drove home. I said, "Bugs, we're batching it again. I got a feeling it might be for a while."

That seemed fine by Bugs. Just like old times. Me and him against the world.

I said, "Think about today, wabbit. I got a runaway daughter back home. I made my thirty-fourth sober day. Heather might be substituting a cause for pills. And Kay Thornberg stepped into the street. Not exactly earth-shaking developments I admit, but you can't always expect cancer cures or manned space flights. Sometimes life's greatest triumphs are taking a step into the street or spending a day sober."

Bugs thought that bit of profundity over.

I passed six liquor stores and seven taverns on my way home. Didn't stop at any. Maybe one day I'd take a drive and not even notice taverns and liquor stores.

Wouldn't Dr. Eli be proud of me then?

EPILOGUE

The hostage situation at Harper Cosmetic was essentially over as soon as the four people inside learned Shannon Harper and George Kemp were dead. I watched a recap of the end on the CNN evening news.

Frank Kelson surrendered almost immediately—he was only there because of Shannon. With her dead he couldn't care less. One hour later Sorrento Gallo walked out, hood off, hands high. At 2:30 P.M. about the time Tricia and her mother were hugging in the street, Cornelia Haas and Susan Chapman emerged, side by side, hands clasped together in the air.

They were thrown to the ground. An army of cops and SWAT troops poured into the building.

Found nobody dead, nothing blown up, although the research lab was reported to have suffered "severe damage." I smiled at that. That's where last night's shots had come from. Larsen had promised the four the moon to get them out. The only thing he didn't renege on was the safe removal of the animals Friends of the Wild rescued from the lab. They were taken to a veterinarian in Waukesha. But that was only because there was no more lab. Eventually there'd be a new lab and new animals.

The CNN anchor then went into details about "this *incredibly* bizarre story," linking the hostage situation in Milwaukee with the two murders in Chicago. He told how the whole thing had been planned by a member of the Harper family. Crimestyles of the Rich and Famous. The media would headline this one for months.

Jack Kaiser and I talked to an Assistant State's Attorney on Monday. He said that with Amanda Truitt's testimony about the threat on her life and because of her age, Tricia Thornberg would be considered held against her will, would testify for the state, and no charges would be filed against her.

The next weekend Full Frontal Nudity played the gig at Cubby Bear Lounge. Opening act for the Beat Farmers. Bill Eli showed up and danced his ass off. He and I sat around after the gig and drank enough Diet Pepsi to float an aircraft carrier, but that's all I had.

Forty-one days.

Two weeks later Kay and Tricia reorganized Animal Sanctuary. No raids this time. Picketing, letters, boycotts, fund raising. Heather joined immediately. A week later she told me Jack Kaiser showed at a meeting.

I decided in time I'd probably get involved too. I'd never hear the end of it from Bugs if I didn't.